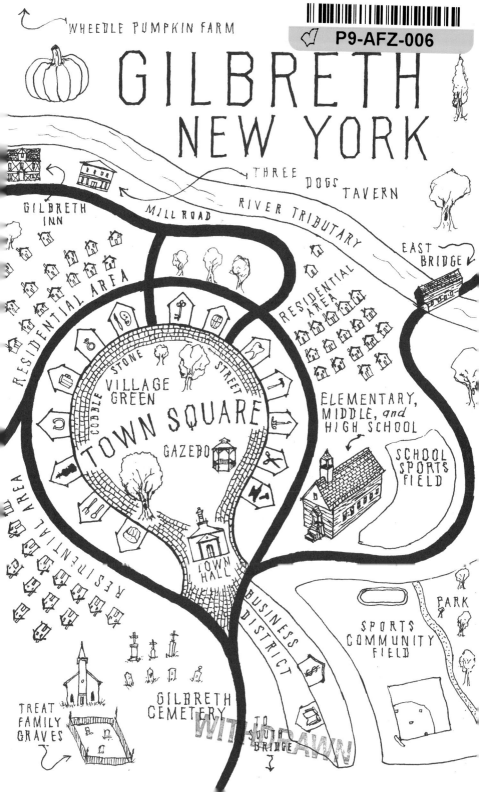

WHEEDLE PUMPKIN FARM

GILBRETH
NEW YORK

THREE DOGS TAVERN

RIVER TRIBUTARY

MILL ROAD

GILBRETH INN

EAST BRIDGE

RESIDENTIAL AREA

RESIDENTIAL AREA

COBBLE STONE STREET

VILLAGE GREEN

TOWN SQUARE

GAZEBO

ELEMENTARY, MIDDLE, and HIGH SCHOOL

SCHOOL SPORTS FIELD

RESIDENTIAL AREA

TOWN HALL

BUSINESS DISTRICT

PARK

SPORTS COMMUNITY FIELD

TREAT FAMILY GRAVES

GILBRETH CEMETERY

TO SOUTH BRIDGE

Under the
Bottle
Bridge

Also by Jessica Lawson

The Actual & Truthful Adventures of Becky Thatcher

Nooks & Crannies

Waiting for Augusta

Under the
Bottle
Bridge

Jessica Lawson

Simon & Schuster Books for Young Readers

NEW YORK   LONDON   TORONTO   SYDNEY   NEW DELHI

SIMON & SCHUSTER BOOKS FOR YOUNG READERS
An imprint of Simon & Schuster Children's Publishing Division
1230 Avenue of the Americas, New York, New York 10020

SIMON & SCHUSTER BOOKS FOR YOUNG READERS
is a trademark of Simon & Schuster, Inc.
For information about special discounts for bulk purchases, please contact Simon & Schuster
Special Sales at 1-866-506-1949 or business@simonandschuster.com.
The Simon & Schuster Speakers Bureau can bring authors to your live event.
For more information or to book an event, contact the Simon & Schuster Speakers Bureau
at 1-866-248-3049 or visit our website at www.simonspeakers.com.
Book design by Chloë Foglia
Endpaper map by Erik Sanko
The text for this book is set in Adobe Caslon Pro.
Manufactured in the United States of America
0817 FFG
First Edition
2 4 6 8 10 9 7 5 3 1
Library of Congress Cataloging-in-Publication Data
Names: Lawson, Jessica, 1980–, author.
Title: Under the bottle bridge / Jessica Lawson.
Description: First Edition. | New York : Simon & Schuster Books for Young
Readers, [2017] | Summary: Twelve-year-old woodcraft legacy Minna Treat
hopes the mysterious messages she finds in bottles under the bridge her
mother died on will lead her to her unknown biological father.
Identifiers: LCCN 2016045822| ISBN 9781481448420 (hardback)
| ISBN 9781481448444 (eBook)
Subjects: | CYAC: Identity—Fiction. | Secrets—Fiction. | Woodwork—Fiction.
| Mothers and daughters—Fiction. | Fathers and daughters—Fiction. |
BISAC: JUVENILE FICTION / Social Issues / Friendship. | JUVENILE FICTION /
Social Issues / New Experience. | JUVENILE FICTION / Social Issues /
Emotions & Feelings.
Classification: LCC PZ7.L438267 Un 2017 | DDC [Fic]—dc23
LC record available at https://lccn.loc.gov/2016045822

For Tara, Joy, Becky & Ann—
Builders & Keepers of many bridges

Acknowledgments

It takes a Gilbrethean village to bring a book into the world, and I've got loads of people to thank.

Thank you to my dear editor, Liz Kossnar, for taking the lead on building a bridge between this story and readers. I'm so grateful for your input and humor and heart, and so very happy to have you as my editorial Captain. PS, you are a rock star.

My agent, Tina Wexler, lovingly builds covered bridges between authors and publishers every day. Throughout my writing journey, she has been a source of shelter and support in moments of joy and uncertainty and everything in between. Thank you, Tina, you kindhearted/clever/bookish bridge carpenter you. PS, we must eat pizza together at some point.

Chloë Foglia is a book designer extraordinaire. Thank you, Chloë, for your talent and hard work! PS, having LEAVES on my chapter headings makes me smile more than I can say.

Justin Chanda and all of the folks at Simon & Schuster

Books for Young Readers do so much for children's literature. I am ever grateful for their talent and spirit. Kristin Ostby, thank you for picking Minna from a stack of ideas and giving me the go-ahead to bring her to book-life. PS, all of you are magic makers.

Thank you to Sonia Kretschmar, who made me want to dive into her beautiful cover and make autumn discoveries with Minna. PS, I wish I owned Minna's T-shirt.

To my critique partners Joy McCullough-Carranza, Tara Dairman, Becky Wallace, and Ann Bedichek, what can I say? This book is dedicated to you wonderful ladies, who joined forces to buy me a laptop to finish my first draft of this story. PS, you inspire me every day and keep me writing.

Adam Andersen—owner and lead carpenter of Andersen Custom Carpentry in Colorado Springs—was gracious enough to give me a tour of his woodshop, patient enough to answer lots of questions, and crazy enough to let me have a crack at his band saw. Any inaccuracies in regard to woodcraft in this book are solely mine. Illustrator Sara Lynn Cramb took a sketch of my fictional village and turned it into an actual map. PS, you were both vital pieces of my writing process.

Linda Fuqua-Jones & Gwenda Rosebush of Palmer Lake Library, I must thank you for your dedication to readers, tolerance for my chattiness and rowdy children, and for the covered bridge popcorn tin—given at a much-needed moment in my drafting process. Diane Fischer, ditto on the chattiness and rowdy children tolerance, and an extra thank you for emergency babysitting. PS, I miss seeing you all.

Over the last several years, the Child Watch staff members of the Tri-Lakes YMCA and Lionville YMCA have provided a nurturing environment for my children while I write stories. Thanks to all of you! PS, I swear I'll start working out more next year.

To Mom and Dad, whose planks are firmly set just behind mine on my life's bridge, thank you for being my cornerstone. PS, come visit and I'll make you some hearth milk.

In every conceivable manner, the family is link to our past, bridge to our future.

–Alex Haley

A Brief Word on My Uncle Theo, Tradition, and Deadlines

Let me start by saying that I, Minna Treat, consider myself to be a very, maybe even an especially, well-adjusted young person. But even I have my limits.

Let me also say that if Uncle Theo dropped one more of his "subtle hints" about me needing to make a decision about a junior artisan project, I was afraid I might blomp him over the head with his copy of *The Art of Subtle Hints: Planting Greatness in Your Child's Garden*. In a balanced and nonconfrontational way, of course.

That's kind of a useless parenting book anyway. The twenty-seven-page foreword is called "A Brief Word on the Fragility of Seeds," which tells you the kind of Hokey you're about to deal with. I have no idea why all those books have to start with "A Brief Word on" or "A Gentle Note About" or "Read This Poem Someone Wrote and Ponder It Before Reading This Book" instead of divvying that sentimental junk up into the rest of the pages, so that people can just concentrate on the must-know information.

All I know is that since me and Uncle Theo were left to each other, he's always wanted to be the best guardian possible, and I love him for that. Anytime I feel even the tiniest bit like having a pity party for one reason or another (talking to you, General Art I paint-a-landscape-any-landscape assignment), I remind myself that in the tragedy and responsibility departments, the past elevenish years have been a real stinker for him.

When Uncle Theo was seventeen, his only sister quit her junior year of college, moved back into their parents' house, and seven months later gave birth to me.

When he was nineteen, that sister died.

When he was twenty-two, his parents died in a car wreck one week after the third anniversary of his sister's death. He was then named the sole guardian of five-year-old me.

Since that time he's armed himself with parenting books and the fiercest determination to put his all into raising me. He does the normal stuff, like food/water/shelter, and the extra stuff, like posting weekly vocabulary words such as *epiphany* and *irrelevant* and *charlatan* on the chalkboard hanging beside the hearth. He even gives sentence examples, like: "Charlatan: In hindsight, it should have been perfectly obvious that the glassblower was a charlatan—after all, glassblowers have a natural ability to blow lots of hot air."

At least once a week Uncle Theo tells me that I am the best thing in his life, and while we are a team, he is the captain, and while he is the captain, I am his heart. And he means it. I think that's the most important thing to know about my uncle. The loving part.

What I do *not* love—because they can be scary and mean and far less necessary than people think—is deadlines. Uncle Theo had told me (only once) that I didn't *have* to participate in the junior artisan contest just because every Treat had entered a woodcraft project since my eight-times great-grandfather Elias Treat and his brothers began it as part of a harvest celebration back in the 1700s.

But then he'd told me (a million times) that it would make the family proud if I *did* enter, and so he'd already signed me up on the off chance I'd like to participate. The projects would be presented on the village's Bonfire Night, the Monday after the annual Gilbreth two-day Autumnfest, which was just over three weeks away. I'd never qualify again, since it was only open to sixth graders.

The deadline wasn't his fault, but it was still there. And it was basically the same as summoning all of our deceased relatives to haunt me day and night, clasping their creepy, invisible hands together while noiselessly moaning, *Loooom-ing deadline, Minna. Pleeeeease don't disapoooooiiiiint us, OooOOOooo!*

According to Uncle Theo, I was more than capable of

deciding on a "special, unique, bold" project. "Embrace the past," he told me.

"Feel its heart beat against your own," he said.

"You're a Treat," he reminded me.

I didn't need another heart beating against mine. My heart worked just fine by itself. And I was well aware that I was a Treat and that my family's past was in me with every step I took.

Sometimes the predictable Treatness of my life gave me a nice, cozy sense of belonging, and sometimes it felt like I was buried under a big pile of well-meaning parenting books and wood shavings, trying to claw my way up to the top so I could reach out a hand to let people know that I was there too and that I had a first name in addition to my last name.

I'm Minna, my fingertips would call out for me, *and I'm here too.*

But who exactly was Minna? I was still figuring that out. Not a big problem, right?

Wrong.

According to *Natural Disasters: Emergency Parenting for the Teen Years*, youth and innocence were basically over once age thirteen hit, and I needed to be as self-grounded as possible in order to anchor myself for the "deluge of tumultuous, volatile changes ahead." If I didn't have complete faith and confidence in myself as a person before the clock struck

Teenager, I'd get swept away by some kind of giant, invisible flood.

So between that kind of doomsday talk and the fact that my thirteenth birthday was three months away, I felt like I was on my own personal deadline for finding out exactly who *Minna* was before the very last autumn of my childhood was over.

Lately, I'd been wondering if my other half, my non-Treat half, was part of the answer.

I didn't know anything about who my dad was. According to Uncle Theo, my mom never even told anyone his name. She just returned to Gilbreth like she'd never left at all.

Question: How do you find the thing that'll make you feel complete when the only thing you're really missing in life is a lost father that nobody else wants to find, and the only person who might be able to help with that particular item is (a) dead and (b) wanted him to stay lost.

Answer: You don't. Not without the help of a magical gateway to the past or a miraculous coincidence or an incredible appearance that would change everything.

I wasn't picky. I'd settle for any of those three.

The Weaver's Prediction

In 1691, William Treat, a London-based maker of fine wood-craft, came down with a stomach ailment that took his life. Before he passed away, he bade his four sons to take heart, to be kind when tested but less kind when life called for it, to befriend danger and embrace discovery, and to avoid meat that smelled like feet. Lastly, he told them to whistle along with the hymns at his funeral because they all had singing voices that sounded like feral cats flung into frigid bathwater.

–From **Gilbreth History: Founding Families & Artisanal Traditions** (Gilbreth Welcome Center, $16.99)

The apothecary shop was a dusky sort of dark, with drawn curtains and narrow wooden shelves stocked with remedies and tinctures and dried herbs. Freestanding candles and oil lamps fastened to the walls sent shadows dancing, reminding me of how unearthly I'd found the place as a child. It was like an enchanted mole hole, a hollow hoard of strange smells and spells displayed among lights flickering in a permanent midnight. I stood waiting, the owner's back to me as he hummed and searched the oils for my uncle's request.

Mrs. Poppy sat in a corner next to a small, ancient-looking cabinet covered in leaf carvings, working small miracles on her handheld loom. She and her sister had a weaving shop down the street, but it was closed on most Sundays. She caught me looking and smiled, holding up her work. "Pumpkin blankets for pets, dear, suitable for anything from dogs to hamsters. The tourists just love them."

I grazed the pumpkin's stem with my fingertips. "It's soft."

Her head bobbed toward her husband. "I was just telling Mr. Poppy that I'm thinking of doing readings this year too. Weavers in my family have been known to have the second sight, you know."

Mr. Poppy snickered, coughed hard, covered his mouth, then wiped both hands on his jacket. He wore his usual working clothes, a Revolutionary War uniform passed down by relatives through the years.

"I heard that, Zeke. Let me practice on you, Minna." Mrs. Poppy grabbed my offered hand and squinted at it, muttering silent words and then licking her lips. She looked up at me in surprise. "You are about to embark on a journey of great discovery."

That was news to me. "I am?"

She frowned and bent her head again. "Or is that great danger?" Dropping my hand, she placed one of her palms over my forehead and shut her eyes. "There will be a great trouble of some kind . . . an accident . . . a flash of light . . . no, a fire!" She opened her eyes and blinked. "A fire?" Swiftly twisting my hand, she examined its side. "And you'll have sixteen children? Oh, that can't be right."

My hand was getting tingly. I jerked it back.

"Hope not," both Mr. Poppy and I said.

She sighed and pointed to a twig frame on the wall. In the middle was a photograph of the Poppys on their wedding day. "Your frame is still up. Do you think you might make a frame for your project, dear?" She asked the question with an easy nonchalance while her fingers busied themselves like spider legs weaving a web. I could tell she was digging for information.

I studied the frame and blushed. "I made that when I was five. It's terrible. And no, I'll definitely make something better than a frame."

She clucked like a mother hen. "I happen to like that frame. Not going to tell me about your project, though? Typical woodworker."

"Typical *weaver*, more like," barked Mr. Poppy.

Every type of traditional art practiced in the village came with its own labels that rivaled astrological charts.

Gilbreth potters were moody. The evidence could be traced back to a 1714 incident involving an unlucky potter who caught rabies from his cat, which had gotten it in a narrow escape from an infected wolf. The potter survived and went on to have a big family, but remained twitchy and morose and unpredictable his entire life.

Gilbreth stonemasons had vicious tempers, first recorded in a journal entry by a weaver who'd made the mistake of insulting a stonemason's technique. In return, the weaver received a stone dropped on his foot, breaking it.

Herbalists were peacemakers, blacksmiths were untrustworthy, weavers were gossips, silversmiths thought they were royalty, candlemakers were nostalgic, glassblowers were impulsive.

And woodworkers . . . well, I hated to admit it, but the label was true: Woodworkers were secretive.

"I like what's in the middle of the frame best," Mr. Poppy called.

"I did look nice, didn't I?" Mrs. Poppy patted her cotton-ball hair and blew a sentimental kiss to the old photograph inside the frame. "I can't wait to see what you'll be presenting at Bonfire Night, dear. You've got talent in your blood, you know." She put down her weaving. "Where's Christopher Hardly? You and that freckly boy are usually glued at the hip."

She raised a drawn-on eyebrow and looked me up and

down. "Don't be in a hurry to grow up. You're not ready for a boyfriend. I was in a hurry to grow up, and what did I get for it? Triplets, that's what, who then moved to Sedona to hawk their father's recipes to reborn hippies."

I stifled a snort. "We're best *friends*, Mrs. Poppy, that's all. We're a very solid friendship crew of two."

She let out a soft, breathy laugh. "Well, I wouldn't worry about him being competition at the contest this year. I heard that he broke another vase the other day. Just a small one, but still." She patted her hair again. "You would never know he's a Hardly."

I stiffened.

This village bred all sorts of talent, but in school we were taught that Gilbreth, New York, had survived and thrived because of two skills in particular: woodworking and glassworking. Fine woodcraft made by my descendants long ago with our heavily guarded techniques, and more recently, glassware made famous by my best friend's descendants when Crash's great-grandfather had a dream and spontaneously whisked his whole family across the country to New York.

My best friend had gotten his nickname back when he started his early training with glassblowing—just observation stuff, but that was still close enough to do some serious damage.

On the day before first grade started, he broke a vase his

father was going to sell for $5,750 to a collector in Baltimore.

Then he broke a sculpture that his mother was working on for a special exhibit at the Metropolitan Museum of Art in New York. He hid in our old tree house for two full days when that one happened. The whole town was looking for him, and I was the one who found him, curled up in a corner with a spoon and a jar of peanut butter.

When he started accidentally breaking projects of his much older brothers and sisters, they started calling him Crash, and it stuck.

He didn't mean to break things. Some people are just klutzes, and it's not like young kids and glass are a real great mix. Accidents happen in every artisan group. That's why Uncle Theo doesn't have a left-hand pinkie finger (circular saw incident) and why Grandma Treat had a major scar on her left forearm (hot tea and nail gun incident). Grandpa Treat had a glass eyeball from when he and his twin brother played too rough with the claw ends of hammers when they were kids.

Still, we lived in a village where children of serious tradesmen were fully expected to carry on tradition or risk being labeled a traitor. Sure, we could go to college, but anyone who didn't either come back to Gilbreth or continue their family's traditional art elsewhere was "lost." Even families like the Hardlys and the Bhagawatis and the Lees, who'd been in Gilbreth for only three generations, had a fairly stringent, unspoken rule of loyalty and legacy.

"Crash will do fine, Mrs. Poppy."

"He better. It's in his blood. If he doesn't improve soon, he'll end up like his lost sister, Lorelei. She got a new job, I heard. Raising money for some college. She might as well be our new mayor—did you hear he wants to plow half of Torrey Wood for subdivisions? Subdivisions!" Mrs. Poppy spit the word out like it was a rotten, slimy grape.

"Here we go, then. . . ." Mr. Poppy arranged his selections on his blending counter and poured a long dose of oil from a wooden flask marked SUNFLOWER. Slowly, carefully, he began adding essential oils by the drop. "I'm glad he sent you to me. Do you know that Treats and Poppys have been friends for centuries?"

I shook my head.

"Oh, yes. It was your ancestor who stood up for my ancestor's daughters when they were accused of witchery after the Maybeck hanging—just for the herbal knowledge in their heads, can you believe that? Elias Treat saved their lives and reputations, cross my heart. In fact, no charge today." With two fingers he tapped the lid. "It's lavender and rosemary, with a hint of sweet orange." He scrubbed at a spot on the counter. "Plus a little hawthorn and passionflower. Helps with sorrow, and also stress in case he's been worried about—"

"Now just zip it, Zeke," Mrs. Poppy said, flashing him a warning glance. "Don't go repeating everything you hear."

"Ha! That's a peach, you telling *me* to zip it." Mr. Poppy

tapped the small jar against the back wall three times, right in the middle of a hanging necklace. Its braided leather cord was strung up and held open with four nails. A tiny, carved wooden horse dangled from the bottom.

"Why did you tap the jar like that?"

"Hmm?" He turned back to me and dropped the small jar into my open hand, his wrinkled hand sinking down to cover the lid. His other hand cupped mine on the bottom as he leaned over, half-moon glasses slipping down his substantial nose. He smelled like cherry candy and tobacco and clean sheets.

"Why did you tap it in the middle of the horse necklace?"

"Brings good health to the patient. That's what my father used to say. He tapped his remedies like that, and his father did the same. That thing has hung there for years, and not one of my relatives remembered who exactly it first belonged to."

I leaned over the counter for a closer look. "It's a good carving."

"It is. Now, this is premixed, but tell your uncle to give it a little shake before he uses it. Drops at the temple, behind the ears, and smoothed over the top of his forehead. Like this." He demonstrated, then waved a hand. "Should take care of his headache within fifteen minutes. It's all on the label. Happy Season, dear. You're a good girl."

"Some days more than others," I said lightly, trying not to stare at his thick crop of nose hair. I nestled the jar into my tool-belt pocket, eager to get back into the light of the Town Square sidewalks. "Thanks, Mr. Poppy. Happy Season."

I had no idea where the Gilbreth saying came from, celebrating the bittersweet time when leaves turned from green to autumn shades on their way toward annual deaths, but as soon as the first trees changed, the phrase mystically appeared. I'd never heard Uncle Theo say it.

A bird flew across my path as I pushed the door open, brushing my face with its wings and disappearing before I could trace its flight. The Hardlys' shop was closed, and I remembered Crash saying something about a family Sunday supply run. I hadn't seen him all weekend. I hurried home, crossing the Village Green.

The sun was already grazing the tops of the trees. Uncle Theo would be waiting, and the fastest way home was through the forest. Selecting a small stone from the ground, I slipped into the sea of trees.

Just before I entered the woods, I could have sworn I saw a flash of black out of the corner of my right eye, moving evenly with me somewhere among the oaks and maples and elms, the ash, birch, and beech. But when I glanced over, it had disappeared.

Are You There?

In 1692 a nearly thirteen-year-old Elias Treat left his home in Gravesend, England, boarding a ship bound for New York with his three older brothers, Tobias, Samuel, and James. Fifty-eight passengers became ill with food poisoning from moldy mutton along the way. The Treat brothers, meat wary after their father's demise, were not among them and were able to build handy vomit chutes from wood scraps, which kept the mess on the ship to a minimum.

–From **Gilbreth History: Founding Families & Artisanal Traditions** (Gilbreth Welcome Center, $16.99)

It was the clinking that made me stop.

My pebble had sailed through one of Whistler Bridge's small, neck-high windows and into the ravine below, which by itself wasn't really out of the ordinary. During school days I only took the Torrey Wood paths if I was running late, and if I was running late, I had to take Whistler as a shortcut, and whenever I took Whistler, I always made a wish.

I'd scoop up a pebble and try to toss it out of one of the windows without pausing. If I threw it neatly through, the wish would come true. If I smacked it against the inside of the bridge, no dice. It was just a stupid game, I knew, but handy for distraction or reassurance if I'd done something like, say, forgotten to study for a math test. Which was rare. Well, rarish.

Tucked deep within the forest near the original Gilbreth settlement ruins, the oldest of Gilbreth's five Treat-built covered bridges stretched across the gently sloped fifteen-foot ravine that ran through the woods like a giant's garden furrow that never got planted. It used to hold a wide creek connecting two of the rivers, but that had dried up long ago.

So there was no water below Whistler Bridge to make a satisfying plunk, only ground, on which my pebbles would thump or thud, or occasionally scrunch into a wad of brush.

But there had never been a clink.

At the curious sound I turned around and stuck my face out the bridge window, searching below in the general direction of my throw until I finally saw the culprit. Tumbled among a bed of weeds and wildflowers was an old Gilbreth-glass bottle. My pebble must have hit it.

I jogged out of the bridge and slid down the ravine wall, puzzling my feet through storm-strewn debris and late-blooming wildflowers until I reached the bottle. A closer inspection revealed a bit of paper rolled up inside.

I'd seen about a million bottles like it before. Like most kids in town, I even had five or six of my own at home, though none had notes tucked in them.

Glassblowing was the shiniest jewel in the crown of our artisan town. No matter which of the local glass families blew it, if it was made here, it was called Gilbreth glass. Gilbreth glass was everywhere in this place. Fancier stuff, yeah, but every glassblower was required to make village bottles through a village heritage partnership. Anywhere from two to five inches high, different colors, each one unique.

The welcome center had a big basket of them to give away for free, and all the school tours that got bused in were given bottles so they could show them to their parents, who were supposed to hop in their cars and come back to blow large wads of cash in the village.

This one was a nice green-blue, but scratched and aged looking, like it had been left there for years and years and nobody had picked it up. It was a ghost of a bottle, faded and fogged over, like sea glass. I took out my tool-belt tweezers (when you're a Treat, random splinters make themselves known at all hours) and pulled on the paper.

When I had the message in my hand, I thought twice.

Treats were good people. People of character. Definitely not peepers-of-bottle-messages-that-didn't-belong-to-them sort of folk.

But darn it, I really wanted to know what that paper said. My morals seemed to be having an off day. According to one of Uncle Theo's more entertaining and informative books, *Roller Coaster: The Oft-Nauseating Ups and Downs of Parenting Kids, Tweens, Teens, and Twentysomethings Who Won't Leave the House*, that could happen. It was normal and not a concern unless questionable choices became a pattern.

I took a breath and unrolled the paper.

The message was just three words, bloated from either groundwater or the previous night's rainstorm: *Are you there?*

I looked around me and saw no one. Of course I saw no one. Clearly, someone had tossed the bottle in the ravine days ago, maybe weeks, or maybe it'd been carried there by a squirrel or bird or raccoon.

The only thing within sight that didn't belong by the bridge was a shovel and rake propped up against a tree far down the trail. It must have been left by Will Wharton, the local maintenance man and my uncle's best friend.

I read the bottle message's words again and wondered who they had been written by and who they were for. I pictured a skinny, bearded, loony man, sitting on the bridge like it was a desert island he needed to be rescued from, so crazy from being alone in the world that he had no idea he'd thrown the bottle into a dry creek bed instead of salty seawater.

A low gust of wind lurking in some corner of the woods freed itself, sending faint mutterings through leafy branches. Muted groaning came from the bridge above me, as though someone was stepping on it or leaning against the side nearest me.

Originally named Whistler Bridge because of my ancestors' tendency to blow tunes while hammering away, the name still worked because of the noises it made when breezes and gusts sailed through spaces in a few time-warped side boards. Depending on the wind's strength, the sounds ranged from warbled whispering to muffled moaning to haunting, high-pitched shrieking that could be heard far through the woods.

"Hello?" I called. Nobody answered, which made perfect sense because nobody was around. It was the wind. Whistling, the way you might expect a bridge called Whistler to do.

The noises all made very nice and tidy and logical sense. I pushed the message back into the bottle, which I tucked neatly into my tool-belt pocket.

Are you there?

It seemed an odd choice of question to just throw into the world. Then again, hadn't that same question been on my mind lately? Directed at my father—my other half? I'd just kept it to myself, though. Maybe the writer of the note didn't expect any answer. He or she had just gotten tired of carrying the words inside.

"Am I here? Why, yes," I said, watching a gaggle of geese heading south overhead in a ragged V.

"Yes," I repeated louder. "Minna Treat *is* here, and she

wants her junior artisan project to go away. But she'd settle for knowing who left this message."

The geese flew on, leaving me with one more secret identity to uncover on my own.

As I scrambled up the closest ravine wall, my foot hooked on an exposed root and I tumbled into a big wad of brush. A thorny branch slashed my forearm, and a thin red line appeared. I sucked it away, and the blood faded to a dull pink scratch.

Wiping a cobweb from my eyes, I struggled free, scooted up to the bridge, and hurried through Whistler for the second time, the ancient boards creaking beneath my feet, sending up small clouds of dry, windswept dirt that followed the wake of my walk, swirling up, almost reaching toward me, smelling faintly of dead leaves and wood dust.

I stuck one hand into my pocket and traced the bottle's outline, remembering Mrs. Poppy's words.

A journey of great discovery. Or great danger.

A great trouble. An accident.

Fire.

Though I was fairly certain that I wouldn't be having sixteen children, I suddenly had the strangest feeling that she'd gotten at least part of her prediction right. Was one of the things she'd mentioned destined to be in my near future?

I wasn't sure I wanted to find out.

Process, Don't Panic

The founders and residents of Gilbreth have a long history of tenacity in the face of disasters, large and small. As their first job off the merchant ship in the winter of 1693, the Treat brothers were hired to make barstools, a vital commission that went unpaid when the pub owner came down with a lethal infection that originated with diseased ticks passed to him by his dog, an adamant bed sleeper. Desperate for food and warmth, Elias traded the twelve handcrafted stools to the man's wife for four bowls of stew and an English lullaby.

–From ***Gilbreth History: Founding Families & Artisanal Traditions*** (Gilbreth Welcome Center, $16.99)

The next morning I woke to the smell of pumpkin spice mixed with animal breath, a little bit of slimy wetness on my chest, the weight of a good-size boulder pinning me down, the sinister hacking sound of an axman chopping, and a crick in my neck, with a small bump right in the middle of the sorest spot.

The boulder weight, animal breath, and wetness could be traced to my drooling dog.

The axman was just my uncle, grunting while cutting a fresh cord of wood from thick, storm-fallen branches in the backyard.

I'd slept on my pillow wrong, which explained the sore neck.

The bump, however, was a mystery that I had an unfortunate inkling about.

"*Off*, Beastie."

Beast was kind enough to lick my face only a few times before launching himself to the floor with a boom that was distinctly more boomish than six months earlier. I would need to cut down on slipping my scraps under the table, which was a shame, because the dog seemed to enjoy boxed pasta and rice dinners far more than I did. Come to think of it, I would need to have a word with Uncle Theo; four nights of Tuna/Hamburger/Chicken Helper in one week was at least two too many.

For now I stumbled to the bathroom with bleary, waking eyes, scratching my skin and trying to blink my sleeping world into reality. Rifling through the drawers, I found a hand mirror and used it to reflect off the wall mirror. Half cross-eyed with effort, I focused on my neck and tried not to gag.

The deer tick was half buried and engorged, meaning it had been feeding for several hours. Ticks were the bane of New York's tall-grass meadows, forests, and scratchy bushes, usually attaching themselves to ankles and legs. I'd never gotten one on my neck.

"Happy Monday to me," I grumbled. I eyed a pair of tweezers but dismissed them immediately—one bad pluck and the head would be stuck in my neck for good.

There were only two solid ways of getting rid of a tick. Painting it with nail polish and waiting for it to suffocate would work fine, but I had school and didn't care to take a tick with me.

Matches, it was. A few seconds with direct fire burning its booty and the tick would back right out where we could give it an execution worthy of a town that had once hanged a witch.

I gave Beastie a good, solid glare. "You looked pleased. Did this thing hop off you and onto me last night?"

Beastie only panted lightly with an openmouthed doggy smile.

After hefting up the bathroom window, I leaned out to yell down toward my uncle. For the last month he'd been chopping like a blizzard was heading our way. For the life of me, I couldn't figure out why he'd be out there when wood was literally spilling from the shed, other than it being the time of year when he started getting quieter and sadder until the anniversaries of Mom's and Grandma and Grandpa's deaths had passed.

But still. All that chopping was suspiciously excessive. I was certain that my uncle Theo had been keeping a whopper of a secret from me for weeks now.

Wearing Grandpa Treat's old plaid jacket and earflap hat, heavy breath forming temporary fog in the early-morning light, Uncle Theo looked like something from a different time. It'd been over three hundred years since my ancestors helped found Gilbreth, but for a moment I felt a soft dizziness wash over me, the kind that comes from living in a village where the past and present blend together so easily and so richly that the future gets swept inside as well, and time just sort of disappears.

Then I screeched for the lumberjack to "please come inside this very second—no, don't finish chopping, thank you very much!"

"Beastie, go make sure he comes."

Beast bounded out of the room. Uncle Theo had gotten him two years ago, thinking that when the dog got to his full size, it would finally be okay to leave me alone at home for an hour while he went on his morning run—the one he'd previously been doing while I was at school ever since he became my guardian. Running the gauntlet, he called it—a wide five-mile circle that went through all of Gilbreth's covered bridges.

He'd gotten the biggest, ugliest, scariest-looking Irish wolfhound puppy he could find, and Beast had turned into a big, ugly, scary-looking full-grown Irish wolfhound whose mission was to defend me, but who was more suited to make friends with squirrels.

Uncle Theo charged into the bathroom, running fingers through his mop of blond-red Viking hair. "What is it? Is it . . . you know." He reached out a hand and gave me hesitant pats on the back. "I can read you that book again. The one with the lotus flower on the cover?"

Oh *Lord*. "*No*," I answered. The last thing I needed after discovering a bloodsucking tick was my uncle giving me a talk about *menstruation* and showing me the cabinet he'd filled two years ago with pads of every size, tampons galore, Advil, Tylenol, Midol, chamomile tea, and my favorite red licorice in case I ever got cramps.

He'd gotten another parenting book, this one called *Mothering Menses*, and had panicked himself into thinking I would get my period and we'd be unprepared and have to go ask a neighbor girl or something like that, and he'd read in *Handle (Hormones) with Care* that embarrassing moments could lead to deep emotional scars.

So instead of that happening, I'd gotten called into the school nurse's office the day after his purchases because she'd heard from her sister, the cashier at the pharmacy, that Theodore Treat was loading up on period supplies. Did I need a woman to talk to about the changes my body was going through? the nurse asked. I did not, I told her.

"It's not that, it's this." I pointed to my neck. "Please, Captain, get this thing out of me."

He looked at my skin as though the tick might leap off me and plunge itself into his forehead. "Okay, Minns, let's process, not panic." I knew for a fact he'd gotten that from his newest parenting book. It was supposed to be instructions for *him*, not me.

He reminded me that I'd gotten ankle ticks almost every year, and there was extra spray in the attic somewhere and that I should be wearing it until the first snowfall. He said it was no big deal. He gently told me, while putting on rubber gloves and mumbling about matches, not to worry, because it would only hurt a little, and yes, it looked like the biggest one he'd ever seen, but it would definitely, almost certainly, probably come out without a trip to the doctor. So I *processed* instead of panicking.

I processed while Uncle Theo returned suspiciously pleased-looking from the attic.

I processed while he lit the match and told me not to move a muscle.

I processed while the flame came close and when he blew it out and pressed the seared end firmly against the evil intruder, who dutifully backed out and was promptly put to death beneath Uncle Theo's boot while I applied a small bandage to my neck.

I even processed while he cupped a hand over my face

and blasted me with a fog of tick repellent, smiled a heavy-hearted smile, and told me that my mom had gotten one in the exact same spot at my age.

"I told her it was a vampire wolf tick and she'd turn to dust in sunlight, so she'd better go live in the attic." He let out a low chuckle. "Then she locked me in the attic for an hour."

It was always awkward when he shared memories of Mom, especially the weirder ones. I never knew what to say. And if he expected me to feel a bond with my dead mother because we'd gotten ticks in the same place, perhaps he was reading the wrong parenting books. Smoothing the bandage, I cleared my throat. "Well, maybe you deserved it."

"Maybe it's a sign," he said, glancing at the photograph of Mom on the bathroom wall. It was bordered by four sticks, connected by wound rainbow string—another frame I'd made several years back. Uncle Theo made sure there was a picture of her in every room of the house, all of them harbored within a Minna-made frame.

"A sign of what?" A sign that Mom's ghost wanted me to have my blood sucked in the same spot as her? Really, I wanted to be fully sympathetic, but he was seriously reaching. And I was starting to notice that despite his staggering supply of books on parenting, not a single one dealt with the fact that I'd lived my entire life without a father.

His eyes lingered on Mom. "Nothing, nothing. Is Christopher coming over for breakfast this morning?" he asked, looking in the mirror and finger-combing his beard. "I saw him walking across the yard about fifteen minutes ago. He jumped like I'd set the hose on him when I called his name. PS, that boy has been killing our milk situation. He chugged three full glasses yesterday, and I didn't have any left for my coffee."

Crash was one of eight siblings, ages ranging from six to twenty-five. His oldest brother had fallen in love with an oil painter from California and now blew glass in San Francisco, and his oldest sister was the "lost" Lorelei that Mrs. Poppy had been gossiping about. The rest of the older bunch were glassblowers who lived in Gilbreth and used the Hardly studio space on Town Square.

Crash had been hanging out at our house a lot this past year. He'd show up in my kitchen before school, slurping down cereal and chatting while Uncle Theo gave me a *Jeez Louise, he's over here again* look behind him.

"He was just cutting through the yard again, trying to make sure Loose Change didn't follow him."

"Loose change? Somebody spill a piggy bank that I don't know about?"

"That's what he calls Lem and Chai. Crash says he's the oops, they're the loose change." Lemongrass and Chai were Crash's six-year-old twin brother and sister, so named because by the time the Hardlys sat down to decide what to call the coming bundles of joy, they were so tired of brainstorming baby names that they simply went with the kind of tea they happened to be drinking.

"Nobody's an oops."

I looked left, then right, then crooked a finger toward him. "Says the man raising the oops," I whispered.

He bent down and took my face between his plate-size hands. "Stop. You were the apple of your mother's eye." He inhaled a long, slow breath, like he was about to Zen himself up before jumping into a pool's deep end. "It was like . . . it was like after you were born, she reabsorbed you into her body, and then her heart became this big blob of beating Minna."

It was uncomfortable seeing my giant, bearded uncle's lips get trembly and his eyes get glassy with a coming emotional flood right after he'd brought up my period and sprayed me for ticks, plus his calluses were making my face itch, so I pulled away and opted for the obvious response.

"That's really gross. And the apple thing makes no sense. Anyway, Crash told me he had something to do before school started, and most people get jumpy around men with axes. And he's a growing boy and calcium is important. And PS, he likes to be called Crash."

Uncle Theo wiped up a few long black hairs I'd shed, then picked up my towel and threw it in the hamper. "I know that. I'm not calling him Crash. And adding half a cup of our chocolate syrup to his milk isn't helping him grow, so don't nutrition-fact me, Dr. Minna. Get dressed quick, food's on the table." He dropped a kiss on my head.

I stood on his feet and gave him a squench, which is like a hug, only tighter. "Thanks." He smelled like wood and sweat and deodorant. I took an extra-long sniff of his shirt, then hopped back to the floor.

"Oh, and have you thought more about what you're going to enter in the junior artisan contest? If you're going to actually submit something, I mean."

He said it too casually, which meant he'd been waiting for the right time to bring it up since he woke up that morning. "You know you don't *have* to. But it's getting late in the game to decide."

It was his hoping eyes that did me in. They crinkle when he talks about something he wants in a joking way, but when he wants it really, really, really bad, the crinkle is followed by a flash of the most open, raw *Puh-leeease, world, it's been a tough few years, just let me have this* one *thing before you find a way to kick me down again* look. And there's not much I can do about it when that happens except melt and nod and agree that he deserves all the things in the world.

"Don't worry, I'm all in."

Relief flooded his face. "I'm all ears if you want to knock around ideas."

"I know you are. How's your headache?"

"Better. So what are you thinking, projectwise?"

"I'm still narrowing it down. There's plenty of time."

"Twenty-one days left, but who's counting? Not me, no sir." Uncle Theo stepped to the door, cringing at the loose, rattling door handle. "Everything is breaking around here," he muttered with a sigh, then shot me a twinkly-eyed grin that looked just a tad bit wilted. "I love you. Happy Monday. By the way, Beast ate your pancakes when he came down to get me, but I put out some cereal. Now hurry up or you'll miss your homeroom and make me look irresponsible when we both know I'm perfect. PS, speaking of perfect, have I told you lately how tick-free and trouble-free and perfect you are?"

I nodded and started to brush my hair into a ponytail. "You have, Captain."

After Uncle Theo left the room, I processed the scrap of paper that had dropped out of his shirt pocket as he bent over to clean up my fallen hair.

Vickerston Realty—107 S. Fry Street

Linda Roberts—Sunday, 2:30 p.m.

Apartment/townhouse—2 bed, 1 bath

Vickerston was a city ten times the size of Gilbreth about three hours away. I was no expert, but it seemed strange for my uncle to have a note about finding an apartment that was hours away when he already had a whole house here in Gilbreth.

Then again, according to *IMAX Nation: How Your Small Child Sees Things in a Big Way*, it was possible that my developing mind might exaggerate and misunderstand the note to the point of making myself upset, even though it could be any number of things, for instance:

Some client who'd called about furniture needed for an office or apartment or townhouse

Another lady who Uncle Theo just *had* to meet, pushed on him by some other well-meaning villager

A scrap of paper that he'd found on a sidewalk and had been keeping in his shirt pocket to throw out but then forgot about

There were tons of possibilities. Limitless, really. Most likely it was a harmless nothing, absolutely nothing to do with his stress headache.

Still, after staring at the note and thinking for a minute, I let Beast give it a good sniff. He gave it one lick and sneezed.

I didn't like the look of it either, so I crumpled the paper and tossed it into the trash. It was kind of wet and blurry from the bathroom floor anyway. Plus, now it had Beast saliva and snot on it. Not the sort of thing Uncle Theo needed to be carrying around in his pocket.

I was doing him a favor.

I was very well adjusted like that.

I was also, I saw from the clock in the kitchen as I ran out the door, going to get a tardy if I didn't hurry.

"Back to Whistler," I yelled at Beast, slamming the door behind me and scooping a wishing stone from the edge of our dirt driveway.

Regarding the Chandler

In 1699 the first covered bridge in Gilbreth was built by Elias Treat and his brothers over a large, unnamed creek in what is now known as Torrey Wood. The bridge materials and many settlement supplies were paid for by Thomas P. Gilbreth, a kindhearted and fully reformed con artist who had traveled overseas with a fortune stolen from a balding pirate desperate for hair tonic.

–From **Gilbreth History: Founding Families & Artisanal Traditions** (Gilbreth Welcome Center, $16.99)

After I tossed my pebble against the wall of Whistler, killing my wish for a brilliant junior artisan project idea to hit me that day, I glanced through the window I'd missed and saw a sparkle.

Another bottle. Again it was nestled among the wildflowers that billowed out from beneath the bridge in blue waves, like a small sea covering the ravine floor.

I hurried down to it. This one was dry and clear, with an unsoaked message poking out, inviting me to read it. It had been thrown or placed there recently.

The chandler can no longer make his own candles.

Another strange thing to stick in a bottle and throw away. A chandler was a candlemaker. We had three chandlers in Gilbreth, but only one was a man—my next-door neighbor Mr. Abel, who also came from a founding family and was the oldest person in Gilbreth.

If it was true that he'd finally gotten to the point where he couldn't make candles anymore, it wasn't a very nice thing for someone to be writing about. I felt a little embarrassed just reading it. Uncle Theo once told me that the day his grandfather told the family that he no longer had the strength or aim to hammer a nail was sadder for everyone than the day he died.

A gust of wind rustled the branches of trees around the bridge. Within the ravine, fallen leaves surged up around my ankles with eerie, almost insistent nudging.

I thought I heard a muttering noise somewhere nearby. I looked behind me. Nobody was around. I even looked up in the trees. It was probably a squirrel stirring. The forest was full of them. Deer, too, but they were mostly shy, and you only knew they'd been around from the piles of marble-shaped poop they left behind.

It definitely wasn't a spirit of any kind. Treats, while having the highest respect for our dead relatives, are too practical to believe in that sort of thing. But still . . .

I felt watched.

And there was a history of the bridge being haunted.

The autumn that Elizabeth Maybeck had been hanged, strange things began to happen in Torrey Wood, where she was buried—people losing things or getting headaches or hearing faint, far-off cries.

A drought followed her death and that's when the Torrey Wood creek that had connected two rivers dried up completely. Two low natural dams gradually built up on either end.

The ravine had been empty ever since.

During the worst of the drought it was said that the forest around the bridge still thrived with life, as though it had some secret water source all its own. Some said that Elizabeth Maybeck's unmarked grave was close to the bridge, and it was her bewitched blood that helped keep the land flourishing near her body.

When the superstitious locals came up with a song about the five bridges of Gilbreth, they gave an especially eerie tribute to Whistler.

Last o'er North Bridge, wealth come soon,
East grants wishes each full moon,
West, leave clear Midsummer Eve,
Come by South Bridge, never leave,
Whistler Bridge, be warned, be warned,

There wait souls of maids unmourned,
There wait souls of maids unmourned.

The final lines of "The Bridge Ballad" were especially creepy during Autumnfest, when folksingers performed it before and after each theatrical hanging of Elizabeth Maybeck.

Plus, those last lines always reminded me of what happened with my mom—but she had a nice spot in the family plot over at the Gilbreth Cemetery, and Uncle Theo spent enough time mourning there for the both of us, so I didn't let the words bother me personally. Too much.

I put the paper back and stashed the bottle in my tool belt, next to the first one, because (a) nobody likes a litterbug and (b) it didn't seem like a particularly nice note and I didn't want anyone else finding it. I'd be doing Mr. Abel a favor by keeping it, right? Right. His candling was his own business.

A turtledove swooped down from the sky, blasting through a leafy branch with a rushing sound while on its way to the dove boxes to eat. A dozen birds were already there. It was late.

"I'm late too," I said, rushing off to school, trying not to think of the other note I'd found that morning—the one that my uncle had dropped. Despite the perfectly legitimate possibilities, I had a very bad feeling about that one.

The Wrong Kind of Woodsmoke

In 1701, Samuel Treat nearly got kicked out of the settlement after accidentally starting a fire in the newly built and dedicated church building. According to Elias Treat's journal, his brother was an idiot who deserved the chin burns he'd gotten when his beard went up in flames. As punishment, twenty-three-year-old Samuel was forced to build wooden stocks, which he was locked in for three days. Village children were encouraged to pelt him with twigs and chicken bones.

–From **Gilbreth History: Founding Families & Artisanal Traditions** (Gilbreth Welcome Center, $16.99)

By Wednesday of that week I was still quietly festering about the unimportance of my uncle's note, which fully explained the small lapse in judgment I had in bringing primitive fire-starting materials to school.

Crash and I had sneaked into Craft Room 3 during the lunch hour because he'd forgotten to soak his basket reeds. Everyone at Gilbreth School was required to take two arts classes per semester, outside their family specialty if they had one. Nobody else was in there, and it seemed the perfect opportunity to test out a different sort of practical art.

"Any new project ideas today?" Crash asked, his eyes steady on the table in front of us.

"Just the one we're working on." Arm muscles burning, I glanced out the tall windows along the wall.

Against a blue sky that looked calm and clear of clouds, branches of the school-yard maple trees swept violently back and forth in the wind. It was the biting kind, I could tell— the kind of strange freezing bursts that swept through Gilbreth this time of year, bringing inevitable changes, touching leaves that stubbornly clung to green and transforming them to blood crimson and pumpkin orange and dandelion yellow, hinting to shop owners that peak tourist season was on its last legs and warning teachers to stock up on hand sanitizer for flu season.

A squeaky chuckle cracked out from my best friend's throat, then burrowed itself down. His voice was changing, which made me feel slightly bothered and anxious, a natural reaction according to *Twitch, Cry, Hide: Parenting Your Child's Reactions to Change*. A hot drink, a mineral bath, and a heart-to-heart chat were the suggested calming remedy, but I was too busy and too self-aware and too at school for that kind of coddling.

"Don't know if they'll accept this as an entry," Crash said. "Maybe if you made a really big one. That would be unique. And bold."

"Don't forget special. Probably not an option, though. Especially if we can't even get this one to work. What are you going to make?"

He shrugged. "My parents haven't said anything to me about it. Maybe I won't even enter."

"You have to enter something." I was about to remind him of his duty to his family when the scent dearest to my heart swirled into my nostrils.

The woodsmoke plume rising from the space below my hands was only a small one, but after eight minutes of taking turns putting consistent pressure on the small hollow I'd carved into a rectangular scrap of pine from the barn, both Crash and I cheered out loud when it finally appeared.

Crash ducked his head and softly blew while I rubbed the starter stick vigorously back and forth in an inch-long straight track toward the shavings to create friction and heat. The scent of burning wood grew stronger.

"Scratch my nose. Please. Then hurry and switch with me, my hands are cramping up."

"Mine are still stiff." Crash leaned toward me and addressed the itch.

"Fine," I said, ignoring a wrist cramp. "Open a window, will you?"

He scooted to the nearest of the three large windows in the classroom and hefted up the glass, then waved at something on the second-floor sill. "Shoo!" Wings flapped. "It's just sitting there." He waved again. "Dumb bird won't go away. It's one of those turtledoves from the wood flock."

"Just leave it. Get back here, please, I need you."

"Okay, okay. Bird, you stay outside."

With Crash taking over blow duty, it only took another minute before a small flame appeared. He added the shavings I'd carved away from the starter stick, thin layers of wood and bark. "Keep going!" He clapped as the flame became a tiny blaze, and the window bird let out a tweet. "That's right, bird," he told it, pounding his chest. "We. Made. Fire!"

Less cheerworthy was the massive breeze that swept through the open window, straight past our small gathering and into the stack of dried field grass and cornstalks belonging to the class. There was a surprisingly quiet *whoosh* and *whomp* sound, and then Crash and I stared in horror at the bonfire we'd created.

Inside the school.

I rushed for the nearest water source, a long plastic bin half full of soaking reeds of various thicknesses. While Crash bolted for the wall's fire extinguisher, I heaved the bin up, struggled to the blaze, leaned my head away, and dumped it over.

Crash lunged to spray the remaining flames and me with white retardant. The door clicked open, and Grace Ripty walked in, a book clutched in her hand.

Grace was the daughter of the new town mayor. Over the summer they'd moved here from California, and she sat next to me in three classes. She took one look at the scene and her mouth dropped open. She just stood there, blocking the door, trying to figure out what we were doing.

She always wore a uniform of heavy necklaces and all-black shirts, pants, skirts, leggings, and sweatshirts and didn't talk much, mostly just lurked around with her hair hanging in her face. She was certainly what Mrs. Poppy might call *a bit of an odd duck*. Then again, Mrs. Poppy had said the same about Crash, so *odd duck* wasn't necessarily a negative to me.

She usually finished her in-class work fast and then whipped out old-looking books. At our last school library day I'd heard her telling the librarian that she only liked to read mysteries.

She took school notes in a regular blue notebook but had a miniature one as well that she kept in her pocket and occasionally took out and scribbled in.

Also, she was one of those people who didn't mind looking right at you for long periods of time. Type-one starers are just staring at something stareworthy, like a car accident or a shooting star. Type twos look at you but don't realize they're so obviously staring. Type threes know that you know that they're staring at you, but don't care. Grace was a type three.

An eighth-grade girl passing by stopped and peered in. "What's going on?"

"Nothing!" I said. "Everything's under control. No need to get help or anything."

The older girl smirked. "Sure. I won't say a word." With that, she hurried back the way she'd come.

I turned to Grace, who had managed to close her mouth. "Would you, um, mind just not saying anything about this?" I asked her.

Grace's gaze swept over the room, settling on me in unnerving intensity. "Okay." She left without another word.

Crash slumped to the floor. "That eighth grader was Angelina Burkoff. She's a blacksmith's daughter."

"Just because she's a blacksmith doesn't mean she's untrustworthy." I took over the extinguisher and sprayed a final blast at the blackened grasses and stalks. "But you're right. She's totally gonna tell. Tag team time?"

"Tag team time," he agreed.

"So the breeze came out of nowhere, did it?" Principal Gunter asked.

She wore a thick blue cardigan over her turtleneck, even though the office was plenty hot thanks to a space heater she had plugged into the corner. The principal had pasty white skin with visible veins that plumped a good eighth-inch high on her hands. She liked to wear layers, and she was always overdressed. There were rumors that she was part vampire, but Uncle Theo said she probably just got cold a lot because being around a school full of kids for the last thirty years had given her circulation problems.

"That's right," I said firmly, trying not to inhale the odor from the clothes I'd put on to replace my fire-retardant-covered jeans and T-shirt. Forgot-to-take-home-to-wash gym clothes, to be precise.

"Angelina informed me that you two should have been in the cafeteria. Why were you in the weaving classroom?"

"It's hard to pin down, really," I told her, keeping my face straight, and keeping my words few and deliberate. *Pants on Fire: 78 Ways to Tell When Your Child Is Lying* was clear about elaborate explanations, evasive facial expressions, and back-tracking being indicative of lying. And there really was no getting out of it. We'd started a fire. "I suppose you could say loyalty had a lot to do with it. Loyalty to the school, loyalty to friendship, loyalty to—"

"Maybe Christopher can tell me," she said, fixing Crash with an impressive stare that had me thinking she'd be a heck of a parent if she ever had any kids of her own. Parenting books loved to talk about eye contact being essential for both empathetic and firm conversations. Principaling books probably did the same.

"It's one of my specials," he bellowed. The Hardlys had

lungs the size of party balloons and were all loud talkers. His voice had always been an uncontrollable blast of noise, and no matter how many times teachers told him to keep quiet during group work, it just wasn't in him to whisper.

"Elaborate," she ordered, blinking a few times. "More softly, please."

"Well," Crash said, "I was soaking my field reeds so they'd be soft and supple for this afternoon's class, because I forgot to do it yesterday. Minna was just keeping me company, and she had this great idea for a . . . for a project. And she'd made this cool thing at home and had it in her backpack and . . ." He shook his head at his lap with the baffled headshake of a boy who'd never been involved in disastrous accidents, which, to be fair, was the case. At least on school property.

It was a solid performance and I let him grovel for a good three seconds. Then I took over, gesturing to the poster on her wall that featured Gilbreth's village motto, a motto that happened to be conveniently plastered on the rinsed and wrung-out T-shirt from last year's Autumnfest that I held in my lap.

"What I made was a tool that people made in the past— far back in the past," I reminded her, placing an open palm over my heart and gesturing to the poster's words with my other hand, like the assistant on a game show that Uncle Theo liked to watch. "'The past tells us where we came from, what we are, and who we want to be,'" I read, lifting my head and looking vaguely into the distance (okay, at the wall) for maximum effect. "I suppose Christopher and I just wanted to try something our ancestors had done. Something that took real skill and . . . and perseverance."

"Perseverance!" Crash said-shouted-echoed, then clapped a hand over his mouth and shrugged an apology. "Perseverance," he whispered.

"Isn't it good to honor ancestors, Principal Gunter? Isn't it," I said, risking an overdramatization that would lessen my argument and tip off the interrogator that I was (a) out of real excuses and (b) not particularly sorry, "almost our *duty* to seek out the past and learn from it?"

She tapped a pencil against her stapler and pursed her lips in a way that told me I'd overshot, just a bit. "Not by starting fires next to a large pile of dried grass and cornstalks in the weaving room."

"Well, no," I admitted. "But we were only trying to—"

"Start a fire," she supplied, nostrils flaring, moving in and out like billowing jellyfish. "You were attempting to start a fire inside the school. Correct?"

"Well, technically . . . okay yes, but—"

"What were you planning on doing after the fire had started?"

"I . . ." Hmm. She had me on that one. "I didn't even know it would work. I didn't think that far ahead."

She nodded, agreeing with me. "Maybe you should have."

"Yes, ma'am," I said, actually meaning it in this particular case.

"Those were for Autumnfest decorations."

Well, as Uncle Theo would say, poopsidaisy. Autumnfest decorations were actually important.

Autumnfest was two straight days of practical folk art demonstrations, historical tours, and public storytellings. Business from craft booths and shops, and commissioned orders during the fest were important sources of income for the whole town. Plus, the witch hangings, acted out by community theater members—four per day so that more visitors could witness the spectacle—were disturbingly popular to watch. Probably like they were in 1600s Salem or 1718 Gilbreth.

"I'll bet the Wheeler Farm can give them more stalks. They grew over twenty acres of corn this year. Crash and I did a two-week apprenticeship in the goat barn this summer."

Crash nodded. "Eight goats got kidney stones while we were there. Do you know what you have to do when a goat gets a kidney stone?"

Principal Gunter frowned. "No. I don't."

"You don't want to," he said gravely.

"You don't," I agreed.

"Getting back to the matter at hand, Angelina informed me that this isn't the first time you two were missing from the cafeteria during your lunch hour. Her younger sister says you never eat there. Care to explain?"

I was prepared. "Fierce individuality is a trait common to many historical leaders. And we're allowed to eat in the library and hallways. We got permission." I did not add that the permission had been granted by the maintenance woman, Mrs. Needham.

"And we have a fear of crowds, maybe?" Crash suggested.

She looked carefully at Crash's special outfit of the day. Every fall when school started, Crash tried out a different costume each day right up until Halloween, when he'd choose his favorite. He'd been doing it since first grade.

My personal favorite was when he'd come to school as Nickola Tesla last September and claimed that Gilbreth was permanently stuck in a time travel bubble, which meant that trying to create your own future was useless, and also that the time bubble made homework irrelevant (he'd forgotten his).

Since he mostly stuck to historical figures and our school was big on the arts and creativity, the teachers never complained.

Today he was wearing a tan sheet toga worn tastefully over a tan shirt and khakis, with a fig-leaf crown resting lightly over his curly brown hair, and a Minna-carved stylus tucked behind one ear.

"Hmm." The principal's eyes flickered across the outer edge of my wardrobe's near-constant companion, a tool belt inherited from Grandpa Treat. Today it held two pencils, tweezers, a twig that looked like a praying mantis, and the two bottles I'd found.

She let out a long, controlled breath from her nose—a principal's sigh. "Never mind. You two have never been troublemakers. But there has to be a consequence." She tapped a finger on the desk and raised a thick eyebrow at the poster, as though expecting it to name an appropriate penance. "You're both entering a project in the junior contest?"

"Of course," I said, summoning a large smile. "Absolutely."

"Good. I remember when your uncle won. That's a lot to live up to."

"Yes, ma'am."

"Speaking of your uncle, will you let him know I'm happy to be a reference from academia? It's for his résumé. He . . ." Mrs. Gunter eyed me carefully and then rearranged the fake flowers sticking out of a root beer bottle on her desk. "He called me about . . ." Her words faded out to nothing.

Fading words to nothing is something people do when they've said too much. Ideally, she should have recovered with a fake sneeze, to explain the awkward pause, and then delivered some sort of excuse, the way Uncle Theo does whenever I walk in on him talking about me on the phone with someone.

Instead Principal Gunter studied us, then studied a piece of paper in front of her. I scanned the words upside down, a talent I'd developed at an early age when Uncle Theo and I had reading dinners and I was either bored with my own book or wanted to know what parenting tips he was learning. It was a request for acorns from a first-grade teacher. Torrey Wood was full of acorns this time of year.

"We'll do that," I said, pointing to the paper. "It says they need the tops of them attached, so you can't buy them at the store. We'll gather the acorns for you. It'll take ages and we'll think about not starting fires the whole time." In the very back of my mind I knew I should be trying to get out of a punishment so I had more time to work on my project.

But the bottle full of flowers had reminded me of the messages I'd found. Gathering acorns was a solid excuse to get near Whistler again. Would another bottle be under the bridge? What might it say? "Right, Crash?"

Crash shifted in his chair. "Um . . . right?"

The principal eyed the two of us for a moment, then glanced at the clock like she was counting the hours until she could go home. "Fine. You two will gather two full paper grocery sacks and deliver them by Monday. I *will* be calling your parents and your uncle, Minna as soon as I get the chance today. Another incident like this will lead to suspension. Christopher, do your weaving assignments on time. Minna, quit bringing flammables to school. Now get to class, and eat in the cafeteria from now on."

"Yes, Principal Gunter," we both barked.

On the way back to class we walked past the hideous painting of mine that Mrs. Bruno had hung in the display case outside of the general art room. There were twelve of us in that class, and all twelve landscapes-of-the-world paintings were plastered there, almost demanding to be ridiculed. Most were okay, but mine was terrible. It looked like something a five-year-old would make.

Crash paused at the case, looking for the one with my name on the bottom. "Maybe you could enter a painting for your artisan project instead of making something out of wood."

"Nope. Treats do wood, the same way Hardlys do glass. Besides, mine's on the far right."

His lips twisted to the side, but he didn't laugh. He even managed to look a little sad for me and my terrible, talentless paint job. "Oh. Yeah. You're definitely a wood person."

"Speaking of which, how about a giant whittled apple?"

"Not bold enough."

"Or a new desk for Principal Gunter, with extra drawers to keep extra sweaters and socks?"

"Not unique."

"A special freestanding wardrobe for all of your historical outfits?"

He shook his head. "Not necessary."

I shook my head back at him. "And you're not helpful. You want to come home with me after school? We could walk down the alley and peek in the back workroom at the silversmith's shop to see if there are any clues about what the Johnsons are making."

Malia and Jaron Johnson were in our class, and they were both my biggest competition for the contest. Jaron had already won some big junior craftsman title and was prone to overwearing his JUNIOR MASTER shirts. Malia was adopted, but seemed to have inherited the Johnson touch anyway. She was even better than her brother.

Crash adjusted his toga. "Nah, they wouldn't leave anything out where people could see it, even through a back window. And I'm busy after school this week." He clapped a hand on my shoulder. "Don't worry. You know tons about woodworking. You *are* woodworking. You'll think of something good. Come on, let's get to class."

I knew I could think of something good. I *did* know tons about all kinds of wood. That wasn't the problem. The problem was that I lived in a town where plenty of twelve-year-olds were already well on their way to being masters of their craft.

My project had to be better than good. It had to be perfect.

Scavenged Corn and a Spy

In 1702 a widower stonemason named Thomas Maybeck joined the settlement with his eight-year-old daughter, Elizabeth. Elizabeth had a quiet nature and a general sadness about her that was alleviated by time spent with animals and the kindness of Elias Treat, who took to carving small birds and whistles for the child. The villagers thought her odd, saying that she read too much, used large words, and seemed to enjoy spying on them as they went about their days.

–From **Gilbreth History: Founding Families & Artisanal Traditions** (Gilbreth Welcome Center, $16.99)

Kicking leaves from the previous night's windstorm off the curb, I stepped onto the cobblestone street leading into Town Square and meandered over to the curved sidewalk that horseshoed its way around the Village Green. Afternoon sun glinted off metal lampposts, and the air was threaded with the earthy scent of Wednesday wood-pulp cooking from Mr. Lee's paper and stationery shop, coffee and pastry smells from the Cutting Board Bakery, and rustic smoke from someone in the neighborhood burning a brush pile.

Gilbreth was like a wavy-edged oval, with wide, shallow rivers bordering two thirds of it. The state-famous Wheedle Pumpkin Farm was just north of the village. An extensive graveyard marked the southern border. The west side was mostly Torrey Wood, with older neighborhood homes like mine and Crash's scraping its edges. The school, post office, grocery, and other businesses were on the east side, and the rec center, park, and sports fields were on that side of Gilbreth too. Town Square and the Village Green were the heart of Gilbreth, smack dab in the middle.

I smiled hello to the owners and artists who had opened their store and studio doors to soak in the perfect autumn weather, my own body drinking in the clanging and pounding noises from the cooper's bucket and barrel shop, the lofted arguments between the ironsmith and his forge, the soft hum of the potter's storefront wheel, and the music slipping into the street from Mrs. Bhagawati's silk shop. I passed the Hardlys' glass studio and peered through the window to see if that was where Crash had rushed off to after our final class of the day.

Both Lemon and Chai wore black cowboy hats and were on the floor, surrounded by papers and markers, getting scolded by twenty-year-old Tom, who'd dyed his hair blue this week. Adam, the oldest of the Hardly kids left in Gilbreth, was in the workshop area, his face covered with a protective mask while he scrubbed at some piece of equipment. Mr. Hardly was pacing the main floor with his phone, stroking his handlebar mustache with his free hand. Crash wasn't in sight.

BAM-BAM-BAM!! The twins had sneaked away from their coloring station, and now four hands and two noses were squished against the glass by my belly. Even when they backed away, their wide eyes, freckled cheeks, matching statures, and pinecone-brown hair, cut just below the ears, made it hard to tell which twin was which. Only the glint of tiny earrings and two missing front teeth told me the one on the left was Chai.

"Where's Crash?" I yelled through the glass.

Lemon helpfully stuck out his tongue and blasted me with a finger gun.

"Don't know," screamed Chai, hopping on one foot, then the other. "It's bottle day for us. Everyone's helping, but Mom and Dad probably didn't want him around to break stuff. Maybe he has a secret girlfriend like *Tommy!*"

Crash with a secret girlfriend at twelve years old? Taking into consideration our crew's place somewhere in the lumpy middle between pariah and royalty in the general social strata of adolescence, the idea was ridiculous. Absurd. Asinine, even, per Uncle Theo's last vocab word.

Before I could think of other places my friend might be,

Tom marched over, cheeks aflame, and grabbed the two of them by the neck like a mama cat, hauling them back where they'd come from.

Lemon squirmed and screamed something about Tom stringing them up in a hangman's noose. I waved good-bye to Chai, who was trying her best to wink at me while also breaking free, failing badly on both accounts.

Outside the bakery Mrs. Willis struggled across the sidewalk to her car, muttering to herself while carrying two enormous burlap bags, one hefted across each shoulder, trapping her long, thick braid beneath in a way that had her head jerked to one side.

She always wore overalls, the front pocket stuffed with herb lollipops. A strong, tall lady with white hair and bright-pink cheeks that always look scrubbed, she'd been known to carry much more while shouting at her husband not to help, that she could handle it. But as she wobbled toward her truck bed, her foot slipped and I saw the accident seconds before it happened.

The offending foot bent and did not straighten, and she stumbled, her knees slamming into the ground before I could do much except quicken my pace.

The bags collapsed as well, one on top of her, the other directly onto a short, poky iron fence that the ironsmith had built around each of the trees placed along the sidewalk. The bag split open, spilling corn into the tree's small dirt bed and onto the street.

"Are you okay?" With effort I lifted the intact bag off her leg while she grumbled away at herself, then stood. "I'm fine, the corn's all . . . gone to poop." She waved a hand at the mess, which crows and small gray birds were already attending to. She reached into her truck bed and pulled out a plastic bin, then bent to gather handfuls where she could.

Squatting down, I lent a hand. "Shoo!" I told the birds. The small ones left, except for one that seemed to think my hand was a sandwich. I shook it and the dove chirped defeat, flicking its wings and settling in the tree above. The crows simply crossed the street and watched from a maple tree.

"Thanks, Minna," Mrs. Willis said, wiping her forehead. "Leave the rest. Birds'll get it. Those ones from the woods are getting bolder and bolder. Are you entering the contest this year? My Michael didn't enter when he was a sixth grader. He doesn't like people knowing what a good baker he is. He's delicate that way."

Her eighth-grade son, Michael, was the opposite of delicate, other than the time his pet guinea pig, Rosebud, had gotten into the street outside the bakery and was run over during Summerfest one year. He'd bawled like a baby and sat on the curb the rest of that week, just staring at the spot where it had happened. But that was an exception.

For the most part, he was a case study in proving that evolution didn't mean you couldn't also act like a caveman. At the moment he and his gang of overdeveloped, underadjusted meatheads were shoving one another on the Village Green close to a group of high school girls who were too old to notice them.

"I'm entering the contest."

She nodded approval. "Did you hear? This year the winner gets five hundred dollars and a trip to New York City to go to a schmancy traditional arts conference to meet collectors. Your uncle will be happy about that. We still miss him on the square." She looked along the shops, to the place where our store had stood for years. "Not the same without a Treat storefront."

Uncle Theo had sold the family shop on Town Square when my grandparents died. Malia and Jaron Johnson's family had won the auction to buy it after they moved here from Boston. At the time Uncle Theo had told me that we'd have a town square shop again someday. But they almost never became available, and even at twelve, I sensed that people who bought cheap toilet paper and didn't fix broken sinks wouldn't have a down payment for an expensive shop stashed away.

Mrs. Willis's eyes were misty as she glanced between the shop front and me. "Are you all . . . holding up? You and Theo?"

I held in a sigh. Every year around this time shop owners said hello to me more, patted my shoulders, gave me little treats and trinkets as Autumnfest approached. I sincerely hoped Mrs. Willis wouldn't start in with a story about my mother. "We're just fine, thank you."

"Take this," she said, passing a lollipop into my tool belt. "It's sage-basil from Mr. Poppy's." She winked. "Helps ward off the ghosts. They love coming out this time of year."

"Yes, ma'am. Thanks." A strange shadow fluttered across the corner of my eye.

Following the fleeting darkness, I saw something move inside Mr. Abel's candle shop. It was a tiny place with pale-green clapboards and a small, iron-caged lamp hanging above the door, squeezed between the bakery and a potter's studio. It hadn't been open as much as the other shops over the last year. Mr. Abel was always around town, though. Day and night he shuffled around Gilbreth with his signature cane and newsboy hat with fur flaps that he pulled down when it was cold.

Mr. Abel was really old now, which was why he came over for dinner a lot and why I went over once a month to help him write out his bills. His wife died last year, right around Autumnfest, and she'd handled all of that. They'd never had any children.

The shop was closed now, lit only by sunlight streaming through the front window. A closer look showed only semifull shelves displaying his goods. Again a dark shape moved across the back of the small room. Huh. Maybe Mr. Abel was in there organizing and didn't want any customers or friends to drop by.

"By the way," Mrs. Willis said, tilting her head toward a spot across the street. "The Ripty girl's been asking about you. Mrs. Poppy told me."

"Grace?" I paused, then slowly turned to see her looking our way from the steps of Town Hall.

Other than the brief exchange during the fire incident, we'd only had one conversation since she moved to town, and that was the day Uncle Theo had come into Mrs. Doring's classroom to drop off my forgotten homework.

Right after class I'd turned from my locker to see Grace's pale face two inches away, her black shirt covered in the bizarre amount of long necklaces she wore, silver and gold chains with varying degrees of decoration. They reminded me of the chains dragged around by that creepy what's his name that scared Ebenezer Scrooge in *A Christmas Carol*.

The one conversation we'd had went like this:

Grace: "How come everyone in this town is so obsessed with arts and crafts and stuff? I mean, a milliner shop? Who even has people make hats for them anymore?"

Me: "Um . . . I don't know. Not me. I don't."

Grace: "Was that your dad? Dropping off your home-work?"

Me: "No. That was my uncle."

Grace: "Where's your dad?

Me: "I don't know."

Grace: "Why?"

Me: "I just don't. Where's your mom?"

Grace: "In Italy."

Me: "Why?"

Grace: "Because she wanted to live in Italy. My dad didn't. I didn't either."

Me: "Oh. Is she Italian?"

Grace: "No. She just took some language classes, divorced us, then left."

Me: "Oh . . . sorry."

Grace: "I have to go to the bathroom. See you later."

And that was it.

I turned back to Mrs. Willis. "Grace was asking about *me*?"

"That's right," said Mrs. Willis. "Yesterday she asked if you'd always lived around here, then went poking into your personals. She was a bit of a pusher with the questions. Gloria didn't tell her anything other than it's impolite to gossip, though." She winked. "Girl's curious about you. Nice kid, but a bit strange. Slouched around the shops this summer like a cloud was hanging over her head."

"Oh." I didn't know what else to say. Some people were just nosy, I guess. "Good to know, thanks."

"I almost forgot, dear. Mr. Willis made you a loaf of nice wheat bread—it's right there on the counter. I was going to have Michael bring it over, but since you're here." She jerked her head toward the shop. "On that table nearest the door, dear."

"Thanks a lot." Uncle Theo and I didn't need handouts, but I wanted the bread too much to argue. I jogged inside the propped-open door, stuffed the loaf into my backpack, and kept walking.

Around a corner marched Mayor Ripty, along with a woman carrying a clipboard. Mr. Abel shuffled two feet behind them.

If that hadn't been him scooting around inside his shop, who had it been? Maybe just my eyes playing tricks on me.

"Hello, Miss Treat," called Mr. Abel, his voice dry and deep and thready, like a dusty, cobweb-filled trunk. He patted me on the shoulder and left his hand there while the mayor chatted with his assistant. His permanent-fixture brown elastic-waist pants always made a sound exactly like branches full of fall leaves rustling against one another. With a face creased and crinkly as a walnut, he got called Rip van Wrinkle by the kids at school. At closer glance I noticed that his other hand was trembling the tiniest bit.

"The chandler can no longer make his own candles," the bottle message had said. Now I felt a little squirmy having read it, like I knew a dirty rumor about him that he hadn't caught on to yet.

"Hi, Mr. Abel."

"And how is your wood project coming? I trust it has Minna Treat written all over it."

The mayor and his assistant were still deep in discussion.

"Can I tell you something?" Mr. Abel wasn't a woodworker, but he knew how to keep a secret. Last year when he wasn't feeling up to trick-or-treaters, he left a full bowl of candy outside his door. Crash and I took every piece, only noticing that we were being watched from the front window after our pillowcases were stuffed. He never said a word to Uncle Theo. I leaned toward my neighbor. "I'm not sure I know exactly who Minna Treat is supposed to be," I whispered.

"Is that right?" He bent to let his forehead touch mine. "Minna dear, if you're feeling lost, you might try looking to the past to find yourself. It's always there with you, waiting to be needed for one reason or another. At least, that's what I tell myself, but then again, at ninety-four, my life is mostly past now." His chuckle was a gravel-filled sound, like the one made by our broken garbage disposal. "Can you and your uncle help an old man out this evening, by any chance? I've got a couple of things I'd love to get out of my attic."

"Sure, Mr. Abel. We'll do it after dinner. You can come over around six o'clock. It's spaghetti night. Again. Just like the last three times you've had dinner with us." I adjusted my backpack straps. "Sorry about that, but it's better than the Tuna Helper."

His eyes creased merrily and he tipped his hat. "Spaghetti's my favorite, Minna."

The mayor caught sight of me and opened his mouth like he was going to say something. But he didn't. Not right away. He just stared for a few seconds with a tilted head and a puzzled pigeon look on his face, before replacing it with an unreadable smile.

"Minna *Treat*? From one of our oldest, most respected

clans! How delightful. Looking forward to the festival?"

I was, but the way he said it made me want to say something rude, which is a natural gut reaction for some preteens and teens when facing authority. There was a whole chapter on triggers and involuntary rebelling in one of the parenting books I'd read. "Yes, sir."

"Sir?" He turned to the clipboard woman. "You see? This is what I love about an old-fashioned town. Ever since I heard about this place years ago, I've wanted to live here. Gilbreth sounded enchanting—the person who told me about it described it as having some sort of magic lingering up its very old sleeve. Nice and safe, too, with a few exceptions that I'm hoping to make improvements on. This place seems like a fit for me, don't you think, Minna?"

Sunlight glinted along his slick streaks of oiled hair every time his big head moved. He and his daughter were outsiders. He wasn't even supposed to be mayor—he just happened to move here and get a Town Hall job right when our old mayor died. Gilbreth mayors were appointed, and nobody else had had the heart to take the job, so he'd volunteered to serve on a temporary basis.

He seemed to be trying hard, based on the informational flyers he kept stuffing into our post office box, with town board meeting dates and ideas to "strengthen and develop" Gilbreth and reminders to buy salt and new shovels for the coming winter. But he had the look of someone who cared too much about his appearance, and he had the soft hands of a man who wouldn't have a clue how to chop wood. He wanted to build subdivisions.

He did not seem like a fit. He seemed like a distinctly unfit Gilbreth mayor with a staring problem. "I've got to get home," I told him, this time leaving off the word "sir."

There was no reason to hurry home with a shortcut, but once again I felt a pull toward Torrey Wood. I hesitated only a second before cutting across the road to the forest, taking the path that led to Whistler.

With a healthy few feet between me and the bridge, I sat on the ravine's edge, listening to birdsong and the hum of fall cicadas.

It took three minutes of looking before I saw it.

This time the bottle was closer to a ravine wall and was yellow brown, almost golden in the afternoon light. And this time I didn't hesitate to lift out the rolled piece of paper, smushing the bottle into my crowded tool-belt pocket while I read the message.

All things lost can be found or returned.

Hmm. Pretty cheesy. That sounded like a line from one of Uncle Theo's more dramatic parenting books.

What kind of person would write things like *Are you there?* and *The chandler can no longer make his own candles* and *All things lost can be found or returned* and then throw them into a ravine, where it was very unlikely anyone would ever read them?

A starling called somewhere in the woods, its high-pitched call sounding almost like a ringing telephone.

Oh no. *Telephone.*

I'd forgotten about the principal calling Uncle Theo. I most likely had a fire punishment coming my way. What was the best way to explain myself? If only I could tell him about an amazing junior artisan project I was working on, he might let the matter slide altogether.

But I still hadn't settled on anything great, and it was safe to say that, after the lunchtime disaster, making a bigger, better survivalist fire-starting device wasn't an idea that would thrill him to pieces.

I picked a few twiggy strands of some kind of wild wheat with dried seedpods still attached. Uncle Theo liked it when I made seasonal nature arrangements for his workshop. September was ending, and ground grasses and plants were starting to fade in color. Except, I noticed, for the wildflowers under Whistler.

In fact, I'd only ever seen flowers under the bridge in springtime, never autumn. And they were always sprinkled along the ravine in a long line, as though someone had scattered a short blue pathway with no beginning or end. These looked the same but were in a large bunch.

Strange, but convenient for me. I gathered a handful of

them, then scrambled up to the path with the bundle clutched in one hand.

My movement was a ruckus to a nearby squirrel, who was already burying nuts for the winter. It scurried up a tree and tittered at me angrily.

"According to *Parenting with Love, Patience, and Bribery*," I told it, "unexpected gifts can be an excellent and genuine gesture that distracts children from remembering to bicker about things they've been consistently bickering about." I plucked an acorn from a low-hanging branch and tossed it on the squirrel's abandoned stash, then arranged the flowers and twigs in the glass bottle.

"Let's hope a nice little forest bouquet will work on Uncle Theo."

A Gift from Beyond the Grave

In 1703 the village of Gilbreth welcomed an eccentric young man named John Abel, who tamed and kept a colony of bees on the east end of Torrey Wood, to make honey mead and beeswax candles. According to Elias Treat's journal entries, he had a big beard, a larger belly, and an enormous ability to find joy in the smallest of things, like sticking a horned beetle in the meat pie of the local farrier, who was known to be a cruel man and a rumor spreader. The farrier would prove to be instrumental in Gilbreth's most famous death.

–From **Gilbreth History: Founding Families & Artisanal Traditions** (Gilbreth Welcome Center, $16.99)

Straightening the flowers, I marched into our yard and passed the stone spring house, then knelt to accept the bounding force and furious licking of my favorite giant gray animal. "Okay, sweet Beastie," I said. "Pour on that cuteness for Uncle Theo."

Up the driveway we went, to the house that my great-great-great-great-grandfather Treat had built. Everything in this village was measured in whiles, long times, and very long times. Treat House had been around a very long time. When Uncle Theo didn't answer my called hello in the kitchen, I looked out a back window and saw the barn lights on.

The barn's stone and oak exterior gave way to packed-earth floors, high beams, and old horse stalls within. The workshop was the place where generations of Treats had honed their trade. They'd been masters of everything from boats to standard furniture to doors like the one Uncle Theo was working on when I peeked inside, inhaling the permeating scents of sawdust and wood stain.

The walls were full of holes from old notes that I'd nailed up for Uncle Theo, and the counters and tables were pocked with pieces of wood scrawled with penciled measurements. One half of the shop was dedicated to a number of band saws, a table saw, a planer, two jointers, a drill press, and a lathe. The machines made everything easier, but for most restoration projects Uncle Theo preferred to use only traditional tools.

I'd handled every tool and had used every machine in the shop, with the exception of the lathe. I'd started at age four with frames made from fallen branches held together with yarn. I'd moved onto simple benches and picnic tables, dabbled in natural and machine-assisted carving, learned joining techniques from the 1700s, then the 1800s, and learned about my uncle's beloved chair making. He'd even had me try sculpturing. They were all fun. They all felt right and Treat-like. I just hadn't discovered which one was *me*.

I moved casually into his line of vision and stood, waiting for him to pause his work and notice me, it being a generally bad idea to surprise someone in the midst of using a sharp tool.

Beast had no such boundary rules, and when he squeezed through the door I'd left open, he let out a sharp series of barks that were heard even over whatever decidedly non-1700s/1800s metal music was pounding through Uncle Theo's headphones.

"Minna!" He took off the headphones. "Give your uncle a smooch. Where's Crash? I saw him crossing the yard again a few minutes ago—he's not with you?"

"Nope. Don't know where he is." I stood on tiptoe and kissed his chest. "For you, Captain." I handed him the bottle and formally backed up, bringing both feet together. I bowed. Just the right touch of class, I thought. "Flowers, to show you that I'm not a deviant child just because of one teeny-tiny incident. And I'm sorry."

A nonpunishing sort of smile broke over his face when he saw the flowers. "Snack for you over there." He sat in a chair beside the worktable and jerked his head to the corner that had been set aside for me since I was a baby. I'd updated it as the years went by, adding a bookshelf and short foot-stool that I'd made myself. An oil lamp of Great-Grandpa Treat's sat on top of the bookshelf for extra light. "Sorry for what?" he asked.

I plopped into my beanbag, threw Beast one of his pre-ferred carrots, and grabbed the bowl of pretzels. "You know what."

"Do I?"

"For . . ." I paused. Hmm. This was clearly a classic case of elders trying to get you to admit something more than what they knew by putting the confession ball in your court rather than accusing you of a single deed. Textbook example from *Spy Dad: Interrogation Techniques from a CIA Operative/ Daddy to Four Girls*. Was it possible that Principal Gunter hadn't called? I smiled sweetly. "You know you're the best, and I'm sorry that I forgot Uncle's Day." Small lie. Tiny. It *could* actually be Uncle's Day, for all I knew. No damage to my character at all.

"Oh? Didn't even know. I happen to have something for you, too," he said, unfolding long legs and standing, stretch-ing his lumberjack arms up, then scratching at the sides of his beard. It was a little wilder and coarser and darker than the blond-red hair on his head—he used to let me see how many M&M'S I could poke into it when I was little. He looked just like the old photos of Grandpa Treat.

He reached into the shelving nearest him and plucked out a brown-paper-and-twine-wrapped gift. "I didn't buy it or make it. It was in the attic. I wrapped it up and was going to wait for your birthday, but that's months away. It's an old, dusty thing I found underneath a bunch of other old, dusty things when I was searching for tick spray." He waggled his fingers and made a ghostly booing sound. "Intrigued?"

Indeedy, I was. I waggled my fingers back at him. "Maybe."

He smiled. "You should be. I'm betting it's full of secrets. Which'll be loads of fun to dig into because you and I don't keep secrets, right?"

"Right," I echoed, staring at the present to make the word sound smooth. I set the flower bottle on a work table and grabbed the gift.

"Minnabean, I found this beside it." He brushed off his hands and dug in his back pocket. "Here." He handed me an old photograph, dusted and faded and somewhat wrinkled from being shoved in a box. It was of Mom next to a Christmas tree, holding a baby me in a chest carrier.

Uncle Theo's hand dropped to the top of my head. "She used that carrier all the time, just to keep you extra close. She'd whisper to you, like the two of you were keeping secrets. Nearly every day she'd walk you through Torrey Wood. She'd strap you in and tell your grandma that she was off to sing you across Whistler. It's almost like her spirit wanted me to find this."

I looked up at him, swallowed a little spit to flush out the uncomfortable tickle in my throat, and gave a nonchalant shrug. "I thought we didn't believe in that spirit stuff."

"We don't. That stuff's for tourists."

"Right."

"Right."

But the thing was, having grown up in a town where people talked about the past like it was still alive—and in some ways it *was* still alive—sometimes I did believe in ghosts. Just a tiny bit. And just sometimes.

I unwrapped the paper and found myself staring at a metal book. Well, not really metal. A regular book with metal plates covering it and a rusting lock keeping it closed tight. It had the number twelve scratched on it. I looked up for clarification.

"That thing is your mom's diary from when she was your age. I don't remember her writing in any others. What a surprise, huh? I know you don't—"

"I don't what?" I interrupted.

"You don't like to talk about your mom too much. Or visit her, but—"

"Just to clarify," I interrupted again, "bodily remains decomposing beneath the soil don't need to be visited. The visiting is for the visitor, not the visitee, because the visitee is deceased. Simple science, which, PS, I'm getting an A in. And I don't talk about her because I don't *need* to. You worry too much." I plastered on a flashy grin. "But thanks." I turned the book over and tugged at the cover. "Do you have the key?"

His smile sank a little. "No. She didn't want me prying, so she wood-glued the metal on, soldered on the chain, and locked it up. I have no idea where the key went. But I figured she'd be okay with you busting into it."

I nodded, ignoring the strange feeling in my stomach. Hunger, probably. But it felt slightly different. I turned the book over, letting my fingers trace the number that matched my age.

"I doubt she'd want me anywhere near it," he added, "but I'm all yours if you want to read it together."

"Not much to do?" I asked. The only table with orders attached was the one he was working at.

He grimaced. "Slow month. Slow couple of months. But, hey, Will brought a half gallon of farm milk over today, and some butter, too. He said you were looking scrawny and needed extra fat. Hearth milk tonight?"

"Really?" My spirits rose. Hearth milk was for special occasions. We'd fill a hanging cast-iron pot with extra-creamy, straight-from-the-cow farm milk and heat it slowly with brown sugar, vanilla, a pat of butter, nutmeg, whole cloves, and a cinnamon stick, bringing it to a simmer over the big stone fireplace. Treats had been making hearth milk for a very long time. It was better than hot chocolate. It was like drinking a warm bed and a soft story.

"You bet." Whistling a few low notes, he fiddled with a vise attached to one of the tables. "Hey, I meant to tell you, I have to go to Vickerston on Sunday for a new edger I ordered and to meet with a professor. I talked to the Hardlys, and you can hang out at the shop with Christopher."

"Everyone will be at the Village Green getting their Autumnfest volunteer duties. And PS for the millionth time, he goes by Crash. A meeting about what?"

He gave a noncommittal head tilt. "The college there is starting a trade department and wanted to know if I was interested in a teaching position. PS to infinity, I'm not calling him Crash."

Aha. So that's what Principal Gunter was talking about. And suddenly the hearth milk made more sense. I was being bribed into submission. I threw Beast another carrot while I debated whether or not to pass along the fact that the principal would be a reference for him. "That's hours away. How would you teach there?"

"It would just be one class—probably on a weekend. And maybe I could pick up some construction jobs—there's a lot of new subdivisions going up around Vickerston."

"You hate framing houses."

He held up a finger. "Not true at all. I love framing old

houses. I only hate framing modern houses."

"Which subdivisions would include, Captain."

"*Anyway*, on weekends you could help the Hardlys by looking after the twins or follow Will around on his projects. Mr. Willis said you were welcome to stay at the bakery and study or hang out with Michael."

Ugh. Spend my weekend with the king of the eighth-grade meatheads? Somehow I didn't think that would turn out well. "Is it an interview? Who interviews people on the weekend?" The words "Vickerston Realty" and "apartment" twittered around my mind. I put the pretzels down. They tasted old. "Sounds like a very unprofessional college, if you ask me."

"We're only talking. You worry too much. A little extra cash would come in handy, that's all. Money's been a little tight lately." He put down his tool and rifled through the sandpaper pile on the edge of the table.

I nodded at his back. "I've noticed."

"You have?"

"You switched to store-brand Cheerios. Same with your soda. Cheap toilet paper and paper towels too. And the garbage disposal has been broken for a month now."

I didn't mention the other items, like the fact that he only bought the good organic milk if it had a 50 percent off sticker because the expiration date was close, or that, while the space heater he'd gotten for my room worked fine, the house's heat being turned off was starting to make for chilly bathroom visits at night.

"Yeah." He looked at the floor. "I'll find more work and get on top of things soon."

I wasn't so sure. I'd heard him talking to Will at their last book club night. The money left by my grandparents was close to running out, and the house was too expensive to keep up with only one Treat and limited commissions to work on. If he had a storefront, he could attract more customers.

"A big commission would save us for the rest of the year, so I'd have time to come up with something," he'd told Will. "Otherwise . . ." He'd trailed off, Will had said, "Sorry," and then they had gone back to talking about their book selection and whether or not Katrina had made a bad decision by slapping Tristan and then running off with his brother.

"You excited about your mom's journal?" His gaze was wary, like maybe it wasn't the best present after all.

"Yes," I said firmly. "Very." But it wasn't excitement tickling my belly. The tiniest bit of anxiety had wiggled its way into my subconscious without me having the slightest idea why.

When I saw that book, I felt thrown off course. I didn't want to read my mother's words. In fact, if anything, that book made me want to find my father. After all, wasn't a living parent more important than one that was gone forever? In *double* fact, I had decided to find him. At some point.

When my life was lacking deadlines. *That* would be a worthy project.

"You decide on a project yet?"

Sometimes I suspected my uncle had a wiretap going into my head. There was a joke about that in a parenting book he'd read, and he'd dog-eared the page. "Nope."

"That's okay. It'll come to you." Uncle Theo smiled and pulled his lucky hammer from his hip flap. "Let's bust this journal open."

"I've . . . got some homework to do first. Can we do it later?"

"Okay, well, hurry up. And then maybe we could discuss the fire you set inside the school. I had a chat with Principal Gunter today wherein I promised her that you're not a budding pyromaniac."

Darn it. Immediately I dipped my head down and clasped my hands together, a prime remorseful position. "It was an accident. And I'm very sorry it happened."

"I would hope so."

"I wasn't thinking." I looked up and hit him with my earnest expression, all wide eyes and chin adorably tilted up to emphasize how very young and innocent I was. "Sometimes the developing minds of preteens can become so focused on one desirable outcome that their developing brains get too flooded with that one signal, and they literally don't have room for other thoughts, namely common sense."

"Don't parent-book me, I'm supposed to parent-book you."

"Sorry." But I wasn't sorry, really. I'd read enough books on parenting kids all the way up through the college years to be able to blast inklings of deviant behavior right in their tracks, along with confidence issues, preconceived notions, emotional distress, lashing out, dealing with awkward moments, and making choices I'd come to regret once I reached a more mature age. Uncle Theo had it easy.

He sighed and shook his head. "Since I understand that you've been given some community service hours fetching acorns, and because, technically, I taught you how to make the offending object, I'm not going to punish you."

"Good choice. I can respect that."

"I can only picture it from what she told me." He laughed. "How long?"

I grinned. "Eight minutes."

He knuckled my head. "Not bad for a Treat. You and me and your mom's diary have a date when you get your homework done. Deal?"

I didn't really have a choice about either of those things. "Deal. PS, Principal Gunter mentioned you and said she's really busy, so I don't think she'll be able to be on your résumé."

I felt a little bit bad when my uncle's face fell, but really, he wouldn't want to work at a college or subdivision, and pushing activities in the name of practicality never makes anybody happy, according to *Who's Driving This Thing? Benefits of Letting Your Children Pursue Their Own Interests.* Clearly, I was doing him another favor. Sometimes it was almost like I was *his* parent.

An hour later I opened to a spot in the middle of the diary. Mom's handwriting was sloppy, which I hadn't expected. I read silently while Uncle Theo watched me with bright eyes.

> On Monday, Lindy told me she didn't want to be friends with me because I told her that mascara looked stupid on her. I said I was sorry (even though I WASN'T), but she's still mad. I sat by myself at lunch all week. I read my history book and acted like I don't care. But I do. Eating lunch by yourself makes everything taste like wood dust.

Well. That was completely less amusing than I'd thought the entries would be. I turned the page, hoping for something more entertaining to not think about later.

> Mom got the wild mushroom plate at the tavern tonight and made us all try some. They looked like swamp sludge and I thought they would taste like feet, but they were

> really good. Like woodsmoke and steak
> marinade. She let me have half. Theo
> pretended to gag on his bite, then really
> gagged, then puked on the table.

Well, gross. The mushroom plate did look nasty—I could vouch for that. I'd never tried it, that's for sure. I flipped to the first page of the diary just to get uncle puke off my mind.

> ~~Stupid journal gift.~~ Might as well use it,
> since Mom's looking at me right now across
> the living room and she looks really happy
> that I'm writing in it. Really happy. Now I
> feel guilty for the stupid comment. I'm going
> to hide this thing in the secret place in the
> guest—room closet. Theo, if you find this and
> are reading it and you find out about my
> secret place and you tell anyone, I swear
> by all that's holy, and all that's not, that I
> will snarfle you while you're sleeping. I'll do
> it before a school day too, so you'll have to
> face a bunch of people while snarfled.

Hmm. Better. My room was the old guest room, which meant that the closet held some kind of secret space. I shut the journal and looked up at Uncle Theo. "Mind if I read this in my room?"

A floorboard was loose. Just barely, and it fit in so snugly that I'd never noticed. Prying it up with my pocketknife, I nearly screamed at the sight of an enormous black spider, poised and ready to pounce over a pile of dusty pencils. I leaped across the bedroom floor. When it didn't come scuttling after me, I looked back. It was in the exact same spot.

I picked it up. "Not bad."

The carving was incredibly lifelike, ready to scare any younger brother bold enough to snoop. I could almost imagine how snorting happy with herself the girl who placed it there would have been, but I stopped myself. No good would come from that kind of imagining. I stuffed the spider back in its spot, popped the journal inside, and replaced the board.

"Back you go," I told it. "You're not the one I'm looking for. You can stay private. I've got better things to think about."

And I did. Now I absolutely *had* to think of a bold, special, unique artisan project.

If my entry was impressive enough to win, I could give him the $500 Mrs. Willis had mentioned for house payments, *plus* Uncle Theo could come with me to New York City and meet those fancy collectors himself. They'd take one look at his portfolio and he'd have all the orders he could handle. Uncle Theo had never actually said what would happen if he didn't get more commissions, but based on recent evidence, I had a nasty suspicion that the words "moving," "teaching," and "Vickerston" would factor in.

If I didn't win . . . well, I didn't want to think about that any more than I wanted to think about Mom's diary. Treats had lived in Gilbreth for three hundred years, starting with my eight-times great-grandfather Elias Treat and his three brothers, who were there from the very beginning.

I wasn't about to let the last of us leave now.

A Brief Word
on Jane Addams

When I was in third grade, I did a report on Jane Addams, a really nice lady who ran a place called Hull House in Chicago. She was an amazing, kindhearted, strong person and did lots of good deeds. I remember looking at pictures of her in books and thinking, *Jeez, how great that Jane Addams was in the world. It's too bad she's not still alive. I sure would've liked to meet her.* But I didn't cry over Jane Addams, and I didn't *miss* her. How could I? I'd never known the lady.

I'd always thought of my mom the same way.

And I think maybe I liked thinking of her like Jane Addams.

In every photograph I'd seen, my mother had *perfect, persevering, pleasant, far-in-the-past historical figure* written all over her pretty face. I'd known her for less than a year of my life and had zero memory of her. The photos of her holding me gave me the strangest, uneasiest feeling—low, fluttering butterflies that I could only get rid of by pretending that someone had staged them—that my grandparents had taken me to a Mother World theme park and plopped me, with my black hair and slight olive skin tone, into the arms of a random blond-haired woman who happened to have a chin dimple like mine.

Uncle Theo seemed to think digging into Mom's journal would be fun for me, but really it would be like reading a Jane Addams historical diary, which was something that I would have to do for homework. I had a winning junior artisan project to brainstorm and a bottle mystery to look into and spaghetti to make for dinner. Oh yes, and a lost father to track down when the opportunity presented itself.

I didn't need any more homework.

Back from the Dead

In 1705 Elias Treat found that by continually feeding two turtledoves the leftover crumbs of his lunch, they stayed behind when the rest of the flock migrated. This would prove to be the beginning of the famed Torrey Wood flock. He named the birds Crusty and Dung.

–From **Gilbreth History: Founding Families & Artisanal Traditions** (Gilbreth Welcome Center, $16.99)

That Friday afternoon, for the very first time since school had started, Mrs. Doring, usually known as Dore the Bore, had every single eye in the classroom fixed firmly upon her.

"*Disasters*," Mrs. Doring said loudly, underlining the word she'd written in capital letters on the whiteboard. "As Autumnfest and Halloween approach, I thought it would be festive to discuss some of the more gruesome parts of our village's history. Of particular interest is the fact that every incident we'll be discussing took place in autumn." She inhaled dramatically. "In *fact*, nearly all of the notable catastrophes in Gilbreth's history took place during autumn." She raised an ominous eyebrow. "Personally, I think Gilbreth is ripe for another one."

"Yeah, right. What are we, third graders?" a voice muttered from across the room.

"*Excellent*," Grace Ripty whispered beside me.

"Today and next week we will cover five of the major calamities in Gilbreth history, both natural and caused by residents. We will discuss implications and long-term ramifications. Take notes, please." Mrs. Doring began scribbling, and within minutes a list appeared.

Mill explosion, 1707

Elizabeth Maybeck execution, 1718

Drought, 1718–1720

Schoolhouse fire, 1727

Revolutionary War, 1782 bottle incident

Bottle incident? What bottle incident? The words reminded me that I hadn't walked through Whistler Bridge yesterday. Would another bottle be there? I was reminding myself of the first three messages when a bird flew into the glass beside me with a horrific bang that had everyone on their feet, shoving their way over and looking at the ground below.

"Disaster!" someone shouted, bursting into maniacal laughter.

I looked at the window smudge. There was no liquidy bird-brain goo or feathers smeared against the glass, like when Uncle Theo hit an owl driving home from dinner one night. There was just a slight discoloring, like a spot of fog that might fade the second I looked away, which I did when Malia and Jaron Johnson nudged their way in on either side of me.

"That poor thing!"

"It's just a stupid bird!"

"You're a stupid bird!"

"That doesn't even make sense."

"*You* don't make sense!"

It was Darian Mackenzie who opened the window without permission to get a better look, shoving the bickering Johnsons out of the way with bony elbows sticking out of a brown-and-green army shirt. He'd gotten it from his aunt, who left Gilbreth to fight overseas. The tallest boy in our class, he had been held back a grade last year because of some immune thing that got him sick. I started kindergarten a year late, so we were the same age. His family owned the local tavern where Uncle Theo and I ate once a week. Some days he smelled like my favorite stew.

"Gimme some space! Come on, people, back it up," Darian barked, like he was heading out the service door with a full tray of pigeon pot pies, which was a terrible-sounding dish the Three Dogs Tavern actually had on its 1700s Traditional Fare menu page.

The bird on the ground was light brown and speckle winged, with a black-and-white patch on either side of its neck. A turtledove.

It had to be one from the wild flock that lived in Torrey Wood. We learned about them in first grade when we took a tour of the forest bird feeders, which had been stocked for over two hundred and fifty years, according to log books from the local museum. Villagers put in the feeders so that the birds would stay here and not migrate. I guess they were desperate for company. Or emergency food sources.

Another name for that breed of bird is mourning dove. The people hundreds of years ago couldn't have known that, though, because wouldn't it be bad luck to keep something with that name around on purpose?

"That thing's dead meat," Darian declared right as the bird woke up, flapped into the room, pooped on my desk, made a direct hit on Mrs. Doring's sleeve, then headed out the open door and down the hallway.

It was the most thrilling moment of my day and by far the most thrilling moment we'd had in social studies this year. Mrs. Doring had a heck of a time calming everyone down, which was also fun to watch.

"Close the window!" she snapped. "That's enough! Get a tissue if you need it for that bird . . . plop, then get back to your desks, all of you, please."

"Getting hit with bird droppings is a sign that you're going to get something you didn't know you wanted," Crash told her. "Aristotle believed that. Shakespeare, too."

"A sign of getting something I want?" Mrs. Doring sighed and rubbed at one ear. "Like a vacation?"

"It doesn't smell," he added. "Some people use it for medic—"

"Christopher, please. Just—just be quiet, everyone."

After closing the door, digging through the grubby cabinets for cleaning supplies, Windexing everything, smoothing her enormous hair bun, and quieting the room with an in-class essay threat, Mrs. Doring got smart about shutting us up. Nothing gets the attention of students like a thirty-minute chat about witch hangings.

"Now," she said, clapping her hands twice. "Get in groups of three and quickly brainstorm five ways that Elizabeth Maybeck's death could have been prevented."

A noisy minute later the room was divided into trios, other than me and Crash. And Grace, who stopped scribbling in her notebook and was now just staring at it.

"Want to join us?" I asked.

Instead of thanking me, Grace turned sideways in her chair. "Have you ever lived anywhere else?"

I felt myself lean away from her, toward the window. "Um, no."

"Never?" she pressed.

I looked at Crash, who was eyeing Grace with a fascinated expression. "No. Why?"

She squinted at me. "You look really familiar and I can't figure it out. There's got to be a reason. There's always a reason."

"They say that everyone in the world has one to five twins," Crash said. "Not real twins, but people who look exactly like us only maybe with a different haircut. It's true," he said, mistaking Grace's puzzled look for interest. "People who look exactly like us are wandering around somewhere like Ohio or Alabama or, I don't know, Italy even."

Her eyes softened just a bit at the word "Italy," and I remembered what she'd said about her mom.

"I can believe that." Slowly, she unzipped her backpack and pulled out a small glass bottle with a piece of paper rolled up inside.

"Hey!" Crash elbowed me. "Is that what you showed me at lunch?"

I'd told him about the three bottles I'd found. He grabbed for the one in Grace's hand.

She yanked it back and held it toward me. "You dropped it in the cafeteria. When you were helping Crash pick up all the stuff he spilled off his tray. It fell out of your belt pocket."

She lofted it just out of my reach, and for a moment her hard-to-read face was soft and open. "Do you believe it? That everything lost can be found or returned?"

Well, chop me a cherry tree. The girl I'd pegged as a blend of Harriet the Spy and Nancy Drew—and the person who would likely be assigned a festival duty entitled Suspicious Creeper with Staring Problem—had hoping eyes.

"I don't know." I snatched it back. "Thanks."

"You're welcome," she said, then turned to Crash and looked him up and down. "Okay, I have to know. Why are you dressed like that?"

I barely noticed his outfits anymore, but I could see Grace's point.

Crash's chin-length hair was gelled and fanned out like he'd stuck his finger in a light socket. He wore a navy-blue, too-big, old-fashioned jacket/coat with a white collared shirt. A crushed-velvet maroon cravat, knotted around his neck, was tucked into the jacket. He'd borrowed Tom's or Jane's eyeliner and made his eyebrow angles dark and intense.

His jaw flapped open, and he swallowed three times before answering. "I'm . . . I'm Ludwig van Beethoven." A reddish neck blush worked its way up to his cheeks.

Grace almost smiled but stopped herself. "Okay."

Mrs. Doring clapped her hands again. "Time's up! Bring me your lists."

"I already finished it. We can use my list." Grace tore a page from her notebook and walked to the line of students waiting to tell Mrs. Doring how Gilbreth residents could have saved a doomed young lady.

"Think she knows you've found a bunch of those bottles under the bridge?" Crash said, his voice booming into the conversation-filled classroom.

Grace, who was halfway to Mrs. Doring's desk, stopped midstep for just a second. Then she kept walking.

"She probably does now." I didn't even care too much. I was too busy poking Beethoven in the chest. "PS, I saw that blush. You don't think she's weird. You *like* her. Watch out for that," I warned. "If you invest your energy into liking girls, our friendship will likely dwindle and fester and wrinkle up like a moldy mushroom. Once you kiss someone, *your whole life changes*."

Crash swallowed. "Your whole life changes? You believe that?"

I nodded. "Absolutely. After you've kissed someone, there's no going back to being a nice little toadstool growing happily on a moss-covered log."

Crash blinked, openmouthed. "According to who? Who would want to be a toadstool?"

"According to me. Okay, and a book on food-related parenting metaphors. And are you saying you'd rather be plucked mushrooms, molding away in a grocery bin? I'll admit that I'm disappointed it's come to this, though not surprised. The books are right, you know." I shook my head at him sadly. "We grow up so fast."

"You're not actually a parent of yourself, Minna." He blushed more, then straightened his jacket. "And don't be crazy. I don't like her. I find her interesting, that's all."

Now his face was approaching tomato red. I didn't like it.

Mrs. Doring began writing the groups' responses on the whiteboard. "Copy these down, please. On Monday we'll discuss the mill."

Grace returned to her seat. "Is there a chance the mill explosion was deliberate?" she asked loudly.

"What?" Mrs. Doring looked distracted. The rogue bird had taken a lot out of her.

Grace repeated the question. "You know, sabotage," she added. "Something planned because of an unavenged act of treachery that happened earlier."

"What a *weirdo*," someone whispered loud enough for everyone to hear.

Now, I was well aware that name-calling was the hallmark of immature persons with little self-worth, but I didn't necessarily disagree. Grace was a mix of silent and bold, which was a strange combination, like she didn't care enough about what people thought to talk to them but then didn't care enough about what people thought to keep quiet, either.

I'd felt her looking at me, almost studying me, a bunch of times since school started, and she never got red or looked away when I spotted her in the act. She didn't look mean, necessarily. But she didn't smile, either. She was unnervingly hard to read, like the *Mona Lisa* painting that Crash carried around last weekend when he was being Leonardo da Vinci.

"No, Grace. That's unlikely. We'll talk about it next week." Mrs. Doring dusted her hands as though she'd been writing with chalk, not marker, and looked at the clock. "That's all for today. To those of you working on an artisan project, the countdown calendar is over the door. Seventeen more days until Bonfire Night presentations!"

Ugh. I was sorely tempted to rip the countdown calendar off the wall and shove it down the throat of the next person who asked what I was making.

Glancing around the room, I speculated about what the others were doing for their projects and wondered what on earth could be special, bold, unique enough to win.

A lifelike sculpture of a hunting owl?

A replica of the president's Oval Office desk?

Hand-carved salt and pepper shakers that looked like witches, with heads that would turn around in circles when you ground the salt and pepper?

If only I knew what everyone else was making, maybe I'd

have a better idea of what I was up against. But it was tradition for entries to be a secret to everyone but the entrants' families until Bonfire Night. Maybe Crash and I could go to Mrs. Poppy's together and ask if she knew anything about the other junior artisan projects.

I turned in my seat as the bell rang and the room burst into a frenzy of scraping chairs, backpack stuffing, and elbowing for the door.

"Hey, Crash," I said. "Can I borrow your notes? And do you want to come with me to . . ."

But Crash was gone, rushing out the door with the rest of the crowd. Mrs. Doring fiddled with papers at her desk, white remnants of poop stain on her sleeve.

I joined the hallway throng and wove in and out of students popping after-school gum, cracking jokes, or sprinting for the one bus that serviced everyone who lived beyond walking distance. I wasn't in a hurry but wished my famed Treat height would kick in sometime soon so I could pick out the quickest path.

Far ahead I saw a green-jacketed student pause at the open door while the crowd surged past. It was Grace Ripty, and she was gazing steadily toward me with that type-three creeper stare, a tiny pencil in her hand hovering over her small notebook.

It was like she was taking notes on me.

Like she knew some secret about me.

Or maybe she'd smelled tick spray on Monday and had developed some theory about me that she would put into her very own mystery novel.

She lifted a finger and pointed to my right, up toward the ceiling. I looked, and there was the turtledove, perched above the art case displaying a bunch of sixth-grade work labeled 6TH GRADE: KINDNESS & RESPONSIBILITY.

The drawings showed kids sharing lunches, picking up litter, and everything in between. My own drawing showed a really bad stick figure helping my neighbor pay bills. I blinked once, twice, three times, then turned back to Grace. But she was gone, swept away by the other students.

When I looked again, the bird was gone too. I caught a glimpse of it flapping wildly against the walls of the hallway, flying around a corner that would lead it deeper into the school instead of to its freedom.

A Miraculous Occurrence

In 1707 the village supply of gunpowder was moved to the stone mill. One disastrous afternoon a cat rushed into the building. One gunpowder barrel was open, the lid having been removed so that the powder could be transferred to smaller kegs. The cat knocked over an oil lamp, resulting in a fatal explosion. Elizabeth Maybeck was the owner of the cat. She was badly scarred and lost hearing in her left ear. Elias Treat visited her and brought her a small wooden carving of a kitten. The millhouse was rebuilt, and its wheel was eventually transferred to the new mill location in 1801.

—From **Gilbreth History: Founding Families & Artisanal Traditions** (Gilbreth Welcome Center, $16.99)

Full of natural light and swatches of bright colors and swing music and a smell like fresh apples, Loominary Weavers was the opposite of the apothecary shop. When I pushed in the glass door, Mrs. Poppy and her sister, Mrs. Baer, were already waving from their seats in front of two giant wooden foot looms.

"Hello, dear!" said Mrs. Poppy, standing and stretching her back. "Judith and I were just talking about you."

Her twin sister, with matching cotton-ball hair and dangly earrings, nodded in sympathy. "We were. You're really starting to grow up, you know. A girl shouldn't grow up without a mother figure. I was just telling Gloria that your uncle should really call up our niece. She's over in Vickerston and—oh!" She paused when Mrs. Poppy delivered a sharp elbow to her side. "I just meant Minna's growing up, that's all." She took off her glasses and peered at my chest. "Don't worry, you'll catch up there. Your mother was quite—"

"Okay," I said quickly, before she could go on. "That's fine. Thank you. I'm actually here to see Mrs. Poppy."

It suddenly occurred to me that maybe I should soften her up before asking for classified information about my competition. I looked around the shop, searching for something to comment on. A Gilbreth Welcome Center badge sat on a side table near the loom. It said, GLORIA POPPY, LOCAL HISTORIAN.

I widened my eyes. "Wow, you're a historian?"

She smiled and nodded gracefully. "I certainly am."

Mrs. Baer snorted loudly. "A few Autumnfest lectures to clueless tourists and you're a historian? You're the local *gossip*, more like, Gloria."

Mrs. Poppy glared. "Takes one to know one, Judith." She let out an annoyed harrumph.

This wasn't going well. I needed her in a good mood. My eyes settled on empty soda bottles on top of the sales desk. *Perfect.* "Speaking of history, do you know anything about a bottle message incident during the Revolutionary War? We're studying it in class next week and I'd love to know some things ahead of time."

Mrs. Poppy brightened, gave her sister a satisfied sneer, and cleared her throat. "I certainly do. I can't rightly remember who came up with the idea, but during times of secrecy and war, people used bottle messages to communicate battle plans. Young boys were usually recruited to place them and pick them up to avoid suspicion."

I sat down on a bench along the front windows. "How young?"

Her eyes softened. "About your age, dear. In 1782 ambushes were set on all five of the bridges. The other side had planted messages of their own, indicating that important meetings should take place at each of the bridges in the dead of the night. Instead of surprising key battle leaders, the ambushers ended up shooting five Gilbreth boys who were sent to collect the bottles. It was just terrible."

"Terrible," Mrs. Baer agreed. "They stopped using that method afterward."

"But"—Mrs. Poppy held up a finger—"another tradition

sprang up in the eighteen hundreds. Love notes. Men courting women would leave poems and such for the girls they liked. My generation did it too." Her eyes twinkled. "Mr. Poppy once wrote me the sweetest little verse."

War secrets and love notes? The bottle messages I'd found didn't sound anything like those things.

"*Speaking* of love notes, do you know what I found in Kaley's school notebook?" Mrs. Baer shook her head in disgust. "Apparently, she's in love with someone named Caden. *Love*, at age twelve! It's enough to make me happy I'm not a parent of a young one anymore, I tell you what."

Kaley Baer was the granddaughter of Mrs. Poppy's sister and she was in my grade. It was the perfect intro to my real reason for coming into the shop.

I stood and walked over to the loom. "So, Mrs. Poppy, you know how you were asking about my artisan project? I was wondering if you'd heard, in passing, what anyone else is doing this year. It's just—"

"Oh, yes!" Mrs. Baer interrupted. "Any hint of what you're making, Minna dear?" she said, her voice full of syrupy sweetness.

"Don't bother, Judith," Mrs. Poppy said. "She won't say a word. None of them will." She let out a laugh and motioned to a locked door that I happened to know led to a small workroom. A small taped sign read, STAY OUT, GRANDMA AND GREAT-AUNT GLORIA! "Your own granddaughter won't let you in to see what she's working on." She turned to me. "That girl took a six-foot loom and half of the supply closet of yarn and fibers, and keeps the door locked. Won't say a peep. It's like she thinks we'll blab it around town or something. Nobody will tell us anything."

Well, darn.

Mrs. Poppy peered out the front window, a look of disgust on her face. "What *is* that strange boy wearing today?"

I turned but caught only a glimpse of a navy jacket and wild hair.

"Did you hear about his sister?" Judith asked. "She just got her *fourth* job this year. Can't remember what the job is. What's the job again, Gloria? And does she get fired from all those jobs, do you think?"

"She doesn't get *fired*," I told them, wishing Crash were there to stick up for his own sister. What had he been up to lately? "She works in fund-raising as a consultant," I told them. "People hire her for short periods of time."

"Oh." Mrs. Poppy seemed a bit put out that there would be no firings to report. "That does make sense. She's working in the Alumni Office over at Camden College." She put a hand over mine. "That's where your mother went to school, you know."

I managed a smile for her. "Yes, I know." *Seriously.* Why did everyone bring up my dead mother all the time and never say a word about my father? I was about to leave, when her words, specifically "Alumni Office," registered. An acorn of an idea smacked me on the head so hard that I actually stumbled. I thought of the turtledove's poop and how Crash had said it was a sign I would get something I didn't know I wanted. His assessment was a little off. The piece of information I'd just received was something I'd had in the back of my mind my entire life.

"You okay?" Mrs. Poppy asked.

I was more than okay. "I'm fine. I've got bendy ankles, that's all. I have to go. Bye."

As I pushed open the door, a fragile seed of hope was sprouting. *All things lost can be found or returned*, one of the bottle messages had said.

What if I could find my father? Maybe then everyone would stop bringing up my mother every Autumnfest. And more importantly, I could ask him to loan us some money until Uncle Theo could get more commissions lined up. Then he wouldn't have to take the job in Vickerston, and we could stay in Gilbreth, where we belonged. Plus, I wouldn't have the pressure of making a winning artisan project!

I'd still have to make something worthy of the Treat name, but if I didn't win, I'd have another way of keeping us in the village. Uncle Theo would never take money as charity, but this wouldn't be charity—it would be *family*. My family.

Grinning from ear to ear, I approached the street, and a burst of navy blue slammed into me.

It was Crash, sweaty faced and breathing hard.

"There you are! What are you running around for? I need you!"

He smiled hugely. "You do?"

"Yes! Well, really, I need your sister. What were you doing after school?"

He rubbed at his arms like they were sore. "Nothing. Just stocking stuff at the shop."

If he'd been at the Hardlys' shop, why had he popped out of the alley on the other side? I could have asked, but I let it go. It didn't really matter and I had a far more pressing question. "Why didn't you tell me Lorelei is working at Camden College? In the *Alumni* Office?"

His smile faded. "I didn't think about it. Why does it matter?"

"You didn't *think* about it? Why does it *matter*?" I shook his shoulders, rattling his goofy hairdo. "Crash! Don't you get it? Oh, never mind, I've got a plan. Do you have your cell phone with you?"

He pulled it from his pocket.

"Good." I grabbed his hand and marched across the Village Green, plopped us both down in the empty gazebo, and told him my plan.

After speaking to his sister for several minutes, he cupped the receiver, shook his head, and handed me the phone. "She could get fired for this," he whispered.

"She won't." I spoke to her and put in my plea. When I

heard typing instead of a spoken response, I knew I had her. "Lorelei?" I finally asked when the clickety sound halted.

"You said he was a junior with your mother? There were three hundred and fourteen males enrolled as juniors the year your mother withdrew. I'll print the list and bring it home this weekend. Physical addresses only. No phone numbers or e-mail addresses. If you or Crash tells anybody, I'll get fired and sued, and my family will lose their glass-blowing business trying to keep me out of jail. I hope this is worth it."

"Me too."

I hung up the phone. It was done.

"How are you going to find out which one is him?" Crash asked.

"I'll worry about that once I get the list. Want to come over and hang out?"

"Sorry, can't." He looked across the Village Green at the Town Square shops. "I've got to check in with Mom and Dad and do my homework at the shop. I'll meet you tomorrow to look for acorns."

"I thought you just came from the shop."

He brushed off his outfit. "Do I look okay?" At my nod he grinned and saluted me, then marched off toward Hardly Glass without another word.

"See you tomorrow," I called, but he didn't turn, just raised a hand and kept walking.

~ ~ ~

There was a briskness to the air that made the forest leaves smell like the wintry end of autumn, crisp and hollow. I quickened my pace and began to whistle softly to keep myself company, noting the number of acorns on the ground for the taking. Crash and I would have an easy time gathering a two-bag harvest the next day.

"Minna!"

Darian's clothes hid him well, and it took me a moment to find his smile and raised hand. He backed out of a spray of bushes near a tumbling of trunks that had fallen long ago and were now growing all manner of mosses. Three canvas bags were draped over his shoulders, a slip of greens peeking out of one. His fingers and hair were covered in earth, and his lifted hand held what looked to be a mushroom. He was foraging for edibles for the Three Dogs menu.

"You and your uncle coming to the restaurant tonight?" he asked, wiping a dirty hand across his forehead. Grabbing one of the bags, he gave me a hesitant, slightly tired smile. "Mushrooms are going to be good and fresh." He stood and hiked over to me. "I was meaning to ask you—do you want to go to the Wheedle farm with me and my mom on Saturday to pick some apples and get pumpkins?"

Two leaves were embedded in his hair, and before I thought better, I reached over and up and snatched them away, brushing his ear with my fingertips and thinking how he was at least three inches taller than me, which was a nice sort of height difference. A flash of heat hit my cheeks. "Sorry, you ... those were stuck." I'd never noticed Darian's ears before, but having touched one, I realized they were a more comfortable place to look than his face. They were nice ears. A little pointy, like a forest elf's. "I can't. Crash and I are gathering acorns. Punishment for the—"

"For the fire," he said with a grin. "That was pretty crazy, Treat."

"Right. Um, thanks anyway." I put my hood up, wondering if I should order something new at the tavern the next time Uncle Theo and I ate there. Definitely not the mushrooms or the pigeon pot pie.

"You doing a junior artisan project?" Squatting, he searched and skimmed the fallen limb with careful fingers, coming up with a tiny white mushroom.

For the love of nongeneric cheese puffs, why was everyone hounding me?

"Yes. And *no*, I haven't decided what." Wincing, I realized I'd inadvertently struck him with a verbal slap, which is when young people take emotional agitation out on undeserving people, furniture, or pets. "Sorry. My uncle's been bugging me about it a bunch."

"That's okay. I'm not entering. I don't really have any skills."

I pointed to the bags hanging off him like strange, bulbous

brown fruit. "You could make a basket of edible things from the forest. That's a skill."

He looked down, then up at me, then down again, twisting the delicate stem between his fingers. "I don't know."

I wasn't about to force the issue—the last thing I needed was another entry to worry about. "Well, bye."

Following the path and watching the graceful, coordinated figure eights of the Torrey flock with my eyes, I bumped head-long into Will Wharton at the entrance to Whistler.

"Oh! Sorry, Will."

"That's all right. I was daydreaming too." He'd just stocked the dove boxes on the other side of Whistler and was carrying a load of millet, safflower, and cracked corn. "You doing all right, Miss Minns? You finding everything you need—for your project, that is?"

There was a serious bent to Will's eyes that made me feel see-through. Like I was trespassing in the woods with a big sign that said, I DON'T HAVE A PROJECT IDEA AND UNCLE THEO'S KEEPING A BIG SECRET FROM ME AND I'M TRY-ING TO FIND MY FATHER BEHIND HIS BACK.

"Still deciding," I told him. "Deciding between really great ideas is tough."

He tipped his hat and sauntered past me, the half-empty seed bag sloping down his back.

Instead of finding a great idea, I found another bottle under the bridge, with another message inside.

Behind the baker's oven, it said.

First the chandler and now the baker? Gilbreth had a coffee shop and a tea shop, both of which served baked goods, but the Willis family's Town Square shop was the only official bakery. What could possibly be behind their oven, and who was the message for?

A chittering set of squirrels chased each other up a dove-box tree. They both ducked inside the little house, which was stocked with seeds and suet, and where I imagined they were gleefully stuffing their stretchy cheeks to a chubby bursting.

Are you there?

The chandler can no longer make his own candles.

All things lost can be found or returned.

Behind the baker's oven.

Were the messages just some sort of random personal journal, thrown from the bridge? Or was there something more? Clearly, nobody was meant to find them . . . or were they? It was hard to say, but even with my looming project deadline, they were definitely getting my attention.

Mayor Ripty had said he thought Gilbreth was the kind of town with magic up its sleeve. But this wasn't magic. It was just an odd mystery that I didn't really have time for. I had more-important things to think about—like keeping my family in Gilbreth by making a perfect woodcraft project.

There was a decent chance that I wouldn't find my father for weeks. And even when I did, the logical side of me realized that he might *not* turn out to be rich and willing to give me and Uncle Theo a family loan.

So I still absolutely had to nail my project. But how on earth do you make a winning project when you don't know what the competition is making?

What I needed was a spy. Not a creep-ish, Grace Ripty kind of spy. And not a clearly-banned-from-project-information Mrs. Poppy kind of spy. A spy nobody would suspect. Maybe a couple of them. Maybe two small and cute spies who were named after tea and could appear fairly innocent when it was in their interest to do so.

Yes, I would recruit Lemongrass and Chai Hardly to spy for me. Spying wasn't against the rules because nobody had thought to include it in the rules. Not a single parenting book I'd read could ding me for poor character when I wasn't breaking any rules.

Besides, just brainstorming that idea had made me feel refreshed, invigorated, and motivated. According to *Healthy, Happy, Hopeful Teens*, those qualities put me well on my way to success. I ran home and ripped through every container in the pantry until I found an old half bag of chocolate chips.

Patting a baffled Beast on the head, I flew back out the door and ran for the Hardlys' shop, mentally preparing myself to beg. True, they were cute, but Lemon and Chai were tough. I had a feeling I'd have to bargain more than a stale bag of chocolate.

A Puzzling Pattern

Between 1711 and 1713 Elias Treat's brothers began pressuring him to marry and start a family. Instead he supervised the building of two more covered bridges, which allowed easier trade access to the north and west. After a heated debate, a three-day waiting period, and a final voting day, the bridges were named . . . North Bridge and West Bridge.

–From ***Gilbreth History: Founding Families & Artisanal Traditions*** (Gilbreth Welcome Center, $16.99)

While the majority of Gilbreth was blanketed by maples and elms and walnuts, Torrey Wood was the only place full of oak trees, making it the ideal place for the punishment ordered by Principal Gunter. Crash and I meandered through the forest on Saturday, occasionally sacrificing handfuls of nuts to a game of war. Today he wore a black robe that looked like it belonged at a graduation ceremony and a hat that looked like a poufy beret. His gray-white beard, attached with elastic, reached down to his chest.

"Did you see that?" Crash pointed to a growth of trees near the settlement ruins, along the running water that was eventually crossed by West Bridge. "Something dark. Almost like a black deer." He turned and frowned at me. "We don't get bears here, do we?"

The settlement ruins of the original village of Gilbreth consisted of a cleared space in Torrey Wood, now mostly grown over into a shaggy oval of meadow. Old cabin timbers still scattered the area, and it had been a good place to play pirate back when Crash and I were young enough to believe that random pieces of metal and scraps of old pottery were treasures.

"Nope. It was probably someone's dog."

He shrugged. "I guess. You need more help with wood-craft ideas?" Uncurling fingers from fisted hands, he counted silently. "Sixteen more days." His eyebrows shot up. "Oh! I forgot, your little spies have some information for you. What did you promise them, anyway?"

The twins had indeed driven a hard bargain, but mostly for my dog. "They have the right to use Beast in their plays over the next year and can dress him in whatever way he'll put up with. And I threw in my emergency licorice. It's just been sitting there." It was old, but I figured licorice was like Gilbreth's bridges, made of the kind of stuff that lasts for years.

"Classy. So Collin's doing a blanket with a New York Giants logo. Should be easy to beat that. But"—he held up a finger—"guess what the Johnsons have planned? Malia's going to cast a full imitation set of the cutlery used at White House State Dinners, and Jaron's doing a copy of some silver jug that Paul Revere made. Their parents are letting them use real silver, too."

That was Very Bad News. How was I supposed to top that?

"Let's take the deer paths to the bridge. We can take a break there."

He grinned. "Checking for more bottles?" He bent to pick a long piece of forest milkgrass up from its roots. "The chandler one just doesn't make sense. He's still good at it. I mean . . ." He shook his head at the ground. "That message is wrong." He struck out on a narrow pathway, ducking under trees and twisting through thick brush.

"Maybe." I wrinkled my nose past brambles, wishing I'd put on a healthy dose of tick spray. "But I wouldn't miss the flower candles he makes—he brought a rose one over last year as a gift. They make me think of bathroom spray."

Crash's head jerked up and he stopped abruptly. "You don't like them? You said over Fourth of July that you loved candles."

"No, I said that I loved sparklers and the smoke smell they left behind and that I wished candles worked the same way. Those smelly candles are the worst, except for maybe the pine-scented ones. You okay? Are you in a bad mood because of the artisan project? Are your parents all over you about it now?"

"No." He stared at me for a moment, sucking and chewing on the milkgrass's root, his eyebrows furrowed. "They still haven't said a word. I'm not blowing any glass for the contest."

"Oh, you'll change your mind." I shifted the half-full acorn bag in my hand and nudged him forward. "Keep going, please."

But Crash remained still. Then he pointed at a person sitting beside Whistler, her feet dangling into the ravine on the opposite side of us.

A short stack of books beside her, Grace was casually throwing rocks at the side of the bridge, which made me upset, but in a healthy, processing kind of way. I was experiencing a very normal, very acceptably high level of irrational possession.

Had Grace been the flash of black Crash had seen back at the ruins? Was she been spying on us?

She looked up at our approach. "Hey." She stood when we reached the bridge. "What are you doing here?"

I hefted up my bag. "Acorns," I said. "Why are you here?"

"Just taking a walk. Stopped here to read." She pointed to the book pile, then looked at Crash for a moment, unblinking. "The astronomer guy? Galileo?" she asked. "We studied him last year."

He straightened his beard. "I'm Nostradamus."

"Don't know him." Grace bent for ammo, threw another rock, and tilted her head to the bridge. "My dad heard something about someone dying around here. I heard it was haunted. I read a book once about a haunted bridge. Five people died before they realized that the rich-man character was inviting friends over for drinks and then using a time-delayed poison on them so they'd die right in the middle of a bridge on their way home."

Crash's mouth dropped open. "Why would someone do that?"

"Revenge," Grace answered. "All those people had bullied him and pushed him off the bridge when he was a kid. Anyway, this one kind of looks like a death magnet. Have you guys heard about someone dying here?"

Of course I had. It was a ridiculous question to ask me. But Grace didn't know that. Crash started to speak, but I silenced him with an arm across his chest. "Yeah," I said. "We've heard about that."

Grace stared between us, maybe sensing something unsaid but not sure what to do about it. A slightly hurt look came over her face while she fiddled with a pocket that held her small black notebook. She smoothed her expression, turning it into a blank statue face. "Fine. You don't want to tell me, that's okay." She bent down and gathered her books.

According to *78 Faces Your Adolescent Daughter Will Wear and What They Mean*, putting up a "stone face" might appear to be a deliberate barrier, but it's really an involuntary expression, one that's an invitation for parents to whip out their emotional chisels and figure out what hotbed of emotion is simmering beneath (the author was very big on mountain/lava metaphors). I'd gotten very good at avoiding stone face since reading that book.

"Grace, sorry. Sometimes we forget that other people in the world haven't lived here forever. Right, Crash?"

He didn't answer.

Grace rotated. "I've moved twelve times in the last eight years. Everybody's lived somewhere longer than me." She inspected her nails. They were pumpkin colored, which made me think maybe she liked colors other than black. "My dad's a city improvement consultant and a safety inspector. He fixes places."

"Gilbreth doesn't need to be fixed," I informed her.

She stared at Whistler's faded side, to places where the boards had warped. "He says this bridge is really old and maybe it should be torn down if the town wants to sell part of the woods."

"The town would never do that. The bridge is a state historic site." I spoke in a very calm voice, reminding myself that it wasn't Grace who'd tattled on us during the fire incident. She could have but didn't. For that kindness, I resisted the urge to bare my teeth. "Your father can't touch it. You can't tear something down just because it looks old."

She shrugged. "He's had historic things torn down before. Safety's safety. And the settlement ruins could be safety hazards too. I get it, though. I heard your family built this bridge and a lot of the original town. Makes sense that you're defensive."

My left eye twitched. This girl was testing the boundaries of my maturity level. "Actually," I told her, "I happen to hate this bridge. The ruins, I'm somewhere between neutral and fond of."

"Wait, the ruins would be a hazard to who?" Crash looked to his left and right. "The deer?"

"A hazard to people. The stocks are still there with those rusty iron things hanging off them. Somebody could get tetanus."

"We like tetanus," Crash said, crossing his arms over his chest. "Tetanus made us best friends."

I clapped him on the shoulder. "That's very true."

When we were in first grade, Mrs. Hardly came over to the barn workshop to order a farm table. I dragged her son into a corner and, without asking, pulled off his shoes and socks and poked both of our big toes with a rusty nail I'd found on the floor. Before he could cry out, I slapped a hand over his mouth and told him parents never thought to look at toes, then pressed our tiny wounds together to become blood brother and sister. I wanted a brother or sister so badly that I'd demanded Uncle Theo find me one the previous Christmas. He hadn't delivered, so I'd decided to take things into my own hands when a good candidate came along.

For an extra measure of bonding, I swept my finger across the floor beneath a worktable and rubbed it into Crash's tiny wound so that he'd get wood dust in his blood.

Instead it gave him a nasty infection, and we both had to go get tetanus shots. He didn't cry and he didn't rat me out for coming up with the idea. We'd been best friends ever since.

"Huh. Well, okay then." Grace blinked the baffled look off her face, pressing her lips together and glancing at the top of Whistler.

"Your dad sounds like kind of a dope," Crash said.

I elbowed him. "Shut up, Crash."

But Grace nodded. "He is, about some things."

Even though I wanted to agree, the fact that she'd said it first threw me off. I inhaled deeply through my nose for six seconds, a settling technique used to avoid rash responses that I'd learned from the parenting book *Temper, Temper*. After all, it wasn't her fault she was an awkward conversationalist with an inherited staring problem. She deserved a little patience. "I'm sure your father is smart. I'm sure you're smart too."

She shrugged. "I was in the gifted programs in all my

other schools," she told us. "There's no gifted program here."

"That's because we're all gifted," Crash said, his face straight. "We're gifted in knowing lots of things about Gilbreth that outside people don't."

Grace narrowed her eyes. "I know things."

Now *she* was getting defensive, which was natural. According to several books, an approach of a soothing voice and a sense of togetherness would take care of that. I didn't really care for her line of questions, but it would be wasteful to ignore my conflict resolution skills.

"Of course you do," I said, nodding in agreement. "*You* know things, *I* know things . . . even *Crash* over there knows a few things. We *all* know things." I smiled widely at her and tilted my head to a forty-five-degree angle to convey friendliness and interest, even though her piercing and slightly confused staredown was giving me the willies. "We're actually probably more alike than we are different."

She stepped forward, fixing me with an intense look, like the one she'd had on her face that day at our lockers. "Are the bottles for you?"

I exchanged a bewildered glance with Crash. "We don't know."

"Who else would they be for?"

"We don't know," I repeated.

"Well," she said, "you both should be on guard." Reaching a finger behind her ear, Grace untucked her dark hair and let it swing over her face in a curtain. Then she turned and cradled her books as she left, taking soft steps instead of the stomps I expected.

"Okay," I said. "Well, thanks," I whispered to her retreating figure. "You'd make an excellent school principal–slash–television detective."

"Told you she was interesting."

"She's kind of forward. A little bossy, too."

Crash grinned. "Like you."

Well. That was just plain rude. Summoning confidence and a stern look for the child who'd just attempted to undermine my authority, I quoted *100 Self-Affirmations for the Highly Involved Parent*: "I'm not *bossy.* I'm the *boss.*"

I looked at the tree cover Grace had disappeared around. I wondered if she'd spend the rest of the day alone. She sat by herself at school lunch, reading her goofy mystery books at the corner table. Maybe she was fine with it, but I couldn't help but think of the first entry I'd flipped to in my mom's diary—the one about how sitting alone at lunch made everything taste like wood dust.

Even though she seemed to veer a little on the dark side of things with all that mystery novel reading, maybe she'd be a help in figuring out what the bottle messages meant. Plus, I really wanted to know why she always stared at me and what kind of stuff she wrote in her notebook.

"She *is* interesting," I said to Crash. "In fact, maybe we

should think of opening up a spot on our crew."

As I turned my head, a streak of sunlight passed through gently waving tree branches. There was a flash in the ravine—a single instant of brilliance—then nothing.

I slid down the ravine and searched until I saw the bottle.

The blue of it nearly blended in with the wildflowers. A piece of paper was rolled up inside but half sticking out.

He looked at the bottle in my hand. "What's that one say?"

I read it aloud. "It says, 'In the tavern's barrel room.' That's it."

"That's it? Real deep." He walked over and flicked the message. "Is it instructions? What kind of treasure hunt is this?"

"I don't think it's a treasure hunt. It's just . . . I don't know." I looked away from his face, up at the bridge, then at the trees with the dove boxes. "Somebody littering or something. Have you ever seen anyone else hanging out down here?"

He shook his head. "People use the bridge to go *over* the ravine, you know. I don't know any trolls. But it's kind of weird, huh? A pattern of mysterious bottles with mysterious messages. I say we investigate. Maybe it's a code. Or a map. To gold!"

"Unlikely prediction, Nostradamus. This is not a pirate movie. It's probably just a kooky high school student doing some kind of experimental poetry. Remember last year when that girl glued words made out of Twizzlers all over town?"

He ignored me. "They *have* to mean something." He stroked his fake beard. "The baker's oven and the tavern room ..."

"I don't know how we would look behind the baker's oven, but do you want to see if we can get into the barrel room and look around when we're done with acorn duty? We can leave the bags here and pick them up on the way home."

"Sure. I bet we'll find something. I should've dressed like Sherlock Holmes." He dug a hand into his pocket, producing a fistful of change. "It was my week to do laundry. I found a buck eighty in Dad's pants. Want to hit Marzetti's first? We can split a slice."

Neither of us got paid for chores, but Crash's family had a laundry rule that anything you found in pockets was up for grabs. "Sounds good. PS, Sherlock Holmes is just in books. He's about as real as the bogeyman."

Crash looked up at the bridge. "Hey, Minna, you don't think ..."

"What?"

"Nothing. I was just thinking maybe it's one of the ..." He reddened. "You know what they say about this time of year. Mischief-makers and maids unmourned and all. And there's that witch we hanged."

Ghosts. He meant ghosts. Probably Elizabeth Maybeck's ghost. Or maybe the ghost of the bottle messenger boy who'd been shot at the bridge. Or maybe he meant another, more recent ghost, one I didn't care to think about.

I cleared my throat. "Elizabeth Maybeck was never a witch, and ghosts are just memories of experiences you've had, or stories you've been told, manifesting themselves as apparitions, usually because you feel guilty or sad or scared about something else entirely," I told him. "That's from *Imaginary Friends and Other Childhood Manifestations*. Chapter five, 'Nightmares and Ghosts.' Treats don't believe in ghosts," I told him.

"Hardlys do."

"Yeah? Well, Hardlys and their glass business stink," I told him.

"Treats and their stinking wood stink worse." He grinned. "And the only thing they know about is woodworking, so they're all doomed to stink forever. What do you say to that?"

I gave him a serious nod. "I say arm yourself with acorns, Hardly."

He bowed. "With pleasure. Bigger half of the slice goes to the winner."

"Fine. Hope you're not hungry." With my very best sneer, I let loose with the first blow.

A Brief Word on Things
I Know Other Than
Woodworking

I know how to say the alphabet backward in six seconds, which is fast. Try it.

I know that bowling alleys made with real wood are usually made of ash.

I know that dog gas is terrible if your dog has eaten spaghetti and sleeps in your bed.

I know that my mother came home a few months into her junior year of college. She told my grandparents that she was ready to start woodworking. They were happy.

When it became clear she was pregnant, they asked about my father exactly one time. My mother told them that he was in her year at school, that there was no relationship, that he was going to study overseas, and that he wasn't ever going to know about me. My grandparents decided that any boy my mother didn't want anybody to know about wasn't worthy of being my father.

They never pressed her, and when I asked Uncle Theo

about it, he said there was no chance of finding him. Crash was sitting beside me when that chat happened, both of us dipping peanut butter crackers into glasses of milk.

Then Uncle Theo said something that's echoed in my memory ever since.

He said that even if there was a chance of finding my father, he would never take it. Never. He said that he would always honor my mother's wishes.

My cracker slipped from my fingers, sinking to the bottom of the glass when my uncle told me that.

And that's how I know that nobody in my life has ever wanted me to have a father. They decided for me that having an unconventional family was enough. And it has been. It *is*. A sibling would be nice, but I don't want a father any more than I want a mother. I have my uncle—my Captain—and he's all the parent I need.

But enough about that. I also know how to whistle loud and make a sound like a dolphin. The whistling comes in handy more than the dolphin imitation, but Crash likes the dolphin better. Who am I kidding, I do too.

Barrels of Darkness

In 1714 Elias Treat, who lived in a small cabin by himself, tripped down the steps of his root cellar, knocked his head against a bushel of vegetables, and lay there for two days and two nights before he woke up with a bump on his head, a strong dislike for potatoes, and an inclination to install a safety railing. He then built railings for every root cellar in Gilbreth, free of charge.

—From **Gilbreth History: Founding Families & Artisanal Traditions** (Gilbreth Welcome Center, $16.99)

Two steaming paper plates slid across the order bar, glowing red under the heat lamp as they slapped against our hands with double *thwap*s. Crash yowled when a corner of cheese hit his palm, then lowered his voice to an apologetic grunt when Mr. Marzetti leaned out from the kitchen.

"Wassamatter, you don't like fresh?" Not waiting for an answer, he waved a hand in the air, mumbling about kids not appreciating something or other.

"Thank you!" I called, ignoring leg pain from my budding acorn bruises.

Saturday was dollar-slice day at Marzetti's Pizza Cauldron and Chimes, and with the spare change Mr. Marzetti let us have from the tip jar, we'd bought two slices of wood-fired oregano dough and homemade marinara topped with a trio of mozzarella, provolone, and parmesan, each one approximately the size of the pool table triangles at the back of the restaurant.

"Ho, Minna, one more!" Another grumble was followed by a third plate streaming out at top speed. "Take that to Gene at his usual table, will you? Crash, grab him a cola from the fridge out there. He likes the bottled ones."

I spun, and sure enough, there was Mr. Abel, sitting at a center table for two, fork and knife on either side of his paper placemat. The plate of spaghetti and garlic bread was heavy, but I managed to heft it over and plop it in front of him. "All the things on the menu, and you got spaghetti?"

Mr. Abel took off his hat, tucked a napkin in at his neck, and put another on his lap. "Told you I liked spaghetti," he said to me. "Evangeline liked it too."

"How's the Bonfire Night tale coming along?" Crash asked, twisting the soda lid and setting the bottle down.

The evening after Autumnfest the whole village gathered at Town Square for a big bonfire made up of that year's gallows. One lead storyteller was chosen each year to pass along a tale that had never been shared. This year Mr. Abel had been chosen. Sometimes it was a sad story, sometimes strange or eerie, sometimes funny. Usually a combination. Bonfire Night was just for the people who lived here year-round. It was cozy and fun and felt like, for one night, my family wasn't just me and Uncle Theo.

He switched his crinkled gaze over to Crash and took a small but messy bite of noodles. "My tale, Christopher, is a work in progress. I'm still not sure how it'll end, but I'm looking forward to figuring it out over the next couple of weeks." He grunted at his plate. "Good spaghetti here. Evangeline never could cook." He chuckled, then coughed, and his eyes teared up. "Never could. What are you making for your junior artisan project, Miss Minna?"

I swallowed the urge to scream and managed a polite smile. "Not sure. Mrs. Poppy thinks I should do a frame."

Instead of laughing along with me, Mr. Abel nodded. "I've got one of your mother's frames hanging in my kitchen, as you know. She used to make those twig ones just like you did."

"It would have to be one fancy frame to win, Mr. Abel," Crash said.

"It would indeed. Maybe another idea, then. Frames are important, but their purpose is to protect and celebrate and hold together what's inside. It's the middle that counts. That's the essence."

My stomach let out a loud gurgle. "Well, that settles it," I said. "No frames from me. I'm awful at painting and photography. I wouldn't have anything to put in the middle."

"Oh, I bet you would. Now you two go eat."

We picked a corner booth. Tiny colored lights were strung along the walls, and the faint sound of Vivaldi's *Four Seasons* played in the background. Marzetti's only played Vivaldi, as a sign over the order counter declared; Sinatra requests would result in an upcharge. A pivoting fan swept over the corner displaying Mrs. Marzetti's handmade wind chimes and bells every thirty seconds, giving the impression of fairy spirits twinkling.

"Okay," said Crash. "No frames. How about a fancy stool?"

I took an enormous, dangerously-close-to-scalding bite and took my time considering. "No. Wooden clogs?"

"You're not a cobbler. What did your uncle make?"

"He made a 1690s Windsor chair reproduction that nearly fooled an antiques dealer. The dealer said that he could sell it for over twenty thousand dollars if only that exact chair had been made about two hundred thirty years ago in Philadelphia. Uncle Theo told the guy that his parents had one at home that was made two hundred forty years ago, and he got all excited, but Grandpa had told him that chair wasn't for sale. He said too many family members had sat in that chair over the years. So now I have to come up with something as priceless as a chair full of Treat butts."

Crash whistled. "Good luck with that."

"Thanks."

In between school and other chores, it had taken Uncle Theo three full weeks of work to make a model and complete that finished chair, and Grandpa Treat had called him a wood prodigy. Time was trickling away. If I didn't think of something soon and get to work, I'd be turning in one of my twig frames currently hanging in the barn. Which would impress exactly nobody.

I crossed the room for more napkins. When I returned to the table, Malia Johnson was in my seat, her brother standing next to Crash. My ears felt prickly at the sight of them and their wunderkind silversmith fingers.

"Hi, Minna," Malia said with a wide, easy smile. Her hair was straightened and back in a simple ponytail, but I'd seen it in a million different styles, all great. And she was always incredibly nice and sunny.

If I didn't know that jealousy was a manifestation of feelings of inadequacy, I might possibly be jealous of Malia Johnson. "Hi."

"We were just telling Crash how the lost bird was seen in the library yesterday. Can you believe it's still stuck in the school?" She cleared her throat when I didn't answer. "I bet you're totally going to win the junior artisan project, whatever you make. I can't believe you built that mini farm table for the kindergarten classroom last year. The details were so pretty." A corner of lip disappeared into her mouth, and she nibbled. "I'll probably mess up when I cast mine."

"Hope so," Jaron said.

Her brother had stolen my line. I opted for a nicer one. "I doubt it."

"Thanks." Her grin fell and she jumped up. "Oh! Sorry, didn't mean to take your seat."

"Or my family's shop?" I blurted out, blushing furiously and feeling as though I was about to start sweating buckets. Or had I already? Crud, my armpits did feel a little moist. I hadn't meant to say that out loud.

Jaron frowned. "What did you sa—?"

"What?" I said quickly, reaching over to knock my water over. "Oh!" I cried, shooting help signs Crash's way.

Malia rushed off for napkins and helped sop up the mess. "We've got to go," she said, making a face. "Mom's taking us to go shopping in the city. Good luck."

I waited until the two Johnsons were at the door, then leaned toward Crash, raising my eyebrows. "Did you hear that?"

"Yeah, she said 'good luck.'"

Fixing my eyes on Malia's retreating figure, I shook my head. "Who goes all the way to the city for shopping? Rich people who have plenty of money because they stole your shop, that's who. She was rubbing it in."

"Rubbing what in? I thought you didn't care about that."

"I didn't until Uncle Theo went job hunting three hours away."

"Didn't they pay your uncle for the shop?"

"Petty details," I snapped, then slurped the half inch of water that hadn't spilled from my glass. "Besides, too many compliments are usually indicative of insincerity and are a precursor to your children either apologizing for a major mess-up or wanting something big from you."

"Stop with the parenting." He grinned. "They want you to lose, that's what they want. They're just digging for information about your project—that means they're scared."

"I like that better. Let's stick with that. What did you tell them?"

"That you're deciding between a carving of Mayor Ripty's face and a set of two hundred fifty walnut toothpicks. Figured that would keep them on their toes."

I nodded approval. "Well played."

Three Dogs Tavern was one street off the square. We crept along the alley behind it, making our approach from the back.

When we were little, Crash and I had spent summer days exploring the alleys behind Gilbreth's shops, spying on any craftsmen doing work in their small backyards, and wading through the giant trash bins full of treasures—pieces of wool, giant flour sacks, chunks of badly soldered metal, colored glass, paint jars with enough left to paint on cardboard boxes with broken brushes. It was a world of its own.

"Hey, look!" Down the narrow lane a rear door was propped open, and two men were rolling ale barrels out of the smaller of the tavern's two back doors and down a makeshift ramp. "It's our lucky day."

We waited until the men's backs were turned while they struggled into an open truck down the alley, then we darted up the ramp and through the door. A moment later, one of the workers trotted back up the ramp and removed the door jam, leaving us inside.

The room was larger than I expected, with rows and rows of wooden barrels, each one up to our necks and three feet wide. The door leading into the restaurant was propped open as well, and I saw Mr. Mackenzie standing with a clipboard next to . . . Mayor Ripty?

"*Hide*," I whispered. "*Hurry!*"

Just as Mr. Mackenzie laughed loudly and started clomping into the barrel room, Crash and I split, him scurrying to one side of the room and me to the other. Squeezing between a barrel and the wall, I peeked out to see . . . Grace?

Where was Crash? I peered carefully around the other side of the barrel, keeping myself low, and spotted the edges of his shiny black shoes. A second later he peeked back at me with panicked eyes.

"Not much of a tour to give, Mayor, but I appreciate you being interested. Most of the barrels you'll see have been reused since the late eighteenth century. . . ."

The three of them walked up and down the rows, coming dangerously close to Crash.

"Quite the history," Mayor Ripty said. "You would think there were ghosts roaming this place."

"Just a few. Don't worry, Mayor. The ghosts mostly show up when it's dark." Mr. Mackenzie prattled on about the fermentation process, while I tried to ignore the cramps in my thighs and sneaked a glance at Grace, whose curtain hair made it impossible to see her face. Praying that Crash wouldn't attempt a whisper, I closed my eyes and tried to wish them out of the room so we could investigate.

In the tavern's barrel room.

There had to be *something* in here worthy of a mysterious bottle message. The only things I could see were barrels and the ceiling. Other than lots of aging ale and worn beams that had drip marks I suspected to be from a bird who'd sneaked in at some point, there was nothing.

"Thinking of job growth . . . what we need is some new commercial businesses. Maybe a franchise or two. There's all that land just being used for pumpkins on that one farm— think of the revenue a subdivision could bring!"

One set of footsteps stopped abruptly. Even unable to see, I could tell Mr. Mackenzie's expression was not a friendly one. "Gilbreth is about celebrating tradition, Mayor."

"Well, it's on the docket to discuss at the next board meeting. Towns like Gilbreth that don't evolve end up becoming ghost towns. I've seen it before." He cleared his throat. "So, I saw Theodore Treat at the local real estate agent's office the other day. Are the Treats selling?"

My legs went numb. Risking an embarrassing encounter, I painfully shifted to the right. Grace Ripty was practically on top of me, leaning on the barrel I hid behind.

"Not that I know of." Mr. Mackenzie's voice was genuinely puzzled, which was good.

"I'll keep my eye on it. We may not end up staying long," Mayor Ripty said, ignoring a haughty noise from Grace's direction, "but I've always wanted to own a historic home."

Great. Just great. First our shop was sold to the highest bidder, now our home was being stalked by a greasy-haired outsider! Just as the trio's footfalls led back to the door, and just as I was festering about the right way to bring up that conversation snippet with Captain-slash-Secret-Keeper Uncle Theo, the lights went out.

And the door slammed shut.

It was darker than dark, blacker than black, and there was a very faint humming sound, almost like breathing.

"The ghosts mostly show up when it's dark," Mr.

Mackenzie had said. But he had clearly been making a funny joke. Hardee-har-har. The noise was probably a temperature regulator of some kind.

Probably.

There was a thickness to the air that made me think of how many years the barrel room had been around, and how many people had been there. Could physical things like tables and chairs and barrels absorb the memories they were part of? I didn't know, but sometimes at home I wondered if there were such things as furniture ghosts.

A whimper across the room was followed by a series of thumps and muffled groans.

"Crash?" I whispered. "Get the lights."

"*You* get the lights. I don't know where they are."

"Neither do I. Just head toward the door into the tavern."

Slowly we made our way by feel to where the group had exited. The texture of the wooden door was . . . odd. It felt damaged somehow.

I tugged on the knob. No good. "It's locked," I whispered. Running my hands on either side of the door, I felt for a light switch. Nothing. "The light switch must be on the restaurant side of the door. What do we do?"

"Hold on." Shuffling was followed by a grunt, a quick scraping sound, and a flame. In his hand Crash held a lit match and a tiny dipper candle. "Just in case—"

The door opened at a violent speed, smacking both of us

to the floor. Grace Ripty, her hand lingering in the restaurant, flipped on the light, jammed the door with a stopper, and fixed us both with her most curious of stares.

"Hello. Dad and Mr. Mackenzie are out by the tables. I told them I left something in here. Which I did. On purpose." She strode over to a barrel and picked up her pen and notebook. "I saw your shoe," she said to Crash, matter-of-factly looking his outfit up and down. She turned to me. "And you're a mouth breather."

"Most people are," I responded smoothly, standing up.

"I meant a loud one. What are you two doing in here?"

Crash glanced at me and stood up. "We found a bottle at the bridge, and it said to look in the barrel room," he blurted out.

"More bottle messages?" She crooked her finger at us and stepped closer. "Like I said, you should be careful with that kind of thing. Secret messages can be tricks, you know. Have you read 'The Cask of Amontillado'? Somebody ended up getting tricked into going somewhere after getting a message, and then another person buried him alive." Once again she was giving me the serious gaze of a museumgoer. Examining me.

"Grace!" Mayor Ripty's voice called from somewhere beyond the open door.

She startled, blew out a breath of air, then raised her

eyebrows at us. "I'm assuming you want to go out the back door?"

I nodded. "Please. And please don't—"

"I won't tell," she said quickly. "Just go."

Crash and I dashed out the back door, ran down the alley, and were soon catching our breath near the Gilbreth Inn's trash bin.

"I don't . . . I don't . . ."—Crash inhaled deeply and sank to the ground—"I don't wanna get buried alive. Especially without any treasure."

Flopping beside him, I let my head fall onto his shoulder. "Don't worry. She was just trying to scare us. I wish we'd had more time to look around."

"Gah!" Crash scooted into me as a flash of red jumped out from behind the bin.

"Stick 'em up!" It was Chai, a red handkerchief tied jauntily around her neck. She laughed and slurped on a long straw sticking out of a ginger beer bottle.

Lemon sprang beside her, a matching handkerchief pulled up over his nose, his finger guns at the ready.

Crash sighed and put his hands up. "What are you doing here? Where'd you get the money for that soda?"

Chai bowed, rose, and smiled widely.

Lemon pointed to the empty space in her mouth. "Her missing teeth make her cute. Cute people get free stuff a lot." He frowned and examined his sister's gums. "Shoot, I think

I see one coming. Maybe we can knock it out when it grows in. My turn." He grabbed the soda and sucked away.

Chai skipped over and curtsied. "Ms. Trawley ordered a vase for her sister. Mom let us walk down here with it and said we could check the bins for treasures on the way back. No food or sharp things. She's timing us, so we gotta get back. What are *you* doing here? Mom and Dad need you."

Crash brightened. "Really?"

Lemon poked him in the stomach. "Yeah, you're supposed to take us home and feed us. You've been sneaking out of chores for the last couple of weeks, you weasel. What are you doing now? We saw you running out of the tavern."

"Nothing," Crash said. "We weren't doing anything."

"Nothing at all," I agreed.

"Lies!" Chai shouted gleefully, rubbing her hands together. "Pony up!"

"What?"

"You have to buy our silence. Like in the cowboy movie Janey was watching last night. It's called *blackmail*."

"I know what it's called." I fought away a smile. It would be targeted as a weakness in negotiations. "You've already got dog rights. What do you want?"

Chai put both hands on her hips. "I want my *own* dog. A yellow dog. I'll name it Crocodile Dog."

Lemon rearranged his handkerchief so it was over his eyes. "Robot duck."

With mighty effort I held in a heavy sigh. "Sadly, both of those things seem unlikely."

"Fine." Chai stabbed a finger against my tool belt. "That," she demanded. "Give it to me. I want to wear it as a necklace."

My hands crept over it. "It's a belt. It was my grandpa's belt. The one who *died*," I added, hoping to gain sympathy.

She narrowed her eyes and pursed her lips, as though I'd made a grave mistake by pointing out the obvious. She took a deep breath. "DAD!" she yelled. With her Hardly lungs, I wouldn't have been surprised if he could hear her a block away. "Guess what Crash and Minna did?"

It took all I had not to slap a hand over her mouth. "*Fine*," I growled.

"We accept the terms." Lemon whipped his hand over and yanked mine up and down a few times. "By the way, Talia Stunetti is still deciding on a project. Rae Thomas is weaving a story blanket—she could be trouble for you. Teddy Chen is building a sculpture from iron pieces—either a dragon or a basketball player, he hasn't decided. Oh," he giggled, "and Michael Willis wants a puppy."

"What?"

Chai took off her handkerchief and swung it in circles. "We overheard him at the park. He threw a Frisbee and it hit Ms. Trawley's dog. He actually apologized and then petted her dog and said he wished he could have a puppy."

Lem nodded. "He looked like he was about to cry. It was great. I wish I'd had a camera. You know—for blackmail."

Ten minutes later the belt was gone, along with Crash's promised collection of historical figurines, to be used as Lem's army in some game both of the twins were hush-hush about.

Based on their intel, my chances of winning the junior artisan contest were disappearing as well.

And based on Mayor Ripty's question about Uncle Theo, a move away from Gilbreth was closer than I thought too.

"Well," Crash said helpfully, "we've got the bottle messages, at least. Hopefully, they'll lead us to enough loot to buy our stuff back."

I wasn't so sure. "Catastrophe," I muttered.

"What?"

"That was last week's Uncle Theo vocabulary word. Maybe the bottles will lead us to something helpful. But maybe," I said, thinking of Grace's more morbid assessment and Mrs. Poppy's scattered fortune-telling, "they'll lead us to a catastrophe. Remember what Mrs. Doring said?"

He nodded grimly. "She said Gilbreth was ripe for another big one."

A fierce wind came out of nowhere, one of the freezing Gilbreth blasts. It blew Crash's hat right off his head.

A paper flyer blew against my leg. It was an advertisement for the Elizabeth Maybeck hangings during

Autumnfest. The sky had grown overcast during our time in the barrel room. Clouds stalked one another overhead, and thunder grumbled from somewhere in the distance. It was far-fetched, but could it be true? "Crash? Do you think someone is leaving bottles as some kind of . . . trap?"

Crash caught and resettled his hat. "I guess we'll find out."

Liar, Liar

In 1715 Elias wrote of his fondness for Elizabeth Maybeck, now a twenty-one-year-old young woman who was almost magically gifted in animal care but was mostly ignored by villagers unless they had an ailing chicken. When her father collapsed in the middle of Whistler Bridge one day, she was unable to revive him. Some villagers whispered that she surely could have saved him with her healing skills but chose not to.

–From **Gilbreth History: Founding Families & Artisanal Traditions** (Gilbreth Welcome Center, $16.99)

At ten o'clock on Sunday morning, fifteen days until my looming deadline, I answered a knock on my bedroom door to see a serious-faced, black-suited, tall-hatted, bearded mini man with a pumpkin pancake in his hand.

"Abraham Lincoln?" I guessed.

Crash nodded. "Predictable, I know. But recognizable. I

was going to do John Adams, but nobody knows him." Crash patted his pocket. "Got the Gettysburg Address right here."

"You're dedicated, I'll give you that. Remember when you studied forgery so you could be that handwriting-copier guy?"

He grinned. "Frank Abagnale Jr. He got away with a whole bunch of other stuff too." He jerked his head back toward the pack he was carrying and wiggled his eyebrows, which looked extremely odd because he'd glued wads of blackened cotton ball on top of his own eyebrows. "I've got your list in here. Lorelei says hi and to remind you that you're dead if you tell anybody."

A numb, burning feeling hit right behind my eyes, and I felt my heartbeat flutter. I swallowed hard. "Got it. So we're really going to find my father, huh?"

He tipped his hat and spoke in a slow, low, wavy voice. "Seems so, ma'am." He tossed the bag onto my bed and unzipped it, revealing a stack of white paper. "Could be a life changer. Nothing like what the citizens of America went through during my term in office, but you've pulled pickle duty the past three years at Autumnfest, so I expect you know about facing adversity."

My fingers grazed the top sheet. "This is crazy. Somewhere in there is my dad." I turned the page and glimpsed a row of names.

"How are you going to get in touch? Sorry she didn't give you the e-mail addresses."

"That's okay. I'll figure it out. Maybe I'll send letters and include our phone number." Letters would get pretty much anywhere within three days.

Crash stepped over to my bookshelf and shook the lumberjack piggy bank Uncle Theo had given me years ago. The few coins inside clinked weakly. "How are you going to buy that much paper and envelopes and stamps? That would be like . . ." His eyes rolled up while he calculated. "I don't know, almost two hundred bucks."

Well, shoot. I hadn't thought of that. An invisible weight settled back onto my shoulders, like the entire Torrey Wood flock had decided to nest there. "The junior artisan contest winner gets five hundred bucks. Instead of giving it to Uncle Theo to help with house payments, we'll send the letters after I win, and within a week I'll have a dad. Hopefully, a rich one. That's a solution *and* a backup plan. Problem solved. PS, I don't think Abe Lincoln was Southern."

Crash reddened. "It's my best accent, but you're right. Illinois or Indiana. He was a soft talker, too." He sighed. "Probably not the best costume choice for a Hardly."

"You look great." I pinched the stack between my thumb and pointer finger and flipped gently through. The paper stuck at the *W*s, and I found myself staring at the name Will Wharton. A tingle crept up my neck and lingered. "Crash, did you know that Will Wharton went to college?" He'd never mentioned it to me and neither had Uncle Theo. Then again, why would they?

"Nope." Crash reached into his pocket. "Here. I made this for you. For good luck picking something cool for an Autumnfest duty."

The lump of glass felt sticky from Crash's sweaty hand. "Thanks."

"I made you something else, but you wouldn't have liked it. What do you think? They wouldn't let me use Mother." He sighed. "I don't think they'll ever take me off Junior. I'm still not blowing any glass for the contest, by the way. I'm not meant to be a glassblower. Not that I care."

He cared. Mother was the larger of the glass furnaces the Hardlys had in their workshop. He'd used Junior, the small one the Hardlys used for school demonstrations and training. I knew Crash wasn't the glassblower he should have been, even being only twelve. Crash knew it too. It was something that we didn't talk about, though. He'd get better, I was certain. He was a late bloomer. He just needed practice. I stared at the hollow blue blob. "This is pretty, thanks. What is it?"

"What's it look like?"

The blob looked like a blob, with a smaller blob on one end that had a poky blob sticking out. "Um . . . a bird?"

Crash grinned at his shoes. "Yup. Remember when that bluebird family had a nest right above the old tree house?" His grin fell slowly. He looked out the window like he was searching for that memory. "The dad bird stood right next to the mom while she was on the eggs. She didn't really need him around, though. She built the whole nest herself."

"I remember."

"You think you'll find him—your dad?"

Picking up the papers, I had the sudden urge to go through the entire list and see if one felt like a life-completing, fatherly sort of name. "I need to stash this somewhere." I slipped into the closet, then tossed a pile of dirty clothes over my shoulder and lifted the loose board.

"Whoa, cool! It's pretty tight in there."

I agreed and took out the diary, throwing it on my bed to make room in the hiding spot for the collection of names.

"What's that?"

"Nothing. Just a diary my mom wrote when she was twelve. It's nothing."

"Huh. You never really talk about her." He picked up the diary and opened it, which made me twitchy, for some reason.

"I said it's nothing." I snatched it away and tossed it again.

Uncle Theo stood there beside our farm table, wearing a suit, of all things, grinning like a goofy, six-foot-five-inch child on his first day of school. "My Minna. How's my favorite tick-free girl? Ready to pick something good this year?"

I swore last year that I'd be hanged on the gallows I helped build if I drew pickle-booth duty or bellows girl for the blacksmith furnace. The pickle booth left your hands reeking for days, and the blacksmith was very nice, but he liked to be "authentic," which meant skipping deodorant and going without a bath for days before Autumnfest. Pumping the bellows was stinky work.

"There's no way I'll pull pickle duty for the fourth year in a row," I told him. "I'm hoping to be an execution heckler, thank you very much. Or work the hay maze. Or maybe a stable helper. It's not fair that the girls can't do that. I can always put my hair up, and there's no reason I can't wear a boy's costume. I'm going to hold a protest if I pull a good boy role and they don't let me do it."

He raised a hairy eyebrow. "Really? You're coming along nicely, Minna Treat. I take all the credit."

I eyed him suspiciously. He'd trimmed his beard. I didn't like it. "Why are you so dressed up? You said it was just a talk."

He straightened his jacket. "Do I look okay? Do I look like someone who could teach a college course?"

I looked him over. "You do. But I thought they wanted you to be in a workshop."

"They said that they'd be interested in having me maybe teach a local history course elective as well. Can you imagine me in a classroom as Professor Treat?" He grinned.

Hmm. This clearly called for affirmation, but my adolescent brain really didn't care. My uncle making money was good, but making money at a job that required us to move was not what I had in mind. I fought back a negative answer and went with a neutral response. "Maybe. I have an excellent imagination."

"Maybe?" He let out an overlong sigh, pinched the bridge of his nose, then let the back of his palm drape across his forehead. "*Maybe*, she says. I knew girl drama was coming, but still, it . . . it feels so sudden."

I gave a snort of disgust. "Boys have drama too, you know. I know what goes on in boy locker rooms. Chapter thirteen of *Mean Girls and Bully Boys* says hormones can wreak havoc on morality impulses, so when you have an already jerky kid to begin with and add in the stress of running a timed mile in gym class, then—"

"Minna, stop." Uncle Theo licked syrup off his upper lip and put his hands over his ears. "I don't need to hear it. But speaking of running, where were you running off to last night, Christopher? It must have been nine o'clock when you ran across the yard. I saw you from the barn window."

Crash jerked out of his chair and jogged to the refrigerator. "Had to get something from our shop for Mom, that's all. It's not that far. Hey, did you know that Michael Willis started growing chin hair in fourth grade?" he said, his head inside the fridge. He emerged with the milk jug. "Maybe his parents buy that hormone milk." He studied the label on the jug in his hand. "Hormone-free cows. Good choice, Mr. Treat. Fight the good fight against puberty as long as you can. I'm not looking forward to it myself."

"I don't need to hear about puberty from you, Christopher. Put the milk back." He turned to me and tilted his head toward Crash. "Who *is* this guy, by the way?"

"He's Abe Lincoln," I said.

Crash straightened his lapels. "*President* Lincoln, please. Show some respect."

Uncle Theo saluted. "Nice to have you here, Mr. President." He dug into his pocket and handed me a small carving of a frog. "For your collection, madam."

I wasn't fooled for a minute. It was the exact same thing that my bouquet of flowers had been a few days back—a distraction meant to keep me from dwelling on him being a lie-of-omission liar. Still, it was a very cute distraction.

I gave the carving a critical eye, turning it this way and that, holding it close, then far. It looked real enough to jump. I gave it a kiss on its froggy mouth. "I love it. And I love you."

"You hear that, Christopher?" A hint of a smile lifted his whiskers and he wiped away a fake tear. "I've trained her so well." He knuckled my head. "Keep your lip kissing to my carvings for another ten years, got it?"

"Got it. Anything else you want to tell me?" I asked in

my best casual voice. "About, say, your trip to Vickerston?"

He busied himself with erasing the chalkboard and blowing his nose for an impressive five full seconds, then turned innocently. "Hmm?"

Hmm was exactly what I was thinking. Deflection, a technique usually employed by preteens and teens who were hiding something. "Nothing," I told him.

He swallowed the last of his coffee, set the cup in the sink, and kissed me good-bye. "By the way, any breakthroughs on the project front?"

"Yes, actually. I'm keeping it secret and working in the woodshop at school." The complete, total, 100 percent lie slipped out of my mouth so easily that I knew it had been there all along, just waiting to be used.

Uncle Theo's face lit up in an awful way, like the sun was rising over the world after a long night. And my lie was the thing that had made it happen. "That's great! I can't wait to see it."

I'd never before been in a position where somebody's happy face made me feel like I needed to run into the backyard and projectile vomit a bucket of guilt and pancakes, but that was my body's exact reaction at that moment. Luckily, my mind was able to hold things together.

Crash gave me a funny look, which I ignored while plastering a big smile on my face and looking my poor lied-to uncle right in the eye. Though I was unable to recall one at the time, I was sure there was some sort of contingency in the parenting books that would justify my blatant falsehood as forgivable, maybe even admirable considering the stresses my developing self was facing.

"Dishes in the sink after you two finish eating. I've gotta get to my interview. I'll be back by nine at the latest. Wish me luck."

"Luck." The door slammed and I turned to Crash. "So, have you figured out a money plan yet for the stamps and letter supplies?"

He stuffed his face with a final bite. He chewed for a long time and finally swallowed. "I'm working on it. Have you really thought of a project?"

I ran my pointer fingers through the remaining syrup on my plate, squishing and swirling it into shapes that flowed into one another and melted away. "I'm working on it."

"Minna?" Crash took off his hat and fiddled with it. "Why'd you lie to your uncle just now?"

"Lies," I informed Crash, wiping my hands and adopting my most severe *I've read more about child psychology than you* look, "are told for many reasons, not all of them bad ones."

"What's your reason?" he asked.

I considered the question. "My woodcraft muse needs breathing room or I'll never think of anything." I popped one last bite of pancake into my mouth. "Besides," I said, "some lady left a message on the phone, calling from an apartment complex in Vickerston, asking if he was still interested in seeing a unit, and he still hasn't said a word about moving to me. So he lied first."

"Maybe it's nothing. He would have said something if you were really going to move. Why don't you just ask him about it?"

It was a logical question. The truth was that if I didn't ask, then I didn't have to risk hearing Uncle Theo actually say that we were moving. Once he said it, he couldn't take it back. So while I didn't appreciate being lied to, I think I preferred it to being told the whole truth. At least until I'd come up with a project or father that could keep us in Gilbreth.

"I shouldn't have to ask, that's why."

"Whatever you say." Crash opened the fridge again and poured a glass of milk that would have made Uncle Theo cringe. "What about a frame for a project? You could make a really nice one, and Mr. Abel was wrong—you wouldn't have to put anything inside it."

I kicked at the floor. "Why does everyone keep talking about frames? A frame isn't going to win anything! My dead ancestors would roll over in their graves and die again if I showed up with the Treat name slapped on a *frame* for my official junior artisan project. No, it needs to be something excellent, and starting something 'just because' is a waste of time."

Crash started to frown, then his eyes softened. "You don't have to choose a project for your family, Minna. Do it for you."

"There is no *me* when it comes to this stuff. Only last names. You're a Hardly, you know that. Besides, really, I *am* doing it for me—so I can stay here."

Honest Abe, sixteenth president of the United States, tipped his hat my way. "Good enough for me." He frowned. "What did he say about the phone message?"

"I erased it before he could listen to it. I'm very well adjusted like that." I stood. "Now let's go get our Autumn-fest duties. If we pull pickle duty again, I might just decide that it's okay to move."

Festival Duties, a Smaller List, and a Larger Crew

In 1718 farrier Henry Salt sold a badly shod lame horse at a high fee to Elizabeth Maybeck. Elizabeth cared for the horse, which she deeply loved, and restored it to full health. Fearing a loss of business for both the dishonest sale and not being as skilled with horses as a woman, Mr. Salt cried witchcraft. Elizabeth was publicly scorned, given a brief trial, hanged, and buried in an unmarked grave in Torrey Wood. A trial witness later remarked that perhaps they'd been hasty, that Miss Maybeck had just been good with animals and smarter than the farrier. Elias Treat was asked to build the gallows. He refused.

–From *Gilbreth History: Founding Families & Artisanal Traditions* (Gilbreth Welcome Center, $16.99)

The Village Green was a loose swarm of people wandering the huge lawn like a bunch of colorful ants with no agenda. Parents chatted and strolled; children bumped in and out while playing tag; the teenagers sauntered, eyeing one another with bored expressions. The Cutting Board Bakery had a booth right near the gazebo with free pumpkin buns and coffee, and the Gilbreth Historical Society had a long table with rows of watery lemonade and iced tea.

Sipping lemonade, Crash and I mingled through the crowd, speculating about where our names would end up on the enormous FESTIVAL DUTIES board set up inside the gazebo. Grace Ripty was in there reading a book, propped on a leaned-back chair.

As though detecting my presence, her Stare-O-Meter went into full throttle. She even put down her book. Beside her on a card table sat several wooden pumpkins, carved by my great-aunt Iris, filled to the brim with festival duties separated out by age group.

Volunteering wasn't *required*, but most people liked to get involved and all teachers gave extra credit to students who participated during Autumnfest. Once you selected a piece of paper indicating your role, you reported to the blacksmith or chandler or cooper or whoever, then were sent off to the emporium for costuming. But for now everyone was waiting.

"Hi, sweetheart!" Mrs. Willis said, rubbing me on the back as we passed.

"Minna!" her husband said. "Have a bun! You're looking too thin."

"No, thanks," I said, looking up at Grace, who was staring strangely between me and Mr. Willis with a cocked head and curious expression. Then she buried her nose in her notebook and wrote down some kind of secret nothing.

Crash nudged me and nodded Grace's way. "Is she writing a novel or something?"

Will Wharton passed by, carrying a microphone and extension cords. "Hey, Minns Binns," he said, a wide smile breaking across his face. His long hair was done in a single braid like mine.

"Hi, Will." *Boy, he's nice,* I thought. *And he lives alone, so Uncle Theo and me could cram into his tiny house and not have to move. He really would make a great . . .* I shook the thoughts from my head and took out my braid, weaving my fingers through the twists to free it.

Crash and I settled in the shade of a large shagbark hickory tree, and Darian Mackenzie plopped down beside us, the tray of free chicken wings he'd been distributing nearly empty, except for a stack of tavern coupons. He looked ready to crawl into bed. "You guys want the rest? I'm supposed to be passing them out, but stupid Michael Willis and his gang took about twenty of them. I hate those guys."

I took a wing and pointed to the flat area in front of Town Hall, where the mayor was clearing his throat into a microphone.

"Attention, Gilbreth! I've got an exciting announcement." He gestured to the wooden pumpkins and giant sign-up board in the gazebo. "I know you're anxious to see how you'll be participating in this year's Autumnfest, but first, I'm both saddened and pleased to let you know that Gene Abel's shop property is opening up on Town Square."

The adults in the crowd snapped to attention—Town Square properties were typically handed down by families or by recommendation and were hard to come by. There were shops off the square, but there was a definite honor and tourist benefit to having a place directly around the Village Green.

While the citizens of Gilbreth all looked toward Mr. Abel, their murmurs giving way to a respectful moment of silence for the passing of his shop, my mind drifted to the bottle message that had predicted that the chandler's skills were all used up.

Somebody had known.

"As Mr. Abel has no family to pass his chandler shop along to, he's suggested a contest to fill his spot. Anyone wanting the store may sign up within the next two days. The deposit and first month's rent will be paid for by Mr. Abel. The participants must produce an original work, showcasing their skill, which will then be judged by myself, Mr. Abel, and all shop owners on the square on Bonfire Night, at the same time as our junior entries are judged."

"Whoa," Crash said, elbowing me. "There you go! If your uncle wins—"

"We definitely won't have to move," I finished for him, warmth rushing through me. And for the first time I really felt like that was completely true. There were *three* possibilities for saving us—me winning the contest and showing my uncle's portfolio to New York clients, me finding my father and getting a loan, and now, the best possibility of all, Uncle Theo winning a Town Square shop. I stood, wanting to launch my arms to the sky in celebration.

"You're moving?" Darian asked.

We both ignored him.

Crash shook my shoulder. "And maybe the Johnsons would trade spaces with you, and you could get your family's real shop back!"

I stepped out of tree shade into the sunlight. That was a long shot, for sure, but so was me making a winning junior artisan project. Not that I had to worry about that *quite* as much now. With three chances, one was certain to land on target.

"Come on, let's get closer." Grabbing Crash's hand, I whisked us through the crowd straight toward the gazebo so we could get our assignments quickly.

"Each participant will have judge visits to ensure that the work is original and brand new, not a previously produced piece. Entry forms are in my office in Town Hall and must be received by Monday at three o'clock p.m. Good luck to anyone entering. Okay, young citizens, now line up for your Autumnfest volunteer duties!"

While Grace Ripty sat beside the pumpkins, alternately looking bored, reading a book, and sneaking glances at me and Crash, I reached a hand into the AGES 12–14 pumpkin and grasped a piece of paper, then followed directions by handing it to the volunteer instead of reading it myself. "Minna Treat," I told her, taking my last sip of lemonade and throwing the cup into a wooden crate marked TRASH.

"Minna Treat," she repeated, turning to the board with a marker. "Pickle duty."

Pickle duty?! I made some noise, a cough perhaps, then stared, stricken, at the lemonade spit spray I'd left darkening the back of poor Mrs. Finnegan's white blouse.

She twisted her neck, trying to look down at the wet shadows. Raising a hand to shake her shirt gently back and forth as best she could to dry my shock, she offered an apologetic smile. "I was only kidding, dear. Punkin Dunkin' booth at the park. Saturday, ten o'clock to two o'clock."

I turned to Crash, who raised his hands and eyebrows. "What's that?"

"It's new. Grace here thought of it!" the woman said brightly. "You dress up as a pumpkin and people pay a dollar to dunk you. The money goes to town restoration projects. Costume's over at the emporium tent. Getting dunked is straightforward, so there's no instructor to visit. Head to the site fifteen minutes before your shift time, and the assigned adult will tell you what to do. We'll provide towels to dry off."

Miserably, I nodded. It was bad form to back out of a task. "Thanks, Grace," I muttered, freezing in place as Mayor Ripty swept back up the stairs. I hadn't noticed before that his T-shirt had the words "Camden College" printed across it.

A prickle crept up the back of my neck as I remembered him saying that he'd moved here because somebody had told him that Gilbreth had magic in it. I tried rubbing the prickle out, but it was a stubborn little rascal.

"Something wrong?" Crash whispered.

I shook my head and kept my eyes on the mayor, who leaned over and gave his daughter a kiss, then turned to me and Crash. "We're going to have more people than ever at Autumnfest this year. I've used the marketing budget to advertise all over the state. We're letting our best artisans know so that they'll have plenty to sell." He winked. "So whatever knickknacks woodwork people make, just be sure to have plenty more than you usually do."

"My uncle doesn't make knickknacks." I kept my voice even. "Neither do the Hardlys. In fact, I'm not sure anybody does in Gilbreth," I said with a big fake smile.

"Ah. Perhaps 'knickknacks' is the wrong term."

"Perhaps," I answered.

He scratched his chin, and a deep wrinkle formed between his eyebrows. "Grace, I've got to talk to some folks, but I'll be around."

"She'll be here for at least the next hour," said Mrs. Finnegan.

Mayor Ripty looked over at me and Crash, his eyes lingering on Crash's tall hat before returning to his daughter. "Okay, well, after that you and your friends are welcome to play at our house."

Grace blushed as he left. "Sorry about the dunking booth, Minna. I can take your place if you want."

"No, that's okay."

Crash pulled general duty, which meant he could pick whatever he wanted. He nobly wrote his name underneath mine, filling the second spot. Then he grabbed two large pieces of pumpkin brittle and handed me one while we waited in the costume line. In exchange for our slips of paper, we were handed two bulky bags stuffed with puffy orange cloth.

"Let's take these home," I said, poking mine as we the crossed the square. "We can keep them both at my place and get ready together."

Crash tipped his hat. "Sounds good."

We reached the bridge and scooted underneath for a bottle check. Crash spotted it first, a purple one about five inches long. He passed it to me.

I got the paper out and read the words: "'Above the coo-per's door.'"

A cooper was a bucket and barrel maker. Gilbreth's coopers were the Trawley family. Their shop was one of the oldest on the square. Puzzled, I handed the message to Crash and scooted up to the bridge. "Okay, so what does that one mean?"

He scrambled behind me. "How would I know? It means there's something above the cooper's door." His eyes bugged out, which meant he was excited, so my ears were well braced when he shouted, "Treasure!" He stabbed a finger at the message.

"Crash, I really doubt there's treasure, and I doubt even more that it'd just be hanging out over the cooper's door. And who says the messages are even for us?"

He shrugged. "I don't know. I guess it depends on who's writing them?" He scanned the exterior of the bridge as though somebody might be hiding.

"At least this one has something that doesn't involve sneaking. We can go take a look."

"Sounds good. Do you want to invite Grace? Or do you just want it to be us?"

I sighed at his pink cheeks. "Sure, let's invite her."

Even though I didn't appreciate getting pumpkin duty, I dealt in facts, mostly about the emotional roller coaster of growing up. I was not a sleuth. And Crash, well, enthusiastic as he might be, I think he was more interested in what outfit he'd need for the part. No, I decided that Grace Ripty, strange as she was, might just be the person we needed to solve this strange set of messages.

We walked home in silence, listening to birds and crunching leaves. I ran up to my room, dumped the costumes, and pulled up the closet floorboard. Beneath it was the stack of papers. I sifted through them to the *R* pages, and there was the name and Gilbreth address: David Ripty.

The new town mayor had gone to college with my mom. I didn't like that idea at all. I felt like crossing him off the list right then, since it was ridiculous to think of my mother ever dating a slimy-haired town improvement inspector. Not that everyone wasn't entitled to their own hair product and occupation choice. But still.

A careful flip through the pages revealed exactly four Gilbreth PO. box addresses:

> Charles Mackenzie
> David Ripty
> William Wharton
> Alfonso Willis

I felt a tingle—a spark that made me wish I had one of Grace's notebooks to jot the names down in. Everyone on the list was a brown- or black-haired man.

Two had bigger noses like mine (Ripty and Wharton).

One had a jerky son (Willis).

One had a son who seemed nice (Mackenzie).

One was an outsider that I didn't like at all (Ripty).

One was practically family already (Wharton).

All were pretty average height. All were within walking distance.

No way. First of all, even after only a few conversations with him and having had zero conversations with my mother, I was certain the mayor was not a possibility. And surely, any potential father who'd always lived in Gilbreth would have made himself known to me.

"Absolutely not. Makes no sense at all," I told Beast, who Crash had sent up the stairs to get me.

But then I lost my breath.

About a year ago, during one of their book club meetings, I'd heard the back end of a conversation in which my uncle and Will talked about how Mom had been love crazy at college—how she'd dated so much, declaring that she was going to marry this person or that person, that nobody quite knew who was her friend, who was her boyfriend, and who she'd just dumped. She'd always worn her heart on her sleeve, Will said, giving it away time and time again. Was it possible that one of the Gilbreth names *was* my father, and nobody had ever found out that I was his child?

Even if there was a chance, which clearly there was not, I couldn't just walk up and ask them if they'd secretly dated my mother a million years ago. They'd immediately contact Uncle Theo, who would probably have me psychoanalyzed for delusional accusations. I needed him focused on the Town Square shop contest.

A Gilbreth father made zero sense. Zilch, zip, nada. All it did was help me eliminate a few names. My gut rumbled a disagreement, then knotted up with a sharp pain, and I had the strangest, flitting, fluttering feeling that what I was looking for, what I needed to find, was closer than I'd ever imagined.

But maybe it was only because a single pancake and a chicken wing were all I'd had to eat today. I took a pencil from the desk drawer and firmly crossed out each of the four names. Three hundred ten possibilities to go.

Then I lifted the paper stack from my two-hundred-year-old desk, slipped it into my backpack, and stared at the metal-bound book on top of my bed, wondering why my mother had left behind a diary from her twelfth year, but not something that would tell me who my father was.

I shook away the thought, ready to switch back over to bottle-message investigation mode.

Above the cooper's door.

Pushing open the back door, I saw Crash slipping down the final rungs of the old tree house. "What are you doing up there?" I called. "That thing's falling apart." I pointed across the yard. "Hence the new tree house?"

"Just looking," he said, hurrying over, with one hand holding on to his tall hat. "I . . . thought I saw another bluebird nest up there. But I didn't. Let's do this. And maybe try not to get locked anywhere this time."

I told him about the Gilbreth names. We both had a good laugh. Because it was ridiculous to think that the piece of me that was missing was right here in Gilbreth.

"Hey, Crash, do you think Mr. Mackenzie's nose looks like mine?"

He took off the hat, holding it between his two hands in a solemn manner. "Do you *want* your nose to look like Mr. Mackenzie's?"

"*No.* I mean, it's a fine nose, but no. No, I don't."

"Good. Because it doesn't. Your nose looks like it belongs exactly to you."

But if I wasn't mistaken, Crash was still taking an awfully close look at the center of my face.

"Hoist the sails, crew member Lincoln," I told him. "Set the course for Town Hall to fill out a contest form for my dear uncle, then over to Grace, then to the cooper's shop."

He snapped out of nasal-inspection mode and switched it for crew mode, saluting heartily. "Aye, aye!" he cried, and then everything felt normal again.

Sort of.

Above the Cooper's Door

In 1720 the only known case of accidental domestic homicide in Gilbreth occurred when the neighbor of Elias Treat hit her husband and her brother-in-law over the head with a cast-iron pot after they came home late from Three Dogs Tavern, having gambled much of the money meant to buy a heifer, a hog, and five goats. The only other multiple homicide recorded in Gilbreth history was the horrific attack at what is now the Trawleys' cooper establishment.

–From **Gilbreth History: Founding Families & Artisanal
Traditions** (Gilbreth Welcome Center, $16.99)

The front door was locked.

The cooper's shop was one of the buildings originally built on the square, with the west-facing wall made of rough blocks of time-hewn fieldstone and the rest made of solid oak. It was on a corner where a street met up with Town Square's circle.

When I knocked, there was no answer. A brief jog along the street and survey of the Village Green told us that Ms. Trawley was in the midst of giving a barrel-making demonstration, surrounded by a handful of kids who'd be helping her during Autumnfest.

"Above the door," Grace muttered, peering up. She'd looked more than surprised when we asked Mrs. Finnegan to let her go, but also pleased.

The door was a relatively new one by Treat standards, built by my great-grandfather and painted a midnight blue. Outside the one front window was a flower box stuffed with yellow and red autumn mums. Above the doorframe was a rusty horseshoe with a sprig of herbs in the center, and above that was a window.

I reached up and tugged on the herbs. "What's this?" An empty bucket stood beside the doorway. I turned it over, stepped on top, and lifted the sprig of short green needles. A deep set of letters and numbers was beneath it, carved neatly between the sides of the horseshoe: T. TREAT—1710. It figured that one of my relatives had built this shop.

I could practically hear the carved name growling at me to go home and work on a woodcraft project that would be worthy of the family. Before it could make me feel too guilty, I let the herbs drop back over it.

Grace scrawled the letters and date into her small notebook. "Rosemary, I think." She sneezed, then jotted down the message and the word "rosemary." "Do any of the other messages relate to the shop or a door or rosemary?"

"No." I glanced around the side of the building. "But there's more than one door."

The back area of the cooper's shop was surrounded by an unlocked fence. Inside the fence was a tarped area stacked with wood and tools, a grassy area with dog dishes and toys, and a gravel path leading to the back door. Nothing was over it at all.

"Back to the front door?" Crash asked, his first words since Grace had joined us. He kept sneaking looks at her, which was annoying. I needed him to focus.

"Front door," I agreed, hurrying back to the shop entrance. "We've got to be missing something. Or else it's about the rosemary."

Grace snapped her fingers. "Above the door," she said. "There's a window there, which means there's a room. What if the thing we need to find is in the room?"

I shrugged. "Then we're out of luck."

She grinned and pointed to the side of the building. "There's a window on that side. It was open when we ran past just now. You could take a peek?" she suggested.

"Me?" I knew that window. It was a good fifteen feet up. "Why?"

"If this were a book, Ms. Trawley would be hiding something. If we waited, she'd let us in, then distract us with cookies or by having us look at a photograph that didn't mean anything, while she shoved all of her bloody knives and suspicious ropes into the closet and slipped any incriminating notes into her bosom. We should take a look at the room without her knowing."

A snort wiggled out before I could stop myself. "Did you say 'bosom'?"

"Suspicious ropes?" Crash asked.

Grace tugged on her necklaces and dropped the laser eyes. "I read historicals, mostly."

"Historicals." Crash stared openly at her and nodded, then slipped me the elbow. "See?" he tried to whisper, failing miserably. "Interesting."

She certainly was getting chattier than she was in class, I'd give her that. "Let's just wait for Ms. Trawley and ask her a couple of questions. She's nice."

"So are most of the criminals in my books," Grace insisted. "They lead two lives, and one of them is dedicated to offering people cookies so they don't find out about the second one. And you should be the one to climb up there," she said, "because you scrambled up the gym rope like it was nothing and I saw you climbing the biggest oak tree in the Village Green over the summer. There weren't even any branches for ten feet and you made it up. It was amazing."

Her attention to detail was the amazing thing. The combination of stalkerly creepiness and flattery was confusing. "I only did it because Michael Willis dared me."

She smiled. "So I dare you."

"I'll have you know," I told her, trying to keep my voice firm with a hint of severity (advised in several books for parents dealing with situations calling for gentle admonishment), "that dares posed in peer-pressure situations, *particularly* those promoting deviant behavior like, say, breaking and entering, not only increase anxiety in the average child, but can lead to dangerous and even fatal results."

"Oh." Grace frowned and looked at her shoes. "I was . . . I'm sorry, I was kidding. Kind of."

I tapped her shoulder and cleared my throat. "Luckily, I am not an average child. I am a Treat. Crash, on the lookout, please."

He saluted and aye-ayed me as I approached the side wall, hidden from Village Green view. I fought ivy to wedge my toes into decent footholds and within moments had my fingers wrapped around the window's ledge.

"Hurry up," Crash warned. "Someone's going to turn the corner in a minute."

Pulling up hard, I hauled myself into the room, half expecting to see a bloody knife lying on the floor.

Instead I looked around to see a very normal bedroom and living quarters. I hadn't realized that Ms. Trawley and her wife, a local weaver, lived over her shop. There was a queen-size bed covered in a beautiful blue embroidered quilt, and a desk with neatly stacked papers and pens placed in a tall red box. There was a dresser with a pile of folded shirts and pants on top, along with a foot-high leafless iron tree with necklaces dangling and a small jar of loose change. A round woven rug covered most of the wood floor. Everything looked neat. Clean. Nothing much of notice.

"Minna! It's Ms. Trawley, she's—*oof!* Grace, why'd you—"

Dying to peer out the window, I froze while Grace's voice sang out clearly, "Ms. Trawley! We were just, um, hoping to, well, have a little tour." There was a faint tapping noise, I guessed on her notebook. "I just need a few notes in here for a school project, and I'm totally going to be late if I don't interview one more, um, crafty person. And then Crash and I are going to the *library* to finish the report."

Did she want me to meet them at the library? Realizing they were around the corner at the front door, I peeked out the open window and looked down. Descending the wall would definitely be more challenging than coming up. Not a great option. Despite it condemning me as an official thief, I tossed a penny out the window, into the side street.

Slowly a foot scooted its way around the corner, followed by an anxious-faced Crash. I pointed down and shook my head. He nodded and returned to the conversation.

"Sure, dear."

"It won't take long and the questions are easy. For

instance," Grace said quickly, "why do you have that horse-shoe and rosemary over your door?"

"The horseshoe's always been there. This used to be the blacksmith's shop, so it was for advertising, probably. Then after the triple murder the building was sold to my family."

"Triple murder?" Even from the room above, the delighted tone of Grace's voice was unmistakable. "What triple murder?"

"Oh, it was terrible—during the Revolutionary War a soldier on the wrong side of the war demanded tools and shelter, and the blacksmith of the time refused both. He and his two sons were stabbed to death in their sleep that night, right upstairs, above their own shop. It was a family who'd already lost nearly all their relatives to some sort of pox the generation before. Such sad losses. Anyway, the rosemary's a nod to the past. Rosemary for remembrance, my mother always said. I hung it there on the day she passed away and replace it whenever it starts to look raggedy."

The front door clicked and opened on the floor below me, and I heard slightly muffled dialogue. "Oh. Would you care for cookies? Tamarin Willis dropped them off and—" A series of sneezes from Grace cut off the rest.

Well, crud buckets. Buckets and barrels of cruddy-filled crud.

While I technically wasn't burglarizing anything, it would look odd at best and criminal at worst if I were found in the Trawleys' bedroom with no explanation. The accidental fire at school, I felt, was strongly defensible, but this . . . well, if Uncle Theo had read to chapter 8 of *Time Out: Actions and Consequences for Your Beloved Preteen*, I would no doubt have a grounded and uncomfortable and possibly therapy-filled few months ahead of me.

"Let me go change," Ms. Trawley's voice rang out, "and I'll be right down."

Footfalls fell on the stairway.

If I flung myself across the hall to the bathroom, Ms. Trawley would have a first-rate view of me. Who knew what she'd accidentally do when she came across an intruder? Had she ever learned to process, not panic? It seemed doubtful, and her ginormous arm muscles were approximately the size of my head, which could spell trouble for me if I startled her. This was a woman who curved steel around giant wooden slats for a living, for goodness' sake!

Oh *Lord*, she'd crush my skull! And I'd die with a reputation of burgling a house, bringing shame galore to the Treat name.

After desperately searching the room, I dived under the bed, only to knock my forehead on wooden drawers concealed behind the comforter. The small closet was stuffed and might be the place she was headed.

I positioned myself behind the door, thinking maybe when she came in, she'd stand in front of the closet, so I could slip out.

I held my breath.

"Ow!" a voice boomed, the noise echoing so loudly that it couldn't be anything but my best friend, Crash, using the apex of his loud mouth. "My foot!"

Grace's voice came next. "Ms. Trawley, come quick! Crash just, well, crashed over some tool in your backyard! I told him to stay put, but—"

"Hold on!" Ms. Trawley called, hurrying down the stairs.

As soon as I heard the back door shut, I hurried down the steps and out the front door, sweating like a maniac and hoping nobody was watching other than Mr. Abel, who gave me a curious, almost amused wave from a park bench on the Village Green.

An hour later we were all lounging on separate sides of the large, cushioned window seat in Gilbreth Library's children's section. There was something comforting about the thick shag rugs, scattered puzzles, oversize stuffed animals, and colorful walls, busy with posters and kindergarten artwork of black cats and scarecrows and smiling pumpkins. It was a happy space, quaint and welcoming. Only the tiny tables and chairs gave me a weird, hollow feeling. Maybe because I couldn't squeeze into any of them anymore.

Grace's eyebrows rose and she sent her type-three stare my way for a minute before she spoke. "What do you mean, another mystery? Other than the bottles?"

I pulled the list out of my pack and handed it to her. "He's in there somewhere. He was a junior at Camden

College the same year my mom was—that's all I know. Nobody knows I'm trying to find him."

Grace flipped through the stack. "But why can't you just tell your uncle? Or just ask everyone on the list?"

I shook my head firmly and explained that we didn't have extra money for stationery and stamps, and that even if we did, Uncle Theo didn't think my father was worth finding.

"Has your dad ever tried to get in touch before?"

"I don't think my father even knows I exist. Hey, um, random question, but does your dad happen to have long pointer toes on his feet?"

Both she and Crash spoke at the same time. "What?"

"Never mind." Ew, ew, ew, I didn't want to picture the mayor's feet, but now I was picturing the mayor's feet! Nasty, hairy Hobbit feet with a long toe on each one and—"Listen," I said, "don't tell anyone about the names. You have to promise. Somebody could lose their job or get sued or both. And now that you know about me using the list, you could be held liable if somebody finds out."

"Really?"

"Possibly."

Her eyes widened, but she nodded. "I promise."

"Grace?"

"Yeah?"

"Why don't you eat lunch with us this week. If you want to," I added.

According to *Inferno: How School Cafeterias Can Be the Devil's Playground*, one surefire way of being emotionally damaged during lunch is to have nobody to sit with. Luckily, I had Crash, and during our first week of eating in the same large room as our peers, we'd managed to survive just fine with only a few isolated incidents not even worth mentioning because the stains came out of our shirts just fine.

She didn't respond, so I tried another approach. "I'm a woodsmith. Crash is a glassblower and random-historical-figure expert," I said, ignoring the guilty look on his face, because sure, he was making blobs now, but he'd be a master in the coming years. "We need you, Grace."

"I'm not good at anything," she said, confused.

"You," I told her confidently, "are a mystery expert. And three different people with three different interests can create a triangle of social bonding that's as strong and iconic as the Eiffel Tower." Or something like that.

On second thought, maybe I was mixing up my parenting books.

"Okay. I'll eat with you. And I'll help you solve your mysteries—the father one *and* the bottle one—on one condition." She hesitated, kicking at the ground. "Invite me to sleep over next weekend." She blushed and looked up. "I kind of told my dad we were friends so he'd back off."

I elbowed Crash before he could bellow something that

would embarrass us all. Instead his stomach let out a huge growl. "Deal."

She smiled again while tugging on her million necklaces. "Now, if I'm going to help solve the bottle mystery," Grace said carefully, a glow of excitement simmering beneath her serious face, "I think we all need to face the possibility that this could be dangerous. *Especially*," she said, "considering that a triple murder occurred in the room above the cooper's door."

I didn't like her line of thinking. "What about the rosemary?"

"Or the horseshoe?" Crash squeaked.

She ignored us. "Is there anyone who might be looking to get revenge against you two?" Her pen was poised over her notebook, ready to list potential enemies.

Crash and I exchanged glances and came up with nobody, other than Lem and Chai.

Grace looked slightly disappointed, then perked up. "In that case," she said, "we're dealing with a benevolent mystery person who's trying to tell you something. Well, either that or a completely random maniac trying to lead you into a trap."

Suddenly I craved a mugful of hearth milk and a nice, nonmystery, non-mother's-diary kind of book. Maybe one about puppies. "I vote for benevolent," I said, my voice coming out hoarse.

She stood up and coughed into her elbow. "Okay, I've got to get home. Bring all the bottles and messages to school tomorrow, including any others you find. We'll have a full strategy session." She frowned. "Fingerprints are out because everything's been touched by you and the message leaver probably used gloves. My dusting kit can stay at home. But I'll bring my handwriting analysis book."

Crash stared at her in open admiration. "You're amazing," he declared.

I felt myself frown, then lifted my lips to turn it into a leaderly grimace. They were *my* bottles, after all, or at least they'd been found under my family-built bridge. That put me in charge. And leaders, like parents, needed to keep control of their groups. Favoritism was as bad for our group as it would be in the case of siblings.

"She's very amazing, yes," I said. "But we're a team now. We're *all* amazing." I cleared my throat and lifted Crash to his feet. "Good work, everyone. Tomorrow's the start of the school week—let's use lunchtime for full strategy sessions."

In the back of my mind I heard the voice of all the parenting books, a soothing yet commanding voice that could equally hypnotize and frustrate a person. It spoke a combination of words from the books—annoying words like "avoidance," "priorities," and "character." Then it whispered that the bottles would do nothing to win me an artisan contest or keep me in Gilbreth.

I silently told that parenting-book voice to shut its cakehole.

~ ~ ~

When I got home, I noticed something I'd missed at breakfast. Uncle Theo had written a new vocabulary word, "procrastination," on the kitchen chalkboard. Along with it was a note saying, *It's never too early to finish the base of a wood project—it gives you more time for the finishing touches. And remember, sometimes simple is best! Love, your loving and incredibly intelligent and only slightly intrusive Captain.*

After heating a mug of apple cider in the microwave and giving the sentences a well-adjusted minute of consideration, I erased the board and climbed the steps to his office space, where I promptly took all parenting books mentioning procrastination and turned them around, giving the spines and titles a much-needed time-out.

I marched to my room, then took off my backpack and launched myself onto the bed, crying out at something digging into my back. Rolling over, I saw mom's journal. The stupid thing was trying to give me a lecture too. Taking a deep breath, I pictured the photograph of my mom that Uncle Theo had found beside the journal. I erased myself and inserted a Jane Addams–ish dress on Mom, then imagined the whole thing in black and white. There. Much better.

I opened the diary.

Mom Memories
and Uncle Dreams

*After Elizabeth Maybeck's death Elias Treat lived in relative
silence for several years. His friend John Abel visited him often,
bringing news of the village, building materials, fresh bread
baked by his new wife, and candles. Elias made pens from the
fallen feathers of the developing Torrey Wood flock of turtledoves, whose excrement he kept a jar of, wiping it across his face
to deter any unwanted visitors who dropped by, wanting a chat.*

–From **Gilbreth History: Founding Families & Artisanal
Traditions** (Gilbreth Welcome Center, $16.99)

JOURNAL OF ELIZABETH TREAT'S
12th YEAR (KEEP OUT, THEO!)

That's what the first page said, which told me that Uncle
Theo had always been the prying type. The entries weren't
dated, and they were all over the place, some just a single

sentence or a short paragraph, some longer, many with blank pages in between. They were all, if I was being honest, the kind of random thoughts that I might write down in a journal. Things like:

> Oh my seesaw, can we just live in the NOW for now? If I get one more dress that looks like it's from the 18ØØs, I'm going to puke in my morning oatmeal.

And this one:

> We found a squirrel body in the walls today, which explains the stink in my room. Theo, if you're reading this, I'm going to roast your toes in your sleep, you toad.

And this:

> Is it defacing public property if you have to perform acrobatic acts to do it and the property was built by your family? Hope not.

And this:

> I took something today. I can't even believe it and I'm not even going to write down what it was. I'm a good person! Or I was. It was stupid and I wish I could have just put it

> back, but she came around the corner, so I
> ran to the woods and got rid of it, so nobody
> will ever know I did it, except me.

I flipped through, just letting my eyes graze over the words lightly, trying not to touch them too closely, or think about the girl who'd held the pen, or think about where she'd been when she wrote them or if she'd had a zit on her nose like mine, because they were just words. Like a storybook in journal format.

Then there was this one:

> I <u>hate</u> sanding wood. Mom says it's relaxing
> and gives you time to think about nothing,
> the same way Dad enjoys ironing. If sanding
> wood and ironing shirts is an adult Treat's
> idea of having a good time, holy cannoli, let
> me never grow up and be an adult.

I turned pages quickly to find another entry before I could think about that one.

"Minna!" Uncle Theo's voice called up the steps. "I'm home! Get down here for a second!"

I threw the journal onto the edge of my desk. "You know, Jane Addams's journal would have been much more organized," I told it. After sipping the last of my cider, I quickly set the mug on top of the cover, far enough back so it wouldn't spill, and turned to the door. A crash and thump sounded behind me. Broken pieces of mug lay beside the journal.

"Minna!"

"Coming!"

Darn it. Lifting the journal with one hand, I picked up the clay shards with the other. A jagged end on the last piece cut my finger, and the journal fell on the floor, spreading its pages like a stuck-out tongue. "Ow, jeez!"

Sucking on the small wound, I glanced at the exposed entry and froze. My finger slipped from my mouth, and a single drop of blood fell and blossomed just above the words:

> I found a bottle sitting on a window of Whistler Bridge today. It had something inside it.

That was all it said.

"Minna!" Uncle Theo's voice called up the steps. "Come down to the workshop for a second!"

I flipped frantically to the next entry, but it was about some boy in her class. The next one didn't mention the bottle message either—it talked about a summer party on the riverside. How could she just mention a bottle and not say what was in it? I flipped back and forth, thinking what a pain my mother was for writing entries wherever she pleased.

"Minna! I need your help for a minute, okay?"

"Okay, coming!" I placed the journal carefully in the middle of my bed and watched it for a second, almost expecting it to come to life.

I walked down the stairs, out the back door, and over to the barn with the strangest sensation. A tugging sort of connection to the book on my bed. Like my mother was trying to tell me something.

"Minnapup! Can you work on smoothing that guy over there so we can start staining tomorrow?"

He threw me a piece of sanding paper with a ginormous smile and directed me to a Quaker-style chair. He'd changed into his favorite T-shirt, a Wanted poster of things that were the nemeses of wood. Despite the nasty-looking fungi and molds and termites and beetles dressed up in cowboy gear, I was happy to see it. Uncle Theo in a suit made me nervous.

But still, he looked suspiciously pleased—way too pleased for someone who should be thinking about how to keep his family's house. He wiped off some forehead sweat and grinned, gesturing to the door he was working on. "What do you think?"

I looked the door over. "I think it's a big rectangle of wood. Specifically, walnut."

"Ha! Yes, but check this out." He passed me a sheet of paper with his sketch. It was full of straight indentations, with delicate swirls of leaves in each corner and a simple design in the center that brought to mind sunlight. It was more than a door. It was more than a loving entrance to a home. It was art.

"Beautiful," I said, then told him about the mayor's announcement, watching my uncle's face and knowing immediately that he wanted that shop more than he would ever tell me. He deserved something of his own but barely even admitted it to himself because he felt so duty-bound to me. I'd learned that from a book that Uncle Theo kept under his pillow called *Balance and the Single Parent: Making and Taking Time for Your Own Goals, Dreams, and Possibilities.*

I had been trying to be nice by making his bed for him one day, completely without the intention of snooping around, but open to finding anything interesting that might make an appearance. That's when I found the book. There were a few others shoved between the bed frame and the wall, too, and a sketchbook that showed a storefront with the sign

THEODORE TREAT & CO.
FINE CUSTOM FURNITURE & WOODCRAFT

I had left the room without tidying a thing. People who put books under their pillows and sketchbooks between bed frames and walls probably don't need the extra stress of worrying about whether their niece-daughters have noticed those things while being nice and making their beds. Plus, who can make a bed with so much clutter in it? No wonder he was a bed slob.

He remained silent for several moments after I told him about the contest. Then he said something surprising.

"I knew Gene was giving up his shop. He didn't mention a contest to see who gets to take over the lease. Maybe because he knew I couldn't do it, Minns. I need to be home for you." He shook his head, then opened his mouth to say more, but I cut him off.

"That's ridiculous! I've got Beast! Plus, I'm almost thirteen, Captain. I'm in school from seven thirty to three. I can come to the store after school if you want, but there's no reason you can't make it work. And I can help you during the summer or do apprenticeships close by. And besides, I already signed you up. Now you have to enter."

He bit his lip, looking at his spare-wood rack. "Two weeks isn't enough to make anything, Minna." He gestured around the shed to the works in progress. "Not when I've got deadlines on these two projects that just came in. They won't pay much, but I've got to get them done. Plus, remember when that botanical garden hired me for outdoor furniture? Then they said they weren't ready to expand yet? Now they want thirteen custom benches pronto."

"I'll help," I said matter-of-factly. "I know you won't let me do the main work, but I can save you tons of time by doing the sanding and staining. And you can push back your deadlines by a week or two."

Uncle Theo rubbed his beard. "Possibly." He grinned. "I never told you this, but a few years ago Gene and Evangeline offered to give me the shop whenever he retired. I refused, saying the barn would be my workshop forever. But sometimes life sends you second chances." A twinkle lit up his eyes. "You know what? I'll do it. What should I make? Maybe a chair or a table or . . ." His face fell slightly. "Now I feel like I'll be neglecting you again next weekend."

That was exactly the point. I needed him busy so he wouldn't realize that I was sneaking around, chasing bottle and father mysteries instead of putting my all into my junior artisan project. I thought fast. "No problem. Can Grace Ripty come over on Friday for a sleepover?"

He didn't look upset, just puzzled. "The mayor's daughter?"

"Yep. We've been bonding. PS, ahem, good sir, perhaps you'll remember that our dear Mayor Ripty is one of the judges for the *Town Square shop contest*. Couldn't hurt to buddy up to his daughter and show her a good time, eh?" I nudged him with my elbow for good measure.

He gave me an appraising glance. "She can come. But if Christopher is hanging out, he has to go home to sleep. Deal?"

"Deal. And he likes to be called Crash."

"I'm not calling him Crash."

"Fine. Uncle Theo?"

"Yes?"

"Would Mom have ever described Gilbreth as having . . ." I reached for Mayor Ripty's words. "A sense of magic lingering up its very old sleeve?"

He chuckled. "Your mom wasn't sentimental enough to say anything like that."

Whew.

He cocked his head to the side. "You know, she'd be happy that you're making girlfriends. It's good to hear you ask about her. Any other questions?"

"No. You get to work on ideas." I shook a finger at him. "There's no need for *procrastination.* PS, are you using any of that?" I pointed to the junk pile, bits and pieces of wood, both high quality and low.

He grinned. "Be my guest, mystery girl. I can't wait to see what you're making."

"Me neither," I mumbled, filling a canvas sack with odds and ends of maple, walnut, oak, and cedar, wondering what the heck I was going to make out of a big load of scraps. But lying to Uncle Theo had left me with an uncomfortable knot in my stomach, and I thought maybe taking some wood to the school's woodshop would help unravel it a little.

"How did the interview go?"

"Great! They want me to teach two classes a week, plus a woodworking course on weekends."

"Were they mad when you turned them down?" I ran a hand over the chair, smoothing it with the sandpaper. "You know, since we live here and it would be too far to commute during the week."

His puzzled eyes blinked, turning into wary caution signs. "You're right. It would be too far." He swallowed what I imagined to be a decent-size ball of guilt for not mentioning us moving. It was impressive, actually. "I told them I'd think about it," he said. "They're giving me two weeks to decide."

"In about two weeks you'll have a shop on Town Square." My own ball of anger dissolved immediately, replaced by a bright and warm sense of relief, even despite my uncle's very blatant lie of omission.

He paused, just a beat. "You bet. And you'll be planning a trip to New York City after winning this year's junior artisan project."

I paused, just a beat. "You bet. Now hurry up and figure out what you're going to make. Nobody likes a procrastinator."

"That's very true." His excited gaze danced over the spare-wood pile. "Procrastination usually only leads one place."

"Where's that?" *Please say victory, please say victory, please say victory.*

"Disaster."

Between a week's worth of lectures on Gilbreth's tragic events, a bottle message leading us to a place where a brutal murder had happened, and the doomed prospect of having nothing better than a frame to submit on Bonfire Night, it seemed that something was building. Like there was a storm on the horizon, and I couldn't do a thing to stop it.

I let out a choked laugh. "Disaster. That's a good one. Thank goodness we don't have to worry about that."

A Brief Word on the Other Treats

In addition to making beautiful chairs, my nine-times great-grandfather Treat once helped build a boat that brought people to America.

My five-times great-grandfather Treat built wagons that brought people to and from Gilbreth.

My four-times great-grandfather Treat built a church for the Gilbreth villagers to gather in and homes for them to live within.

My three-times great-grandfather Treat built beautiful tables and shelves to fill homes and rooms and walls with warmth and character.

Grandma Treat carved salt and pepper shakers and small animals to decorate tables and shelves.

My mom made the grandfather clock standing in our hallway.

Uncle Theo's specialty is chairs.

What will I make? What will I leave behind? Why do

I have to think about my accomplishments being part of a long line of Gilbreth legacies that some future kid will be forced to memorize?

I love Gilbreth and can't imagine my life anywhere else . . . but every now and then I wonder if the generations of artisans who stay in this town aren't secretly turtledoves. We're all kept so nice and cozy and fed on memories that we've forgotten what it means to migrate.

Strategy in Ruins

In 1723 Elias Treat was eating dinner with his three brothers at Three Dogs Tavern when raucous cries came from the barrel room. Upon inspection, they found two of the Mackenzie brothers lying within it, bound and gagged and suffering from nonfatal stabbing wounds. A wagon full of their ale had been stolen. The thieves tried to leave the area via South Bridge but were met by Elias and Samuel, who had anticipated the escape route. Stronger doors and locks were immediately commissioned by the tavern.

–From **Gilbreth History: Founding Families & Artisanal Traditions** (Gilbreth Welcome Center, $16.99)

The following Friday, Crash and I trailed the rest of the class over Whistler Bridge, heading toward the original settlement ruins to eat lunch. Everyone from school had spent the morning doing annual litter pickup in Torrey

Wood, so any tourists who took hikes the following week-end would find the forest pristinely trash-free. Crash and I had volunteered to clean the ravine near the bridge, ensuring that nobody else would find our bottles.

There were just ten days until my looming project dead-line. Uncle Theo had begged for artisan project details seven more times and asked how I was liking the diary five more times; the real estate agent had left four more messages, which I then deleted; and Crash and I had found four more mysterious messages.

That brought the total found to ten, but none of the mes-sages made the least amount of sense, other than the one that called out Mr. Abel for being unable to work. Grace hadn't been to school that week because of a flu bug, and without our mystery expert Crash and I had been at a loss.

"Let's go over the messages while we eat," I said. "I brought them all with me."

We wound in and out of pockets of students, search-ing for a slightly isolated spot. While Michael Willis pelted twigs at a classmate who'd jokingly put himself into the ancient public stocks, Darian Mackenzie wandered the area, squatting down at various bunches of greens and examining them. Malia Johnson sat in a large group of friends, all of them chittering excitedly.

"Remind me again why she and Jaron are even entering the contest?" I whispered to Crash. "It's not like they need a trip to go meet fancy collectors. Really, it's grossly greedy. Don't you think?"

"Do you really want me to answer that?" he asked. He put a finger to his lips and tapped them. "I think you might be lashing out at others because of insecure feelings regarding your own situation." He grinned. "Can't remember which book you said that was from, but pretty good, huh?"

I shot him a begrudging nod and pointed to three stacked logs that were the remnants of a cabin. "Let's sit there."

Even a sunny day couldn't take away the haunted feeling around the ruins. I pulled my lunch and the bottle messages out of my backpack and sat down. "Where have you been after school this week, anyway?"

He sank beside me. "Nowhere. Just doing stuff. My parents had me help Mr. Abel box up his shop. I've had a lot of chores at home. It's my week to do laundry."

That was a lie. He'd paid for pizza with laundry money the weekend before. "You weren't at home when I stopped by yesterday. Tommy was getting dinner to take back to the shop. He said he thought you were with me."

He shrugged. "I was there. Catching up on sleep. You know my house—everybody's somewhere different and nobody pays attention to anyone."

Hmm. He *did* look somewhat refreshed, like he'd been sleeping way better than I had. Crash put down his sandwich and moved on to his chips, looking distracted. I organized the messages on the ground in front of us and was just going to tell him to focus when a shadow hanging over my shoulder distracted me as well.

"Hey," said Grace, with her *Mona Lisa* mouth. She glanced around the old settlement grounds, hands tapping her sides as though she wanted to write down suspicious safety hazards for her dad.

"Hi," I said back, patting the ground beside me. "You weren't in homeroom this morning. Can you still sleep over? Where's your lunch?"

She pulled a thermos from her backpack. "Chicken soup. Dad was paranoid and took me to the doctor again to make sure I'm okay. I haven't puked for two days, so he said I can still come over to your place tonight." She sat next to Crash, bending her knees up and balancing a candy bar on them while she twisted open her water lid. "Why are you dressed like my grandfather?"

He was in a black suit and tie, white shirt, and white wig with an attachable wraparound handlebar mustache. A group of fanned condiment packets were arranged in his front jacket pocket.

"Why do you always wear fifty million necklaces and dress like a ninja?" he joked back, then blushed at Grace's reddening face. He tapped his pocket and gave a hesitant smile. "I'm Henry Heinz." His smile faded a little when she didn't respond. "He revolutionized the ketchup industry—

ring a bell?" He grabbed at the pocket, then reached out a hand, holding a ketchup packet to her.

She glanced over at me and I accepted the ketchup packet. "You look perfect," I told Crash.

He straightened his jacket. "Thank you, Minna."

Grace shook her head at the two of us, then glanced over the messages. "What have you two found out?"

Crash and I looked at her, both of us sinking slightly into the cabin wall.

"Not much," I said. "I thought maybe we'd hang out around the bridge tomorrow and see if we catch anyone throwing bottles."

She nodded. "That's a start. I would have been all over these messages if I hadn't been sick. Let's see." She brought one of the papers close to her face, her lips mumbling silently. "Okay, so handwriting analysis would say that these are all written by the same person . . . an experienced writer of letters . . . confident formation . . . right leaning, which indicates a desire to communicate, but that could be in any kind of way." She frowned and dropped the paper. "He or she could want to be supportive, or could be wanting to control someone." She nodded to herself. "This person could be a manipulator."

"A manipulator?" Crash shouted, earning a few puzzled glances from around the ruins.

Grace focused on the words. "Or friendly. It's hard to say for sure. Let's try sorting."

She started playing with all of the papers, taking out the first two messages and making two columns from the rest.

Column one:
> *Behind the baker's oven.*
> *In the tavern's barrel room.*
> *Above the cooper's door.*
> *Within the miller's wheel.*
> *On the apothecary's wall.*

And column two:
> *All things lost can be found or returned.*
> *Stolen forget-me-nots are always in bloom.*
> *Spirits return during Autumnfest.*

Trees stirred, and branches all around shifted with aching, stretching sounds. Squinting at the remnants of wood and stone structures around me—the stocks, the well, and other lingering imprints of past life—I could almost see a faint mist glide over the ruins.

Spirits return during Autumnfest.

My eyes nothing more than slits, I could picture the village as it once was—almost see lost souls in period dress going about their business as though they were still alive. A tingle—a vibration of recognition—passed quietly through me, then disappeared just as quickly. I slid the remaining messages over to Grace. "What about the first two messages I found?"

She half sighed and half grinned, like it was both a pain and a pleasure to have to explain this to us. "The 'Are you there?' message was clearly to get somebody's attention. And the message about the chandler was found days before Mr. Abel announced his retirement. It was to establish authority—to let us know that the message leaver knows things."

Grace tapped a message against her chin, then pulled out her tiny notebook, eyes scouring the notes inside. "The second group is weird. It's just random thoughts, but they must have something in common. What do you two know about forget-me-nots?"

"Um, they're flowers?" Crash lit up. "I could go to the florist and find out what they look like. And ask if somebody's stolen any?" He looked dubious until Grace gave him a solid thumbs-up.

"Okay, Crash will cover that. This whole first group is obviously instructions for us to find clues. We've been to the cooper's. What was above her door?"

"A horseshoe and rosemary," Crash supplied.

"And a window and a bedroom," I added.

"*And* the name of Minna's relative," Grace quipped. "On the house where a murder took place. So now we need to go to the baker's, the miller's, and the apothecary's, and back to the tavern, and see what we can dig up." She snapped. "Wait a minute! There was an explosion at the mill—remember from the list Mrs. Doring put on the class board?" Grace sucked in a breath. "People died there, too. I read about it."

I shook my head. "But the note says 'the miller's *wheel.*' The only mill with a wheel is the Stunettis'. Nobody's died there."

"Oh." She looked slightly deflated.

"Nobody's died at the apothecary's, either," Crash declared, then frowned. "There's a sign on his wall saying that. Or maybe he just means that nobody's died from his remedies."

Just as I was going to suggest that maybe we should stop talking about people dying, something slammed into Grace Ripty's knees and exploded. Tiny eggshell fragments stuck to her jeans. Someone had tossed a soft-boiled egg, maybe. A wadded-up piece of paper followed. Slowly she reached down and uncrumpled it.

"'You don't belong, necklace freak,'" she read. "'Go back to wherever you came from. Take your stupid dad with you.'"

I stood, trying to estimate the culprits based on the angle the egg and paper had come from. Twenty feet away, next to a tall tulip poplar, Michael Willis was standing on the edge of a group of his chortling meathead gorilla friends, looking at a scruffy wad of twigs. They were all high-fiving. Michael slapped a waiting hand, then turned away and bent, touching a fallen bird's nest.

I stuck two fingers in my mouth and aimed my loud whistle his way. "Hey! Who threw that?"

Crash stood up. "Who threw that paper?" he shouted.

"What do you care!" someone called.

Two seconds after I'd turned to comfort Grace, a sudden blow slammed into my back with a tiny *crunch*. When I examined the offending object, I found a very small and very crushed egg.

"What is it?" Grace asked.

"Turtledove egg," I muttered. Turtledoves lay eggs up to six times during a season in warmer climates, all the way into October, but the flock in Torrey Wood usually nested from April to July, with a few outliers now and then. I thought of Uncle Theo's words about procrastinating from the weekend before.

Some pair of doves had procrastinated until very, very late in the season to make their precious eggs. It wasn't their fault disaster hit, but that didn't change the outcome. Heat burst into my chest and cheeks.

With only a brief moment of mourning for the rest of my sandwich, I launched a peanut-butter-and-bread ball into the air, landing a direct hit on Michael's bulbous nose.

"You'll pay for that, Treat," he growled.

Feeling only a tiny bit of guilt for not asking, I snatched the rest of Crash's bean burrito and fired it into Michael's chest. "I already have to live in the same town with you, don't

I? Isn't that punishment enough? And throwing mean notes and killing small animals doesn't make you tough, it makes you a jerk."

His mouth opened to shout back, but nothing came out. His dark eyebrows sprang together, but they turned up at the insides, like he was trying to hold in something other than an insult. "The eggs were already ruined. I didn't throw them. Or the note."

"That'd be *me*!" one of his friends yelled, taking an exaggerated bow.

Two teachers had made their way back from a bathroom run, and our rumble drifted to a close. Laughing and whispering and muffled words buzzed through the air once again as I sank back into a sitting position.

"Doesn't matter," Grace said, straightening her posture, her stone face smooth as a statue while she shrugged. "That note's probably true."

Crash sat back down. "It's not true."

I didn't know what to say—what can you say about jerks? I was sure one of Uncle Theo's parenting books had covered this, but for the life of me, I couldn't summon the right words.

"I'm bad at art," I blurted. "Just really terrible."

She looked surprised, then puzzled, then amused. She took a bite of candy bar, looking at me in a new kind of staring way. "I know you are," she said. "Even Crash says so."

"What?" I turned to Crash. "You said what?"

Crash gulped. "Nothing! Why would I say that? I wouldn't say that. I'm bad at fitting in. And blowing glass."

"Well, how about a toast," Grace said, reaching for one of my cheese puffs and lifting it into the air. "Cheers to us." Crash raised one beside hers, and they both looked over at me. To be honest, I was feeling a bit muddled by Crash's disloyalty.

Grace lowered her puff an inch, looking embarrassed. "Too stupid?"

It was just a wee bit early for Grace to be leading toasts, being the newbie to our group. But thinking that way would just lead to resentment, which was known to stunt emotional growth. "Not at all," I declared, lifting my puff just a tad higher than hers. "Crash, come over tonight so we can all make a plan."

He bit his lip. "But I was supposed to help . . . you know what, sure." He lifted his cheese puff to meet mine. "I'll be there."

We banged them together like fancy glasses, and I couldn't help but notice that a smile had sneaked onto my face. A crew of three didn't seem like such a big change after all. I wondered briefly what we'd been waiting for all these years, when it occurred to me that maybe Crash and I had been waiting for Grace, and she'd been waiting for us.

After the cleanup we returned to school, and the next period was my freebie. Free periods at Gilbreth School allow older students to go to study hall or to an assigned corner in one of the Specials classrooms to work on something related to that class. You can do extra sit-ups or shoot baskets in gym class, work on a basket or scarf in the weaving rooms, or go in one of the soundproof band rooms to practice an instrument.

I'd signed up to go to the woodshop to wait for my heart to be bitten and smitten by woody inspiration. So far I'd only managed to dismiss possibilities. With the deadline clock ticking, my choices were basically narrowed down to "creative wooden sculpture" or "creative and useful wooden item to be determined."

"Hi, Minna," said Mr. McConnell, looking over the students filing into his classroom.

"Hi." I didn't take woodshop for obvious reasons, but Mr. McConnell had been letting me use his room since I had a weeklong fight with Crash in second grade over who would make a better superhero—one with glass power or one with wood power. We'd both caved after a week, but I'd spent those five days having lunch in the woodshop room. It was my favorite place in the school and it felt like home. Uncle Theo had even signed a permission slip, dismissing the school from liability if I chopped anything off, so I was allowed to use the equipment or even bring mine from home.

"Your uncle going to enter the contest for the Town Square shop?"

I nodded. "He's got some great ideas."

"And how about you? What are you making for the big artisan project?"

I squirmed. "Um, it's a surprise."

"Don't want the competition finding out?" He grinned, raised an eyebrow, and shot me with a finger pistol. "Attagirl. Only about a week left. Must be exciting. It's such a family tradition for you."

"Mm-hm."

"And now you'll be part of that tradition."

"Mm-hm." I gripped a worktable for support, feeling like my whole self was stuck firmly inside a vise.

"I'm sure yours will be a wonder to behold. It's important, you know. Tradition."

Jeez Louise, I got it. "Yes, sir. And actually, I'm going to, um, keep some of the project here, so my uncle won't see it. So," I lowered my voice to an unnecessary whisper, "if he asks you for any details, please just keep it ..." I gave him the shush sign and almost added a conspiratorial wink, but since winking at any teacher feels creepy, I left it out.

He gave me the thumbs-up sign. "Will do," he whispered back, returning to a group of third graders who were using wood glue to make boat-shaped pencil holders.

Adding chunks here and pieces there, I bulked up the frame I'd assembled over the last four days. I could hardly stand myself—I'd given in to peer pressure and made the one thing I'd sworn not to, and it wasn't even a good one!

Ten days until Bonfire Night presentations, and all I had to show for it was a mess.

Standing at arm's length, I saw that with all of the adding in I'd done, the empty space inside looked like a crude heart. A clumsy, damaged heart.

It was only when the bell rang, the classroom emptied, and it was time for me to pack up and leave that I saw the feather in the corner of the room.

The woodshop got swept out every night, so this had to be new. I walked to the corner, with that once-again feeling that I was being watched. A quick survey of the room assured me that nobody was there except me. I bent and picked up the feather—a beautiful thing left behind. A single hollow shaft with perfect white wisps, naturally combed at an angle without having ever touched a brush.

It was from the turtledove, I was certain. Still inside the school somewhere. It had gotten itself into a tight spot and probably felt trapped.

I hoped it would find its way out.

Stewing Plans
and a Sleepover

In 1725 a wood-chopping accident resulted in the loss of Elias Treat's left pinkie toe. He was henceforth jokingly called Old Eli Niner by his brothers and the villagers. In an odd coincidence, the final child of Samuel Treat was born the very same day and had eleven toes, bringing the overall Treat family toe count back to normal.

–From **Gilbreth History: Founding Families & Artisanal Traditions** (Gilbreth Welcome Center, $16.99)

L it only by my great-grandfather's oil lamp, my nook of the barn workshop was thick with anticipation and the smell of hamburger grease, which Crash had managed to spill all over himself while trying to sneak pieces of Uncle Theo's browning chili meat. He'd accidentally knocked the pan off the stove, and we'd been shooed from the kitchen like scavenging birds.

Grace had ditched her tiny notebook for a larger version, and we were making a final stakeout and snooping schedule.

Crash had changed after school and was wearing a black bowed ribbon with long tails that hung against his white shirt and white dinner jacket.

"Okay, I give up. Who are you now?" Grace asked Crash, a small smile brushing her lips upward.

He tapped the white bucket he'd striped with red marker, in which he'd brought his appetizer contribution of fried chicken wings.

"Colonel Sanders," I supplied. "The guy who founded Kentucky Fried Chicken. A little questionable on the historical-figure front, Crash. And you've been doing a lot of food guys lately. Maybe mix it up a little more."

"Is he even real?" Grace asked. "Isn't he, like, a made-up person for commercials?"

"He's just a big lie," I agreed. "Right, Crash?"

"He's not a lie." There was something in Crash's eyes. He was looking at me the way he'd looked at his mother the last time the two of us had stopped at the shop and she didn't even look up to see him. Like I'd missed something and didn't even know it.

But I hadn't. I knew he had a little crush on Grace, but I didn't see a need to sugarcoat questionable costume decisions for that reason. After all, we couldn't have anyone *liking* anyone else and expect to get along. Crews of three didn't work that way.

Grace stepped over to Uncle Theo's unfinished contest entry. Pieces to be assembled were lovingly set on a soft cloth thrown over one of the nearby worktables. She ran a finger over a wooden leg. "You think your uncle will win?"

I looked over the chair pieces. Anyone who knew of such things would see the artistry immediately. Then I thought of Uncle Theo wearing the suit on the day of his Vickerston interview, his eyes bright with the possibility of being Professor Treat, and suddenly I wasn't sure what was right for my uncle. My parenting instincts were bumping into one another like loose pumpkins in a truck bed on a bumpy road.

"You bet I'll win." Uncle Theo stood in the doorway, his head practically hitting the top. "Let's eat, kids. Chili's ready, along with my Treat-family-famous corn bread."

Crash jumped up. "I'm not staying for dinner, Mr. Treat. Thanks anyway." He shot me an unreadable look. "I've got things to do," he said, then just stood there, looking at me.

"Okay," I said, standing as well. He had the bridge shift starting at 5:00 in the morning, so he probably wanted to get to sleep early. "See you tomorrow."

He let out the smallest of sighs, then took a few steps and waved. "See you tomorrow."

"See you tomorrow," Grace echoed, giving him a wink, a thumbs-up, and a salute, which turned his sighing face into a smiley face.

Smiling was better for team morale than sighing. I ignored the twitchy feeling in my stomach. I should have been more of a leader and been the one to make him smile, I supposed, but I was more of a shoulder puncher than a thumbs-upper, and he'd been just out of reach.

By just after midnight Grace and I had played a board game, built a fire in the kitchen and made hearth milk, and watched two movies—all stuff that Crash and I used to do before Uncle Theo read some article earlier this year and decided we were growing out of sleepovers. Not knowing what else to do during my very first girl sleepover, I found myself brandishing a bag of marshmallows, chocolate squares, and graham crackers, and leading Grace up the stairs and into Uncle Theo's office.

Raising both arms, I gestured grandly to the bookshelf in all its glory. There it stood, sturdy and stocked full of wisdom.

"Oh my gosh," Grace said, scanning the titles. "What *is* this?" She giggled.

I cleared my throat. Her tone was a little too mocking for my taste, especially for someone still wearing a gazillion chain necklaces along with pony pajamas.

"It's a parenting bookshelf." I plucked a book out and handed it to her. "Advice on how to raise me to be happy and healthy."

"Wow, this is bonkers." Her fingers grazed the title. "Are you?"

"Am I what?"

"Happy and healthy?"

I looked down at myself. "I think so."

"So no . . . *Angst and Secrets*," she said, pulling that very title from the shelf and posing with it in front of her.

I laughed and put it back. "I'm working through them."

She chewed on her lip and sank to the floor. Looking over the bottom shelf, she pulled out a book entitled *Male Mom: Channeling Dad, Playing Mom, and Being Yourself.* "My dad could use this one, other than the 'being yourself' part. He's not exactly the nurturing type." She put the book down.

I plopped myself beside her. "Uncle Theo tries too hard."

Grace stared at the book's title. "Do you miss her? Your mom, I mean?"

I felt myself blink a few times, then shrugged. "Didn't know her. Come on."

Down the hallway, into my room we went, me realizing that it was the first time anyone other than Crash had been over. I piled dry s'more ingredients on the bed and hopped up beside them.

Grace climbed to the other side of the bed and shifted on the comforter, like something was poking at her. "Oh! Sorry."

She pulled the list of names from beneath her and studied them while I nibbled on a graham cracker and glanced over a sample letter I'd written to send to potential fathers once I had the money. Then, realizing once again that I'd need to win the artisan contest to get the money, I tossed the letter on my desk and tried brainstorming more ideas.

A carved set of wooden cutlery to rival any silver utensils or jug that Malia and Jaron might make?

A hope chest that I could fill with the judges' favorite foods?

A rustic seesaw for the town park?

Grace's head snapped up. "Minna! Will Wharton's on this list."

"Yeah, I know."

"Why didn't you tell me! I met him last week when he came to the house to talk to my dad." She crawled off the bed and stood, tilting her chin to view me from the side. "I could see that. You know, maybe she was his secret girlfriend, but then they had a fight and she had another secret boyfriend at college and—"

I threw a graham cracker at her. "Stop it. It's not him. That's one letter I don't have to send. There are three more that live in Gilbreth."

"What? Who are they?"

I listed them off. "Charles Mackenzie, David Ripty, Alfonso Willis. The tavern owner, your dad, and the baker."

"Why didn't you tell me all this? I'm supposed to be the lead detective!" She sat down again and went through the list, *my* list, her knee bouncing like a jackhammer. She erased the lines I'd put through each of the Gilbreth names.

With a red pen pulled from her pocket, she put a star next to each name, even her dad's, smacking her lips together with popping sounds while she drew.

"Grace, there's, like, zero chance that any of those guys is my dad." An uncomfortable wriggling snaked its way around my belly. "If it was someone from Gilbreth, she would have had to tell them." But a voice in my head whispered, *Maybe she was going to. Maybe she just didn't get around to it.*

Maybe she ran out of time.

Grace shushed me. "But what if it *was* someone from this town?" She waved the pages at me. "*What if,*" she said with such volume that I wondered if Crash was rubbing off on her, "a whole other side of your family is right here in Gilbreth, and somebody knows who it is?" She got up and paced back and forth. "I mean, it's possible, right?" She sucked in an enormous breath and stepped within inches of me. "*Minna,*" she whispered. "What if the bottle leaver isn't leading us toward a reward or disaster? What if the messages are leading us to your *dad*?"

I stopped breathing.

Grace jabbered on about possibilities. ". . . *or* we could secretly pull hairs from their heads or get some blood and do a paternity test! That's what they do on those talk shows."

Great. Now my life was a talk show. Sucking in a gulp

of air, I came to my senses. Grace was just speculating to the point of delusion, something that toddlers and tweens and teens did to justify all manner of desires. I felt calmer having parent-booked the situation.

"I'm not pulling hairs from people's heads. I don't exactly have access to scientific tests. And I think you'll agree that blood is out of the question."

She slumped. "Good point. What else do you know about Daddy X?"

"Daddy X?" I sighed and thought. "Mom said that he studied abroad. Uncle Theo and Will said that she was kind of love crazy in college and dated a lot. She swore she was going to marry a new person every week, that kind of thing. So really, it could be anyone on the list."

Grace grabbed her notebook. "Back to Gilbreth possibilities. What about Mr. Willis and Mr. Mackenzie?"

I told her what I knew.

The Willises had actually gotten divorced before I was born. I was in the Cutting Board one birthday, munching on a thickly frosted cinnamon roll, when Mr. and Mrs. Willis started bickering, and Michael shouted at them to just get divorced again. When I asked, Uncle Theo told me they had gotten married young. Mr. Willis had been taking college classes while they worked at the bakery, and they'd had a lot of fights about her having to run the whole place herself. They'd gotten divorced right before Michael was born, and Mr. Willis had finished his last two years of college at Camden. They'd gotten remarried when Michael was five.

As for Mr. Mackenzie, Darian had told a story during a personal history unit in class about his parents meeting at the tavern during his father's junior-year winter break from college. His mom was just a tourist and they both had to go back to school, but they'd fallen in love instantly. After a few more months, they decided to get married and had Darian within a year. Instead of going back for his last year of college, Mr. Mackenzie started working to support his new family. Darian had finished his talk by saying he hoped to be the first in his family to finish college one day.

Grace gave a firm nod. "Both possibilities, then."

Something strange was whirling around my belly and brain. It felt like the time I'd insisted that children could like coffee too and had three cups of Uncle Theo's favorite kind to experiment with a little harmless boundary pushing. My entire body felt like it was buzzing. All of a sudden the next day's investigations felt a million times more important.

"I hung out at the bakery this summer a little." She picked up a hair elastic from her overnight bag and pulled her hair half back. "Michael is vile, but Mr. Willis seems okay. He'd make a great—"

"Stop." I didn't want any more talk about me and Michael Willis being even half related.

"My vote's for Will," Grace said. "You guys look alike, and he's always hanging around in the woods, messing with the dove boxes and trails."

"That's just his job. Besides, Mr. Mackenzie is in the woods foraging sometimes."

"Is he?" Grace's eyebrow jutted up as she jotted the information down, then chewed on the pen.

"Your dad went to Camden too." I sifted through the papers and said my words carefully. "That'd be funny if he was . . ." I let the sentence drift away, hoping she'd finish it.

Grace shook her head. "Dad only ever dated Mom, so I'm listing him as unlikely. I'll still interrogate him a little when I get the chance. That would have been neat, though. I don't like being an only child."

"Me neither." I pulled the extra pillows off my bed, distributing them among the sleeping bags on the floor. "At least we've both got someone to be roommates with tonight."

Grace stiffened. "Roommates?" She cocked her head to one side, like a turtledove listening for the waterfall of new seed being poured into the dove boxes. She looked at my wall like it was a really hard math problem that Mr. Parnell had slipped into a quiz to see if anyone was reading ahead, then sank onto her sleeping bag, looking lost.

I wondered if I'd said the wrong thing. "Um, I have to go to the bathroom."

When I got back, she was still sitting there, staring hard at my father letter draft. Her notebook lay turned over on the floor beside her. At my approach she shook her head and her eyes cleared. "Sorry about that. I was just thinking of something." Her eyes focused on the corner of my bed, where the diary was sitting out. Every time I'd gone to put it in a drawer, there'd been some distraction.

She eyed me warily. "You probably think I'm lame for inviting myself over." She sighed. "I just wanted my dad off my back. He wanted to know why I haven't made friends." She picked up a pencil, twirling it between her fingers. "As if there's any need. We'll be gone soon."

"You're moving?"

She shrugged. "Probably. He has no idea what it's like to be the new kid in school over and over."

I'd lived in the same place my whole life, but that might be changing soon. "What's it like?"

"It's like . . . being stuck in the same story over and over, and you know how it's going to end each time, so you kind of just . . . stop trying. Dad thought I was depressed or something because I'd only let him buy me black clothes, but I told him it was a fashion choice, and he backed off. Really, I just got sick of trying to fit in." She pulled at the bottom of her pajama shirt. "Everywhere we went was different, and I was tired of trying to catch up." Her head lifted, but her eyes kept their aim at the ground. "So I'm a crew member now?"

I passed her a marshmallow. "You bet. Welcome aboard."

She grinned, then frowned. "I thought maybe you were just being friends with me because you wanted my help with the bottle mystery and with finding your dad."

The graham cracker in my mouth went all clumpy. It gummed up in the back of my throat, and it took three full swallows to get it down. "I thought maybe I was too. But I'm not. I thought you were just being friends with me and Crash to get your dad off your back."

She wove her fingers through a few of her necklace chains. "I thought so too. But I'm not."

"Good. I like your necklaces," I said. And I did. There were so many of them that they seemed like a scary chunk of metals, but up close I could see that each one was pretty.

"Thanks. They're my mom's. She called from Italy once when Dad wasn't home." She traced a pony on her pajama pants. "She wanted him to ship her jewelry over there. I told her I was keeping all of it and hung up." Grace sifted through the necklaces and let out a choked laugh. "Stupid, huh? What would your uncle's books call that?"

I considered the question. "Rebellion-based deviance," I decided. "A justifiable form of grieving for something that's been lost or taken away. You could also scream uncontrollably at your mom or dad, possibly while throwing soft objects. That would be a cathartic and natural reaction too."

Grace scratched at the place where her sock met her ankle. I wasn't sure what to do. If she were Crash, I'd tackle her with a pillow, and then we'd go back down to the kitchen and search for junk food or maybe sneak into Uncle Theo's room and mix up his sock rolls. But she wasn't Crash. I scooted next to her and put one arm around her in a half hug. "I'm sorry, Grace."

She leaned into me, then pulled away. "It is what it is. I'm luckier than some. It's just that since Mom left, I've felt kind of . . . not whole or something. I mean almost whole, just not quite."

"Complet*ish*," I supplied.

"Exactly!" She tugged on a silver strand lying against her chest. "Like I'm missing a link in one of these necklace chains." She looked down and wove her fingers through the chains.

I wanted to make her feel better. "So if I win the artisan project and get money for stamps and stuff, you're going to help me send all the letters?"

She grinned. "Sure—if we don't find him in Gilbreth first. You really get five hundred dollars? Maybe I should enter. I could use five hundred bucks."

I threw a cracker at her. "Don't even think about it. What do you need that much money for?"

"A plane ticket to Italy. I thought maybe . . . Maybe she'd like to see me, but she just can't afford to fly me over there."

Uncertain. That's what kind of eyes Grace had when she said that.

Grace picked up the cracker I'd thrown at her. She tried to toss it in the trash can under my desk, but it missed. "What happened to your mom, Minna? I mean, I know that she died, but . . ."

I hadn't ever spoken the very short, very sad story out loud. I'd only heard it once, from Will Wharton. I'd interrupted a group card game at the age of eight, begging for my dad's name. Both Uncle Theo and Will had been flummoxed. Stymied. Scared. And then I'd asked them something that nobody had ever really explained to me—what exactly had happened to my mom the day she died.

Will spoke the words while Uncle Theo sat on the carpet beside me, his elbows resting on the low family-room game table, his head between his hands.

It was the only time I'd seen my uncle cry.

A Brief Word on Hearts and Inheritance

Heart disease is the number one killer in the world. A nurse from the nearest hospital came into our class in fourth grade with a big plastic heart that split into parts, so you could see how it worked. My desk was in the center of the room, so she used it as a display area, and everyone gathered around. I tried to pay attention to what the speaker was saying, but it was hard to concentrate when the heart was just sitting there in pieces on my desk.

Nobody in the Treat family has had heart problems, except one. Mom was different from all the other Treats that way. She walked around with an undiagnosed heart condition her whole life. Maybe she would have caught it if she had been into sports and lost her breath more often, but she didn't. I'm sure she ran around as a kid and jumped in leaves and stuff, but nobody ever realized that her heart was slowly dying.

I'm not worried about inheriting it—Uncle Theo has me

checked every year, and I'm always fine. I probably wouldn't think about it at all, except for the times when I find myself walking over Whistler Bridge.

That's where she died.

She'd gone for a bike ride, just a normal bike ride, taking the Torrey Wood paths into town to get some fresh bread for a late dinner on the day Autumnfest ended.

Something made her stop at Whistler. Maybe it was dizziness or a sharp pain in her chest. Maybe a sudden loss of breath. She liked to throw rocks out the windows while making wishes there, Will said. I like to think that's why my mom stopped riding. Whatever the reason, she collapsed in the middle of the bridge and never got up.

When Uncle Theo found her, the bicycle was leaned neatly against the wall, like she'd only been pausing to peer out of Whistler's windows for a brief moment, to see where her wishing stone had landed.

Like she didn't have a clue that she wouldn't be coming home to me.

Like she hadn't known at all that she was out of time and was about to leave the world forever.

The Miller's Wheel

In 1801 a new millhouse was built farther down the river to accommodate the growing needs of the village. Giovanni Stunetti, the first native Italian to live in the village, was the most skilled miller anyone had ever known, and he became close friends with the Treat family, whose members were all known to be great lovers of corn bread and grits.

–From **Gilbreth History: Founding Families & Artisanal Traditions** (Gilbreth Welcome Center, $16.99)

Over a breakfast of Readi-Mart Taste-E-Os, Grace and I determined that she would be stationed inside, talking to the sixth Mr. Stunetti to run the mill and making sure he didn't unlock the wheel to start powering the grinding stone. So that left me on my own to do the climbing.

"I'm going home to check in with Dad," Grace told me. "I'll meet you on Mill Road." She hesitated, then gave me a quick hug and ran out the door before I could even think to hug her back.

Uncle Theo was in his workshop, his back turned to me as he worked on benches, his headphones clamped firmly over his ears. After nailing an elusive note to the barn wall that implied I was working on my artisan project, but was vague enough to be adamantly *not* a lie if I was ever questioned in a court of law about it, I walked to the other side of town.

Grace and I had one last check-in, then parted ways a quarter mile from the Gilbreth Mill, me stepping off the road and onto the riverbank.

We'd had a record year of rainfall, and the river water drifted nearly to the top of its banks. Another few inches and the water would drift over the three-foot-wide natural dam and spill into the Torrey Wood ravine. One drought and three hundred years of mud and debris were all that separated the two.

I watched as Grace walked confidently down Mill Road, ready with a notebook full of annoying questions sure to distract the mill's owners.

I'd been to the millhouse and the expanded stone cottage beside it for Talia Stunetti's birthday parties. I wondered if she was making an artisan project. I hoped not.

The Stunettis gave tours on weekends during the tourist months, demonstrating how they used waterpower to grind wheat and corn and other grain into flour, and selling it in their gift shop. It was too pricey for most Gilbretheans to buy on a regular basis, and Talia said they mostly sold to fancy stores and to the New York City farmers' market scene.

The millstone itself was a massive, medieval-looking thing completely enclosed in a tall, cavelike room and was fascinating to watch. But the message had said, *Within the miller's wheel*, so there I was creeping along the riverbank, planning my approach.

I felt obliged to remind myself about *Truths and Consequences'* three self-care tips before I committed to launching myself onto the twenty-foot-tall millhouse wheel.

"Okay, Minna," I said, straightening my tool belt, "remember to take deep breaths, remember that you could always take a day and think this over, and remember to consider potential consequences." I inhaled deeply, decided that waiting another day would be a waste of time, and considered the fact that I could fall, bump my head on an underwater rock, and drown.

I also added a compliment for my own morale. "Minna Treat," I whispered to myself, "you are an excellent climber and always remember to floss, which is rare for someone your age. Now go see what's in the middle of this wheel."

Edging off the riverbank, I tested my weight on one of the wheel spokes. The wheel dipped but didn't fully turn. Slowly, I struggled halfway up, then scooted into the middle.

The thickness of the wheel's beams made it difficult to maintain a grip. My palms were slick with sweat, and I wiped them on my pants, one at a time, trying to get rid of the wetness.

Peering at the center of the wheel, I saw nothing. Well, not nothing. I saw the center knob, which was made of wood. I stuck my hand along it as far back as I could, expecting I don't know what.

Stretching an inch farther, my fingers touched something rough. A raised line of some sort that curved out of my reach.

Adjusting my perch, I peered at the rotation beam, the carved cylinder that helped the wheel turn smoothly.

The sound of talking carried over from the side of the house, low murmurs and one loud narrating voice that could mean only one thing. A tour! Were they coming this way? A light wind confused the sounds, and I couldn't tell if they were coming or going. My wrists were getting sore from holding my awkward position.

The voices grew closer. Why hadn't Grace stopped them? I'd been on the tour before and knew that the big showstopper was watching the wheel churn water, which was actually quite boring, but the sight always got appreciative gasps of delight from newbies.

The rotation beam had been worn and scratched with time. I stepped down a spoke and tried to look on its underside. Craning my neck, I saw an old branding mark, too faded to read, right in the center of a . . . was it . . . yes, another rusty horseshoe. Beside the branding mark were . . . letters? It was letters and numbers. An inscription of some kind. But what did it say?

One of my feet slipped and I muffled a cry before regaining my position.

"And now," a loud, clear voice called out, "let me just run in to tell Mr. Stunetti to release the brake so we can see the wheel turn. Then we'll go back in and see the grinder in action."

Oh *Lord*, they'd come around the corner any second and see me, dangling on the wheel web like a creepy, human-size spider! My strange activities would be all over the town in minutes. If Uncle Theo found out I wasn't busy working on my artisan project, he'd have questions for sure.

But I had to see what the inscription said. Straining to the right, I could just make out the carving: J. TREAT—1700.

That was it? Another horseshoe and a crummy name and date? My ancestors had made about a million things in Gilbreth, so I didn't see what the big deal was. I had to have missed something.

Just as I was making my way across the wheel to step back onto the riverbank and escape the eyes of the tour group, my hands slipped and I fell ten feet. Splashing into the water below, I swallowed a huge mouthful of river.

Coughing and sputtering, I frantically swung my arms and managed to make it to the bank and climb out. Scurrying around the side of the house like a soaked rat, I hid myself seconds before the tour came around the corner.

Ten minutes later I was a hundred yards down Mill Road, squelching along in soppy shoes, planning to cut through Torrey Wood, when Grace shouted. I turned and waited while she ran to me, hand over her mouth.

"I was keeping the millers busy and didn't realize there was a tour until I came out to check on you. What happened?"

I gestured to my body. "And you call yourself a detective? I fell in."

Her mouth hung open and a giggle escaped. "I'm so sorry, it's just, you look . . ." She stepped forward and pulled a leaf from my hair that I must have picked up from the water. "There. That's better." She looked me over and smiled. "I really am sorry. Did you find anything?"

I squeezed my shirt. "Not much. There was a horseshoe around a faded branding mark. There was also a date— 1700—and the name J. Treat. Probably one of my ancestors. Pretty boring."

She pulled her notebook from the bag hanging across her body. For the first time that day I noticed her shirt.

"Blue looks nice with your necklaces," I told her.

She shrugged but looked pleased. "Thanks. I figured

I'd mix it up a little. I'm off to the tavern. I'm going to try talking to a few people if I can't get back in the barrel room."

"Sounds good," I said. "I've got the lunch shift watching the bridge." The wet clothes were starting to make me shiver. "I better go change and check in with Crash. I wonder if he's caught anyone."

Grace shook her head. "He hadn't this morning when I passed by on my way home to check in with my dad, but I wouldn't be surprised if he'd missed something. He was busy cutting lengths of string for something instead of keeping an eye out and didn't even see me coming until I tapped him on the shoulder. He jumped so much that his hat fell off. He was dressed in leather and had a raccoon skin on his head."

I nodded. "That would probably be Davy Crockett. He did that one last year."

"Why does he dress up like historical people?"

"He's just trying out costumes before Halloween. He does it every year. It's kind of like his own personal tradition." But her question made me think. Why did he choose actual people who were famous for different reasons? I'd never asked. It didn't seem important. It had started around the time he got his nickname and was just part of Crash. "So you're going to the tavern?"

She checked her watch. "Yep. And then to the library, and Town Hall for another check-in with Dad, then my bridge shift. You'll send Crash to the apothecary and florist?"

"Yep. Then you'll relieve me and I'll go to the bakery. Then we all meet at the hideout spot to debrief."

"Perfect. Pay attention," Grace urged. She reached into her bag and handed me my very own mini notebook. "Take notes. Anything can be a clue."

When I returned to the house, Uncle Theo was still in the barn workshop, blasting heavy metal music and working on what I sincerely hoped was a contest-winning chair. He'd left a note for me on the back door, telling me to check out the new vocabulary word on the chalkboard.

> Euphoria: The fact that his niece is working
> so very hard on her junior artisan project,
> a family tradition that's been unbroken for
> three hundred years, brings Theodore Treat a
> blissful sense of pride and euphoria. (Boy, do
> I love you, Minna Elizabeth Treat.)

Oh, brother.

Feeling overwhelmed, I rifled through my uncle's bathroom drawer until I found his stress remedy. A few dabs on the temples, and I was ready to catch the bottle leaver, hoping he or she would just show up and be the answer to everything.

What if Uncle Theo didn't win the Town Square shop contest?

Was there really any time for me to come up with a project that would win?

I changed clothes, grabbed some food, and headed to Whistler, with one more question haunting my mind.

Was my father closer than I'd ever dreamed?

19

Possibilities, Muscle Work, and an Unexpectedly Blunt Bottle

Elias Treat's journal continued to reveal that he, who had never married, always held deep affection for and lingering guilt about the deceased Miss Elizabeth Maybeck. It is said that her ghost can still be heard shuffling through Torrey Wood. Some say she's searching for a way to change her life's outcome, and some say she's searching for the farrier, Henry Salt, so that she can have her vengeance.

–From *Gilbreth History: Founding Families & Artisanal Traditions* (Gilbreth Welcome Center, $16.99)

T *his was it.* Far through the trees I saw an indistinct figure creep down the path in a hesitant stop-start pattern that could only mean the person was sneaking around.

Three hours into my shift I'd seen nothing concrete. Malia Johnson jogged through the woods and paused at Whistler . . . to tie her shoe. Then Mayor Ripty showed up with a clipboard. He walked around the bridge, gave it a few kicks that left me cringing, and jotted something down, before wandering in the general direction of the settlement ruins.

An ironsmith's son crossed Whistler an hour later and walked purposefully toward the ruins with a metal detector. Will stomped down the path with a wheelbarrow full of mulch but didn't stop at all. I spotted Darian far off the trail with his father, probably scrounging for edible plants. But that was it.

Now, after a whole bunch of false starts, I was about to catch our mysterious bottle person.

Just a few more yards and I'd be able to tell more . . . yes! I lifted myself ever so slightly out of the mass of brush cover Crash had been using. There! It appeared to be a small man, hunched over, wearing a hooded sweatshirt . . . definitely carrying something. . . .

Oh.

Oh, *no.*

Michael Willis scanned the woods and crept forward, all the way through the bridge. He paused and looked around again. He was going to do it! He was going to leave a bottle message. What on earth could he *possibly* be doing it for?

He reached into his front pocket and pulled out a—

Loaf of bread?

It was a loaf of bread, steaming slightly when he broke it in two. My stomach rumbled as a light breeze sent a dreamy, yeasty scent my way. Licking his lips, and stepping gently over to the dove boxes, Michael Willis began breaking up the bread and trying to throw the pieces on the feeding platform.

"Come on, birds," he said in a voice I barely recognized. "It's fresh. I baked it. Sorry that jerk threw your eggs . . . sorry I didn't say anything."

I stared in astonishment as the lead eighth-grade caveman broke up the rest of a long loaf and then hurried back down the path, proving that woodworkers weren't the only secretive people in Gilbreth. Not by a long shot.

Checking my watch, I saw that I had another hour before Grace showed up and relieved me. Wherever Michael was going, I hoped he wouldn't be baking more bread.

When I arrived at the Willises' bakery, the shop door was unlocked. All of the lights were on, but not a soul was in sight.

"Hello? Mrs. Willis? Mr. Willis?"

The glass case at the front was full of delicate pastries. Behind the counter, the back wall was lined with slatted wooden shelving. The shelves were stacked with baguettes and other loaves, labeled with tiny chalkboards, waiting to be bought. An old-fashioned cash register rested on the counter, one of Mrs. Marzetti's bells beside it. I rang it.

Nobody came.

"Hello?" I called again.

A small hallway led to a water fountain and an empty bathroom. I'd been in the bakery countless times but had never explored the kitchen area. After a final glance around I turned the OPEN sign facing outward on the front door to CLOSED and hopped over the counter.

I pushed through a swinging door to a large room. The back door was propped open, making me think I probably had very little time before a member of the Willis family came back. A large family photograph hung on one of the walls, showing a beaming Mrs. Willis, a proud-looking Mr. Willis, and a semismiling Michael. What if Mr. Willis turned out to be my father? Would they have me pose with them for a new family picture?

For the briefest of moments I imagined myself trading my morning Taste-E-Os for sticky buns and cheesy bagels—and freshly baked Italian bread every night we had spaghetti.

Or would I rather have tavern food, with Mr. Mackenzie as my dad?

What did Will Wharton and the Riptys eat at home?

Before the daydreams turned to other breakfasts and

dinners, I noticed the oven. No, make that *ovens*.

Behind the baker's oven, the message had said. But no less than five ovens were in the kitchen, each of them looking extremely heavy in their spots against the wall. After a few minutes of useless shoving, I realized it was hopeless.

I peeked out the back door to make sure the coast was clear in the alley. It wasn't.

The fringe hanging off the legs and arms of his leather costume jiggled as Crash hurried along, hastily fastening the buckle on the old-fashioned mailbag that he sometimes used as a backpack. The bag was stuffed to bursting with something.

"Crash! Come over here!"

"Oh!" He startled, then jogged over. "Just came from the florist. Forget-me-nots look just like the flowers under the bridge. But the weird thing is that he said—"

"Good work!" I pulled him into the bakery. "Now help me move these ovens—just enough to check behind them."

Grunting and sweating, we managed to move the first two ovens enough to sneak a look behind them. Nothing. We scooted them back in place and started on number three.

"Minna?"

"Mm-hm?"

"Why do you want to find your dad all of a sudden?"

"I just want to."

"Why? You know exactly who you are. Your life is already

planned out and you're *excited* about it. I mean, you want to be a woodworker, right?"

I frowned at him. "Of course I do. I don't want to run off and live with some father I don't know or care about. And if it turns out that my dad does live in Gilbreth, I'll still stay with Uncle Theo, even if we have to move. That's not what this is about."

"Then what's it about?"

I stopped yanking at the stove and wiped sweat from my forehead. "I don't know. I want to know what I am other than a Treat, I guess. You wouldn't understand. I just feel like I'm missing something. And," I said, knuckle-punching his shoulder, "we've got some bumpy years of growing up ahead. Trust me, it could get ugly if we don't feel grounded. We need to feel solid and prepared so we can weather the storms of change."

He blew at a piece of curly hair dangling in his eyes. "But why does change have to be a storm?"

"Want to hear a tragic case study?"

"No. You're already whole just the way you are, you know. You're already . . . great." He shifted and wiped both hands on his pants. "I just mean that you're already Minna."

"I know that. I'm extremely well adjusted," I reminded him.

"I know you are. Hey, I forgot to tell you, Lorelei changed jobs again. She was only at Camden to help with some kind of short campaign. She's in Pennsylvania now. If you hadn't gotten those names from her when you did, the chance would have disappeared. So maybe you finding your dad is meant to be."

"Maybe. Let's get this done."

The third and fourth ovens brought nothing but blank walls as well. Crash was red faced and stunk a little bit. I think he knew, because he kept getting fidgety whenever our skin touched.

The fifth oven was pushed up against a corner. It wouldn't budge and it was practically sealed to the wall.

"What are you *doing*?" a familiar voice rang out. "You sound like a couple of warthogs from that Nature Channel show Tommy was watching last night."

We both jumped and bumped heads, turning more in annoyance than fear. Lemon and Chai stood at the door leading back into the bakery, twin grins on their faces.

"Nothing!" Crash slumped against me. "We just need to get a look at the wall behind the oven. Don't ask why."

"You shouldn't even be here," I pointed out. "The sign out front says 'closed.'"

"The lights were on. It was unlocked. And it's never closed this time of day. You two are up to something."

"Fine, what do you want?" Crash grumbled.

"For our silence?" Chai rubbed her chin and considered her brother. "I want you to cut off all of your hair. And then eat some of it."

Lemon let out a gleeful squeal of delight. "And then glue the rest on your face as a beard and mustache!"

Chai nodded her approval. "Using Mom's hot-glue gun so it really sticks."

Crash let out a groan.

I fixed each six-year-old with my sternest expression. "We all know that's not going to happen. Try again."

They let out twin sighs of disappointment. "Fine," Chai conceded. "When Beast gets old enough to have puppies, we'll take her firstborn." She smiled smugly to herself, then high-fived Lemon.

Beast was a boy. He was also neutered. "You're ruthless," I told her. "It's a deal."

"Good." She elbowed her brother. "Give it to her."

Lemon solemnly handed me a note. It said, in very bad handwriting:

*Talia iz maacking a tinee watr weel and grindeen ston.
Shhh wil probly beet you. Tzo badd.*

"'Talia is making a tiny water wheel and grinding stone. She will probably beat you. Too bad.' Great." I crumpled the note and stuffed it into my pocket.

"So what are you doing with the oven?" Lemon asked.

"Yes, what *are* you doing?" Mr. Willis stood in the back doorway, a puzzled look flashing over his face. With suspenders that were as omnipresent as his wife's overalls, Alfonso Willis was known as a gentle giant with kind brown eyes, a youthful face with a prominent chin, enormous ears, and buzzed black hair. Keys dangled from one of his hands, and the other rested on the shoulder of Michael, who stood beside him, giving me the stink eye. The gentle, bird-feeding Michael had apparently disappeared.

My mouth flapped uselessly. Nothing came out, other than awkward, guilty sputters.

"Oh, Mr. Willis!" Chai let out a dramatic wail. "I threw my magic milky marble, and it went right behind that oven!" She pointed to the oven we hadn't been able to move.

"Nobody was in here and *he* wanted a butter bun and I told him not to come back here." Chai's finger punched the air in her brother's direction, and her eyes rolled in expert fashion. "Minna and Crash told him not to come in, too. They're babysitting us." She fixed me with a mini eyebrow raise that let me know I owed her for that.

Mr. Willis's expression immediately smoothed into understanding. "I'm so sorry. Here, let me look. Michael, put away the rest of those flour sacks in the truck later, will you? Put that one away and then help me move this oven."

I held my breath and gave Crash a squeeze on his waist. They were going to do the unveiling for us. Casually I stepped closer to the corner.

"Lemongrass, Chai, are you enjoying kindergarten this year?"

"Yes, Mr. Willis," Lemon said sweetly. "Everyone loves us."

Mr. Willis chuckled and pointed for Michael to grab one side of the oven. "You know, this bakery used to be the schoolhouse."

Something flickered in my mind. "The schoolhouse that had a fire?" I asked.

He nodded and grimaced while lifting. The oven moved an inch away from the wall. Leaning my head back, I saw nothing. I would need to be closer to get a good look.

"The very one. A man fell off the roof while rebuilding and broke his back and passed away. . . . I can't remember the details, but between the fire and the death, people thought the place was a bit cursed and changed the school location a couple of decades later. Hmm . . ." He stared at the strip of floor he'd exposed, stood up, and stretched his wrists. "I don't see a marble on the floor, Chai. I'm sorry."

"What's that?" Michael asked. "On the wall."

The hairs on my neck stood up. "What is it?"

Michael glared at me. "That's what I just asked. Dad, pull it out a little more."

Mr. Willis frowned, pulled, then brightened. "Well, look at that! My mother bought this oven, and I remember her saying something about a historical marker, but everything in this town is historical and she needed the space." He gestured for me to take a peek.

There it was. Another rusted horseshoe, this time with E. TREAT—1728 carved just above it on a small section of wood planking that hadn't been plastered over.

He snapped his fingers. "That's it. It was one of the original Treat brothers who died. I can't remember which one. Sorry about the marble. But I can certainly fix your appetite. Michael, give these customers some buns, will you?" He winked at me. "Put them all on the house for Minna."

Something about the free bread made me uneasy. Why was Mr. Willis being so nice to me? Then again, I didn't have any money anyway and the twins looked like Christmas had come early, so I accepted a bag of buns, gave them all to the twins, and looked up at the Village Green, where I saw a flash of familiar black and blue.

A bathroom break. That's what Grace told me and Crash, apologizing profusely as we all rushed back to the bridge for a debrief and final spying session of the day. Once we were safely behind the camouflage of brush, she pulled out her notebook. "Crash, you go first."

Crash reported that there was nothing at the apothecary shop, other than shelves and shelves of stuff. "I asked Mr. Poppy, and there are no horseshoes anywhere. I think he thinks I'm crazy now."

"How about the florist?" I asked, remembering that I'd

cut him off at the bakery. "You said the flowers were forget-me-nots."

He nodded. "The weird thing is that they're not supposed to be blooming this time of year, unless they're in a greenhouse or something. It's not natural. He said he's heard of that happening with plants before—they call them ghost flowers because they won't go away when they're supposed to be dead."

Grace scribbled a few lines. "Forget-me-not ghost flowers. That's creepy."

My mind drifted to the superstition about Elizabeth Maybeck's blood—how it had kept the plant life around Whistler flourishing during the drought years. But that was three hundred years ago and probably not true anyway. Probably. I didn't really want to think about it. "Your turn, Grace."

She sighed. "The library didn't really help. The dates weren't mentioned in any of the books. I found out that the Stunettis' millhouse was built in 1801, which doesn't even match the date you saw inside the wheel."

I pointed behind us. "Up by West Bridge are the ruins of the first millhouse. There's no wheel there. Maybe they borrowed parts from it when they built the new one."

Grace's expression was grim. "Remember what I told you? The old mill exploded in some weird gunpowder accident."

Crash twiddled his shoelaces. "Yeah, so what?" he asked,

not looking as though he wanted to hear the answer.

Grace turned to a page and held it up. "Don't you see? Triple murder at the cooper's. An explosion at the mill that killed two people. As for the baker's place, Minna, what did you find out?"

I felt my lips twist, not wanting to share. "There was a horseshoe." I told her the name and date that went with it. "And . . . it used to be the school."

A thump sounded. Grace had dropped her notebook on the ground. "The school, as in the one that caught fire? It was on Mrs. Doring's list too."

I nodded. "And when it was being rebuilt, one of my relatives died."

Grace breathed out. "Three, maybe four locations with disasters, depending on what we can find out about the tavern—nobody told me anything today. And horseshoes left behind. It's like that . . . that"—she snapped her fingers—"horsemen thingie. The Four Horsemen of the Apocalypse!"

"Four horses would be sixteen shoes," Crash pointed out.

"Then more bottles and horseshoes are on the way," Grace said firmly. "Probably with clues leading to more-current disasters, which will lead up to a major disaster that will be happening any day now."

"Alien invasion?" Crash guessed, scanning the sky.

"*A Gilbreth Apocalypse*," Grace whispered.

Crash inhaled sharply. "A . . . a *Gilpocalypse*."

Oh *Lord.* "The Apocalypse is not coming. Or the Gilpo-calypse. You are both ridiculous."

Grace ignored me. "I don't like this. Especially for you, Minna, since the carvings all have your relatives listed."

Crash stood up. His cheeks were flushed and he took a few deep breaths and fiddled with his mailbag. "There's nobody coming from either side. We should go look under the bridge. Maybe someone left another bottle while you were gone, Grace." He took off, not turning around. "Come on."

We spread out, kicking leaves and peeking under fallen branches. It was Crash who finally let out a triumphant shout of discovery. He was directly under the bridge when we rushed over. There, nestled in the bed of forget-me-nots, was another bottle.

"You pick it up, Minna," he said.

He didn't want to touch it, and I got the distinct impression that Crash really thought the bottles were cursed.

I took the message out and read it, feeling my heart drop firmly into my stomach. I blinked, but the words didn't change.

"Read it!" Grace demanded.

"It says . . . it says, 'Minna Treat's life will change at Autumnfest.'"

"The notes *are* for you!" Grace surprised me with a slap to the shoulder. She nodded swiftly to herself. "This is *exactly* what would happen in a mystery novel. Don't you get it? It's talking about your father! Somebody knows who your father is!"

I shook my head. "It couldn't be."

"Well, it's definitely somebody who knows you."

Grace wrote furiously in her notebook for a moment, then looked up. "The change will come during Autumnfest." She looked up and gave me a long appraisal that turned slowly into a type-three stare. "Okay, well, I think that scratches one theory off my list."

I leaned over her shoulder. "What theory is that?"

Her lips pinched together in thought. "Doesn't matter anymore. I think we can definitely say that either your father or someone who knows the identity of your father is leaving the messages. Who were those people on the list from Gilbreth?"

I recited them from heart. "Wharton, Willis, Mackenzie, and Ripty. But there are three hundred ten other possibilities, and plus, everyone in Gilbreth is getting ready for the festival, and I really don't think they're the types to leave bottles."

"People," Grace said, pulling her hair back into a full ponytail, "can keep the most astonishing secrets. The murderer in my last book was an eighty-seven-year-old woman who ran a knitting club and made soup for homeless people."

"Comforting," I said. "Thank you, Grace."

A strangled sound came from Crash, who suddenly looked a little yellow.

Grace rubbed her chin and leaned close to me, like I had the word "clue" hanging around my neck. "Maybe *you're* the location. Maybe the next location is wherever you happen to be."

I wasn't sure I liked the sound of that.

"It could definitely be a trick," Grace said, nodding thoughtfully. "Or a warning. Or it could be Minna's dad. Or"—she held a finger up and lowered her voice to a dramatic whisper—"maybe it's all of those and Minna's dad is a crazy person leading us to disaster. Terrible, horrific, gruesome, *deadly* disaster." Forehead furrowed, she scribbled something in her book. "It's nearly impossible to say. What are we going to do?"

Crash had turned decidedly quiet.

"You okay?" I asked him.

He swallowed twice before answering. "Maybe it's your dad, but what if it's not? Maybe we should just pretend we never found the bottles. Things can stay how they always were. Maybe it's not worth it to want to find your other half if it means finding disaster, too. Think about it. You say it won't, but everything will change, Minna. Is that what you want or not?"

His eyes. They weren't hoping. They were nervous, but I didn't think he was afraid of a big, scary disaster. Not the explosion kind, anyway.

"Crash," I said, adopting my best soothing voice. "Life is messy. Mistakes and disasters are scary, but they're necessary for every living thing that wants to grow and stay alive." I patted his shoulder. "That's from *Planting Greatness in Your Child's Garden*. It's referring to making your kid start using the toilet, but I feel like it applies here, too."

He met my eyes with a soft grin but didn't laugh. "So what do we do now?"

The bottle in my hand was green, with a swirl of white that almost looked like a four-leaf clover. Despite Grace's gloom-and-doom ideas and Crash's hesitancy, it felt lucky.

"I think," I said dramatically, ignoring all three of *Truths and Consequences*' self-care tips, "there's only one week left until Autumnfest. I'm going to do something we should have tried about eight bottles ago. I'm going to write back."

Freed Captive,
Doomed Tradition

Three Dogs Tavern has been host to clandestine meetings of all kinds over the years, held mostly at a table known to this day as Founders Corner. The Treat family were host to many such dinner meetings, which delved into a variety of topics, from sensitive political matters to local pranks involving rotten eggs and loose floorboards.

–From **Gilbreth History: Founding Families & Artisanal Traditions** (Gilbreth Welcome Center, $16.99)

With three days left before Autumnfest, the general art room was starting to pile up with the hand-painted signs from last year, which we'd been freshening up. The signs directed tourists to fresh cider, the hay maze, bathrooms, folk music, meet-an-artisan tents, cash machines, festival information tents, free craft stations, storytelling, and more. Mrs. Bruno looked justifiably exhausted.

"Season of Change," she said, rubbing one shoulder. "That's today's assignment, just paint anything. I don't care what. Who wants to grab me dowels from the other end of the school?"

My hand shot up like a giant beanstalk, along with half the class's.

"Minna, go to the woodshop. Twenty or so should work."

The woodshop was empty and dark on Wednesdays. I sidled over to the cubby where I'd stashed my pathetic excuse for a project. Sanding the edges of the scrap frame had done about the same amount of good as trying to use extra frosting and a twig wreath to hide the chunks Beast ate from Uncle Theo's birthday cake last year.

As I lifted the sad thing to eye level, gauging what color stain might turn the whole thing invisible, I barely registered a dark object hurtling toward me before my neck exploded in pain.

Fireworks burst behind my closed eyes and I bit my tongue. Crying out, I raised one hand to assess the damage and—

BAM!

Throttled again, I dropped the frame, whirling to see a winged thing making a frantic lap around the ceiling before landing on a supply cabinet.

I looked down. Several scraps had broken off when the frame crashed to the ground. The heart at the center was gone, the pieces that had helped form its outline scattered on the ground.

"You . . . you . . . you stupid bird!" I yelled. "You ruined my stupid frame!"

The turtledove swooped down over my head, then up toward the ceiling, where it watched me, pumping its wings to stay suspended in the air. It was trapped and hovering. Scared, maybe. Probably hungry and panicked and mad at itself for blindly flying into the school in the first place.

I put my hands up. "Easy, easy," I told the dove. I took slow steps toward a nearby window, then unlocked the latch and pulled it open. "Go ahead," I told it. "Go home. Unless you feel like migrating with the wild geese. In that case, head south."

Without so much as a thank-you chirp, the bird hurried out the window and flew off in the direction of the forest it had flown away from in the first place.

I shuffled through the rest of the day, feeling as anxious as the bird must have felt the whole time it was stuck in the school.

Mrs. Doring gave us free reading time, which I devoted to polishing my letter draft for potential dads, in case my gut instinct—the one that said he would meet me at Autumn-fest—had been spoiled by too many box dinners and spaghetti nights, and wasn't working at top function.

Dear Potential Father,

Hello! I'm Minna Treat and I was wondering if you dated my mother, Elizabeth Treat, during your junior year of college. Maybe you went overseas (she said you did) and didn't think of her again (which I have always doubted), but she came home that same year (to Gilbreth, New York) and had me! She's dead now, which is sad, but I'm here and am living a perfectly wonderful life with my uncle and my dog, Beast, who are both the best, but we might have to move soon.

Please write back. I don't want money or to suck time away from your current family (if you have one). Just wondering if you're my dad, and if I have any half siblings, and if, now that you know my mom had a baby, you'd like to know that I exist and know where I am, the same way I'd like to know if you exist and know where you are. Also, are you financially stable, and do you have any very long toes on your feet, and do you have any skills I might have inherited? Just curious.

Looking forward to hearing from you OR sorry for wasting your time (depending on whether or not you're my dad!).

~~Best regards,~~

~~Regards,~~

Sincerely,

Minna Elizabeth Treat

PS: My huge and vicious dog follows me everywhere, so if you're not my dad and you're crazy, stay away from me for your own sake.

For what seemed like the tenth time in the last three weeks, Crash took off after class without a word. It was tavern-dinner night, and I'd thought maybe he could help me take a look in the back room to see if anything was there, but he'd gone running out of class like a chicken with its head cut off, which I'd never seen but was something Grandma Treat used to say, and now Uncle Theo says it every so often. Darn Crash for disappearing again. It would be tricky to stage a distraction on my own.

I stepped over path roots in Torrey Wood, stopping by the bridge and taking out the blue-green bottle with my message inside. The first three I'd left said, *Tell us who you are, please,* and *Please! We need some help with the messages!* and *Please come to Autumnfest. I'll be at the Punkin Dunkin' booth all weekend. I don't know what your messages meant, but I'd like to know.*

This one simply said, *Please come.*

Feeling slightly silly, I gave the bottle a kiss and set it right at the opening of the bridge, vaguely wondering if I had become the frazzled, crazy person I'd imagined had tossed the first message off the bridge.

The hearth fire crackled a few feet from my chair, and the air was thick with the scent of oak burning, hearty soups, meat pies, buttery rolls, musty floors, and spices. Uncle Theo sat across from me, talking with Will.

Dark exposed beams spanned the low ceilings, which occasionally creaked with overhead household footfalls of whichever members of the Mackenzie family weren't working that night. Voices murmuring and candlelight flickering throughout the large, open room made for a warm and rustic atmosphere, and the occupied tables and chairs looked as though they had been made in the 1800s, because most of them had been. If there was one place in Gilbreth that was haunted—other than the covered bridges—it was Three Dogs Tavern.

The server turned after placing our dishes on our regular corner table and did a delicate dance to dodge one of his fellow employees with a full tray of plates. The sharp clack and soft clomp of their shoes sounded like they had echoes, as though some friendly, invisible customers were navigating the floor as well.

"This is new for you." Uncle Theo nodded at my dinner selection, then smirked at the empty bread basket. "Good thing you ate those four rolls in case you don't like it."

Utensil in hand, I surveyed the wild forest mushrooms, piled beside a large helping of mashed potatoes I'd asked for as a side. There was no way Mom could be right. The plate of sludge-covered mounds of mushrooms sitting in front of me made me certain that I'd puke the way Uncle Theo had years and lifetimes ago.

I stabbed a forkful of dark-brown caps and stems, plowing a healthy scoop of potatoes on top. I stuffed the whole wad in my mouth. Grabbing a full water glass with my free hand in case I needed to douse the flavor, I began to chew.

The texture was both soft and firm, layered like the thinnest pieces of wood. Uncle Theo watched me, amusement tickling his lips into a wicked grin.

Slowly, quietly, like a twilight fog filling secret hollow spaces beneath covered bridges, came a savory, melting, almost mystical taste. Like someone had marinated damp spring earth and shoots of tall summer creek grass and roasted acorns and moonlight all together. It was like the seasons were turning on my tongue—like the past and the present were alive right there in my mouth. I couldn't quite believe it.

Wild forest mushrooms tasted like Gilbreth.

"You like them?"

Another forkful was my answer, and my cheeks were

puffed to the gills with mushrooms when Mayor Ripty appeared.

"Theodore Treat and William Wharton! Just the men I was looking for. Two more workdays and then we're in it, eh?" The mayor rubbed his hands together excitedly. "I'm estimating at least ten thousand people will show up over the two days, and we need to make sure our infrastructure is secure, don't we? And two logical, salt-of-the-earth men like you are just what I need on my side at next week's town board meeting."

Both men blinked back at him, saying nothing.

"I'm trying to drum up support for the demolition of Torrey Wood for either housing or commercial business. Or a water park." He held a palm up. "Not *all* of it, of course, just twenty acres or so. Think of the growth potential." He slapped one of Will's shoulders. "Less of those pesky trails for you to maintain too, eh, William?"

"What?" The word blurted out of me. "You really want to tear down the woods?"

The mayor mistook my disgust for excitement. "Sure do! If we get that done and maybe add some national business to the scene, I might just save this beautiful town from dying."

"The town's doing fine, Mayor."

He raised his eyebrows. "Is it, Theodore? Is that why I hear that you might be looking for work in . . . where was it? Oh yes, Vickerston." He winked at the rest of us. "That

Mrs. Poppy sure does know everything around here." He turned to me. "And I'm sure you wouldn't mind us taking that bridge down in the middle of the woods. Bad memories for your family. The subdivision plans would lay piping in that dry ravine and fill it right in. No need for a bridge without any water under it, am I right? And really, how many covered bridges does one town need, right?"

I nearly threw my water on the mayor. Barely stopped myself. "Five," I told him. "Gilbreth needs five covered bridges." Suddenly the mushrooms didn't sit so well in my stomach. I pushed the plate away from me.

The unexpected force of my voice took the grin right off the mayor's face, replacing it with an uncomfortably mayorish neutral grimace. "Well, I expect four bridges will do. Minna, if you're done eating dinner, why don't you go give Gracie some company while I chat a bit more with your uncle and then make the rounds." He looked around the room. "There are a few other people I'd like to check in with while I'm here."

Glaring at the mayor and praying he wasn't my father, I excused myself to go visit with Grace.

She brightened at my approach and patted the booth seat beside her, sighing in the direction of her father. "He's always working. Did you get any answer to your bottle messages yet?"

I shook my head. "My bottles are gone, so somebody's taking them, but there hasn't been a new one left behind." I pulled her up. "Hey, since we're here, let's go check out the barrel room. Again," I acknowledged. "When you found me and Crash in there, we couldn't see well enough to look around. The clue said, 'In the tavern's barrel room.' Maybe it has the missing piece we need to understand what the message leaver wants to tell us. I saw Darian clearing tables—he'll let us back there."

"Great!" Reaching back in the booth, she grabbed her notebook and pen, then followed me to the short hallway leading to the bathrooms. Two other doors were along the hallway, one a storage closet, one leading to the kitchen.

I stuck my head in the kitchen door and saw Darian at the big sink, yanking on a power faucet and blasting at a pan before shoving a loaded tray of dirty plates into the automatic washer. "Psst! Darian!"

He turned, wiped his hands on the apron tied around his waist, and walked over. "Hey! What's up?"

"We need to get into the barrel room. Just to look around real quick . . . for . . ." Staring up at Darian's face, half admiring its general niceness and half searching it for similarities, I lost track of what I was going to say.

"History assignment," Grace barked. "Extra credit."

He grinned. "I heard you're working the dunking booth. Give me three free turns, and you're in."

"Deal," Grace answered for me. "But first, what can you tell us about the barrel room—is there anything unusual, maybe even *secret*, about it?" She held the notebook in front of her like a reporter, poised to capture a story.

Darian looked to his left and right, then nudged us closer. "Okay, I'm not supposed to tell anybody this, but . . ."

Grace and I leaned forward.

"It's full of . . ."

"What?" I asked, breathless with anticipation.

"Barrels." He laughed, spraying a healthy burst of saliva. "Come on, girls, follow me." He led us to the back of the kitchen, then turned right and brought us down a short hallway until we arrived at a beautifully carved oak door. He reached behind a low, freestanding cabinet and pulled out a key.

After inserting the heavy brass, he twisted and heaved the door open. When I walked into the barrel room, I saw that the other side of the door was blackened. I hadn't noticed it when Crash and I sneaked in, because by the time the lights went on, Grace had swung it all the way open.

He saw me looking at it. "Yeah, this whole room caught on fire, like, a million years ago, and the whole tavern and all the Mackenzies inside it would've burned to the ground if this door hadn't stopped the fire from spreading until they could put it out. It's superthick. They had to rebuild this whole room, but the door, they left." He handed Grace the key, not noticing the ominous expression on her face. "Just hurry up and put it back when you're done, or I'll get in trouble."

"Thanks, we will." Grace stepped inside.

"Minna," Darian whispered, pulling me back toward him so we were nose to nose.

"Yes?" I said, hoping I didn't have mushroom breath.

"I'm going to do it—the junior artisan contest. I'm making a foraging basket. I was afraid my dad would say it was stupid, but he didn't. So . . . thank you."

"Oh." Fabulous. More competition. It seemed everyone had found their perfect project except me. Still, it was hard not to be happy for him. "Well, good luck," I whispered, turning back and letting the door close behind me.

The walls were all made of stone, cool to the touch. There was an ancient-looking iron woodstove in one corner and checklists hanging from barrels, much like the lists that used to hang from every worktable in the Treat barn workshop. The smell was yeasty and crisp.

"Did you *hear* that?" Grace whispered. "Another disaster. I'm telling you, if we get another location message, we better be extremely suspicious."

"I think you're suspicious enough for all of us. At least nobody died. What's this?" There was a small plaque by the stove. "Looks like a dedication or something." I traced the name and date. "'Masonry, John Turner. Door, Samuel Treat. 1724.'" Beside it was another horseshoe.

"Samuel Treat," Grace repeated. "That another of your relatives?"

I nodded. "One of the four founding brothers. My eight-times great-uncle." The room's light flickered. "Another dead end."

The word "dead" wasn't lost on me. Four locations, all with terrible things associated with them, all with the names of the first Treats in Gilbreth. I was among the last Treats left.

Grace was right. Any new location clue would have to be approached carefully. "Let's get out of here."

Grace came back to our table, where Will and Uncle Theo were eating a dessert, loudly chatting about their latest book club read. Another dessert for me was sitting on the table. I passed it to Grace.

"It's good, but I'm not hungry," I told her. "Try it."

Grace dug a hesitant spoon into one of my tavern favorites, barley pudding with cream sauce and raspberries. "Look at my dad. He's been all over this room, talking to everyone like we belong here."

"You do." Without my thinking about it, the words had come out. And they were true. Grace seemed more relaxed than the girl I'd known three weeks before. Less guarded.

But she took only a bite of dessert, shaking her head sadly. "I bet we'll be gone by Winterfest."

"We might too," I said.

Mr. Mackenzie patted the back of a woman at the next table and headed our way. "Everything okay here?" he asked, smiling.

Mayor Ripty swept by and dropped a ten dollar bill in front of Uncle Theo. "For the dessert," he said. "Least I can do for a family that's been a friend to my Grace."

Mr. Mackenzie picked up the money and handed it back.

"You don't need to pay for that dessert, Mayor, the Treats eat on the house here."

"Oh? All right, then." The mayor awkwardly pocketed the cash, and waved at someone across the room before bustling away again.

What? We ate for free? Why did we eat for free?

Mr. Mackenzie patted Grace on the shoulder. "You like that pudding? I got the recipe from an ancient cousin I tracked down when I was over in Scotland during college." I felt a thick pinch on my thigh.

She stabbed a finger at an open page of her notebook. There was a set of columns headed with the names of people from my father list who lived in Gilbreth. All of them had notes except her father's. She was pointing at the Mackenzie column.

STUDIED ABROAD!!?!? AND TREATS
EATING FOR FREE AT MACKENZIE'S
TAVERN = FATHERLY GESTURE

"Did you enjoy the mushrooms, Minna?" Mr. Mackenzie said with a wink.

Was it a *fatherly* wink? How would I know? I'd never had a father. I felt ill but managed a weak, "Yes, sir. Did you happen to go to Scotland your junior year?"

His face became softer somehow, and his eyes looked just

above my head, stuck in some memory. "I sure did. Second semester. I ended up coming back early, but those months changed a lot of things for me, Minna." He knocked on the table twice, put a hand up in a frozen wave, and walked back toward the kitchen.

"Hey, speaking of that thing I want to talk about," Will said, using his favorite code for changing subjects, "your uncle has been talking nonstop about how hard you're working on your woodcraft project."

"She won't tell me a word," my uncle said, his voice tinged with pride. "She's been working so hard. All that going okay?" he asked me.

"I guess you'll see," I said in a playful voice that sounded forced even to me.

No bottles appeared over the next two days.

Classes were canceled on Friday so the entire school could meet at the Village Green and help decorate for the weekend ahead. We set pumpkins near the sidewalk lampposts, tied dried cornstalks wherever we could, hung signs, and decorated the four outer bridges, which people would drive through to enter Gilbreth.

We marched over to Gilbreth Park in a herd, and Autumn-fested the living daylights out of the area. That's where Crash and I would be stationed.

It was also where I was hoping to get answers, ones that

would blast away all the other trouble that was threatening to bury me up to my irresponsible neck.

It wasn't until we returned to the school to store extra supplies that I realized I'd completely forgotten to take home the terrible artisan frame I'd made. I ran down the hall to the woodworking room.

What I found was a locked door.

Footsteps pounded behind me, and Crash's hot, huffing breath breezed against my ear. "What's the matter?"

I pointed to the door, panic rattling me while I rattled the handle. "I was going to try to fix the cruddy project tonight to make it viewable by the judges. Or if a miracle happened, turn it into something special, unique, and bold."

School would be closed all day on Monday, too, so that students could help clean up Autumnfest debris, especially around the Village Green, where Bonfire Night would be held.

He squeezed my shoulder, both of us knowing that anything I could make in one night wouldn't cut the pumpkin mustard. "It's okay," he said. "Your uncle will be so nervous about the adult judging that he won't even mind that your project isn't there. And he'll have the news about finding your dad to deal with, and then he'll win, and then we'll all live happily ever after."

"We'll live happily ever after in *Gilbreth*," I said, holding out a pinkie finger.

"In Gilbreth," he agreed, linking his finger to mine and giving it a tug.

I pointed to a bundle of limp greens pinned to his chest. "What's that? It looks like a bunch of weeds."

I'd been meaning to ask him about it at lunch, but there'd been a social emergency involving Crash trying to tell the lunch lady that his dad wore a hairnet like hers while he worked and that the oldest evidence of a hairnet was from a thirty-three-hundred-year-old Danish girl called the Egtved Girl, and that before helmets, horse riders with ponytails wore hairnets during competitions because if the riders fell off their horse and their hair got stepped on, it could rip their entire scalp right off.

He blushed. "Yeah, it's a bunch of weeds. I couldn't find anything that looked like a peanut plant."

"Who are you supposed to be?"

"You can't tell?" He frowned and looked down at himself. "George Washington Carver. He studied peanut plants and other stuff. He was a scientific genius."

"So he invented peanut butter?"

"Well, no. But people think he did. And without him, maybe peanuts wouldn't have been around enough for the people who really invented peanut butter. And I like peanut butter. A lot."

I took in a good glance at my best friend and had to smile. "You sure do. Excellent choice."

He smiled at the ground. "Thanks. Get some sleep. You

and I have a big day of being pumpkin-dunked tomorrow. Grace, too. I got an extra costume for her."

It *was* going to be a big day tomorrow, and not because we'd all be soaking-wet squash. We'd find out who was leaving the bottles and why.

My life would change. The message said so.

Years ago I'd lost my mother during Autumnfest weekend. And now—I could *feel* it—I was about to find my father. And I would figure out exactly who Minna was and feel complete. And Uncle Theo would win his Town Square shop.

"Orange will look great on Grace." I was keeping it breezy for Crash, who looked to me to be the rock in our crew, but inwardly I felt like I'd swallowed a bowlful of popping kernels of corn. Because as much as I had a feeling that my life was about to change for the better, I also had the memory of Mrs. Poppy's predictions and Mrs. Doring's voice saying that Gilbreth was going to be hit by some major calamity.

I couldn't help thinking that if something bad happened in Gilbreth, I'd be the first to fall.

On the way home through Whistler, I picked up a small stone and made a wish. I tossed the pebble toward the last window I passed and kept walking, not looking back.

A Brief Word
on Wishes and Truths

When I was three years old, I was crazy about sweets. One day I waited until my grandma's back was turned and pushed a chair against the kitchen counter and climbed up. Then I opened the cabinet above, which contained the Treat house treats. Cookies, chocolates, whatever nibbles Grandpa Treat liked to pretend he didn't eat. I'd seen him enough times, though, to know exactly where to go when Grandma left me on the kitchen floor with some alphabet cards and got caught up on a phone call in the hallway.

I opened the cabinet with my chubby, grubby fingers and tried to haul the plastic lid off of Grandpa's goody stash. Just as victory was close to being mine, my hand slipped, and I lost my balance and fell to the floor, breaking my three-year-old tailbone.

Sometimes you want something so much that you get

desperate, and you start to take risks to try to turn a wish into a truth.

Sometimes it works out.

And sometimes you just get hurt really badly.

Autumnfest

In 1727 the first harvest celebration was held, a day-long event consisting of physical challenges, tradesmen competitions, children's games, friendly gambling, and dancing. The first junior artisan contest was won by James Treat Jr., who took his uncle Elias's advice and made a cabinet patterned with leaves, which was later bought by the local herbalist.

–From **Gilbreth History: Founding Families & Artisanal Traditions** (Gilbreth Welcome Center, $16.99)

There was something special about stepping through Torrey Wood on a festival day, even while waddling through long, grabby tree branches in green tights and puffy orange pumpkin costumes that were so bulky that Crash and I couldn't fit on the wood paths side by side.

"What if a disaster happens?" Crash asked. "Like a freak hurricane or somebody getting hanged for *real* at the witch hangings? What if the dunking booth breaks and we both get stuck underwater and—hey!" He stumbled over a root in the path.

Okay, so I'd shoved him a little to keep him from listing more disasters. "Stop speculating, please. Grace is rubbing off on you. Everything will be fine." I helped him up and brushed off his costume. "Better than fine."

But I wasn't so sure about that. After a breakfast of cereal and a pat on the head from Uncle Theo, who was going to finish sanding his contest entry before manning the gallows, we'd checked again for a reply bottle to my invitation. There was none to be found, but the bottles I'd left had definitely been taken. Unless a curious raccoon or squirrel or turtledove had nabbed them, the messages had been picked up and, presumably, read.

Would the message leaver show up and reveal himself or herself?

Would it be my father?

Would disaster strike?

It was all enough to give a pumpkin a headache.

The sounds and smells sank into me before we'd reached the edge of the forest. Violin, mixed with banjo and other stringed instruments, tickled my ears, and glorious, rustic scents wandered and wisped their way into my nose.

The main stage, decorated in squashes and cornstalks and the first graders' acorn banner, was aflutter with volunteers in

Autumnfest-logo T-shirts setting up cozy rocking chairs for the storytellers and arranging equipment for the blacksmith demonstration.

The kettle corn cauldron was up and running, roasted meat was being turned over open-air spits, and artisans were setting up their wares in booths on the grass—copper kettles and cast-iron pots and handmade buckets and stools and ceramic dishes and candles and paintings and soap and blown glass and pens and pencils made from feathers and sticks.

Even at nine o'clock in the morning the town was brimming with tourists. The parking helpers (dressed festively either in historical dress or as traditional-arts objects like giant glass vases and candles and wooden buckets and knitting needles) kept the cars going to a large lot down by Gilbreth Park.

Food vendors were already serving Gilbrethean specialties like Tavern Barbecued Turkey Legs and Puritan Corn Dogs and every type of pumpkin product imaginable. Pumpkin soup, pumpkin ice, pumpkin-infused turkey legs, pickled pumpkin slices, pumpkin-flavored pickles, pumpkin seed salad, pumpkin bread, pumpkin desserts, and pumpkin drinks . . . it was dizzying.

As we crossed the Village Green, I began to feel strangely jittery. Horses clomping loudly down the street gave me the sense of being chased by someone or something, and the haze rising from a nearby barbecue smoker made me think of a coming forest fire instead of food.

A boom from the cannon stationed at North Bridge startled me off the curb.

"Jeez, you okay?" Crash asked, steadying me with a hand. "Need a breakfast turkey leg?"

"Fine," I replied. "Everything's going to be fine. No eating thirty minutes before swimming," I joked. According to *Laughing Your Way Through Angstville (a.k.a., the Teen Years)*, humor is supposed to defuse tense situations, though it didn't seem to be working.

A small herd of children and adults were being given last-minute coaching at the gallows for the performances they'd give for the next two days. The young lady playing Elizabeth Maybeck stood tall and proud, her long, plain skirt and short bonnet contrasting with the bagel sandwich she held in one hand and giant soda she slurped from the other.

Circling the gazebo with linked arms, three serious-faced older women in dresses, bonnets, and orthopedic shoes sang "The Bridge Ballad" in eerie, high pitched voices.

"Hey, morons!"

Crash and I both turned, a regrettable mistake I immediately wished I could take back. The book *Sticks and Stones* clearly states several times in its three-hundred-plus pages that if you are called names, the best reaction is to (a) ignore the name-caller or (b) look behind you, turn back, then say, "Who are you talking to? You couldn't possibly be talking to me. I am a very self-confident, smart, beautiful person with many interests." Come to think of it, that second option seems like it could backfire.

Instead of taking either option A or option B, Crash and I stared back at Michael Willis, who was dressed in tights, knickers, and a frilly white shirt, and had the bad luck of manning a pickle booth. He looked around to make sure Mr. Gansy was occupied, and lobbed an orange piece of pickled pumpkin at my head. Then he reached into a barrel beside him and chucked a green pumpkin-flavored pickle, laughing like a deranged colonial bully.

I tried to move, but with the bulky costume, I just sort of bumbled into Crash and got smacked in the face.

It wasn't the pain from the direct hit to my cheek or the embarrassment that hurt the most.

It was the stench.

I could already smell the vinegar and pumpkin spices adhering to my skin, sliding down my cheek, stinking like nutmeg and cinnamon-infused pee. A slow burn of hot blood boiled up from some hidden place inside me that clearly wasn't as well-adjusted as the rest of me. Today I could be meeting my father for the first time. It was *not* a day to smell like pickled pumpkin or pumpkin-flavored pickles.

Crash winced in sympathy. "Was that the disaster, do you think?" he whispered.

"You're both disasters," Michael said, a satisfied look on his face as he whipped a orangey lump just over Crash's head.

Daring to step within a few feet of Michael's booth, Crash did a solid job of glaring at him on my behalf, the impact only slightly lessened by the adorable stem-and-leaf hat the costume maker had insisted on. As for me, I had worked the pumpkin pickle/pickled pumpkin station for three years and knew its setup. Glaring wouldn't do.

I waddle-marched over, smiled kindly, and grabbed an empty plastic cup from a stack next to a large barrel marked CIDER. After popping the top off the pickle barrel, I scooped up a cupful of brine.

Holding the cup to the side, I thrust my face toward his. "Listen, Michael. I get it. I understand that your tendency to be awful to people stems from deep feelings of insecurity and fear."

The sneer practically sprang off his face as he sat down on the chair behind him. "Go get dunked, pumpkin."

Tightening my grip on the cup, I managed a deep breath. "Michael, I've read plenty about your type of deviance and have every hope that with proper guidance, self-reflection, and access to stronger deodorant, you can be a normal human being. As a peace offering, I wanted to let you know that Mr. Wheedle's black Lab just had puppies and he's looking to sell them. Maybe your mom will let you have one."

"What?" Michael's blank expression slowly gave way to a hint of longing.

"And as a matter of self-respect," I told him, "I wanted to do this." Swiftly and carefully, not wasting a drop, I poured the entire cup on his lap before he could come up with another insult.

Mr. Gansy, finished with whatever paperwork he'd been busy with, twirled back to his booth and waved at me while his festival volunteer sputtered, fighting dry heaves from the fumes that were wafting from his soaked pants.

"You better not end up being my brother," I snapped, grabbing Crash's hand and waddling away as fast as the costumes would permit. "That," I told my friend, "felt very good. I feel less nervous now." I clapped an arm around his shoulders as we hurried past the square, tottered past the school, and wobbled down toward the park.

Hours later Grace and the booth sponsor were calling out for customers, while I perched on my dunking paddle beside Crash. Both of us were grateful for the sunny day, but I was ready for another towel break. He leaned over. "Quit smiling at everyone like that. You're making potential customers nervous."

A dark-haired man with a chin dimple was standing at the food stand across the way.

I kept my lips stretched and answered through chompy smile teeth, "Making eye contact and keeping your facial expression friendly is an excellent way of demonstrating an open nature, which indicates a normal, happy child. Whoever my dad is, he won't want to introduce himself to a frowning kid with social issues. And I'm not smiling at everyone. Just the dark-haired people."

"That's, like, ninety percent of the population. And the bottle leaver might not be your dad."

Grace tossed me a cinnamon doughnut hole from the still-steaming bag she'd bought from the Cutting Board Bakery booth. "The bottle leaver's probably not actually your dad, Minna. I mean, I know I said that before, but it's probably just someone who knows something."

"Yeah," Crash said. "And he or *she* might have any color of hair. And what about bald people?" His target was hit and he plunged into the water below us.

Shoot. I hadn't thought of that.

"Minna, you're off for the next half hour," our adult sponsor said.

Uncle Theo had given me fifteen dollars for food to get me through lunch and dinner, but I couldn't leave the booth for fear of missing the bottle message leaver. I'd trapped myself there.

All week at school Grace had reverted to the Stare Face McGhee she was from before, sneaking glances at me and then looking at her notebook with such concentration that I wouldn't be surprised if she turned out to be some kind of government-recruited spy who was sent around the country to solve mysteries. I'd thought I saw a corner of a photograph glued into the middle of her notebook, but when I'd asked, she'd gotten red, slammed it shut, and changed the subject.

She was the same way now at the dunking booth, which I had chalked up to her feeling bad about thinking up such a punishing sort of Autumnfest duty.

But as she ran over to her backpack, flipped through her notebook to that same place right in the middle, and eyed me again, I couldn't help but feel a chill unrelated to my soaking-wet vine-green tights.

Grace, it seemed, was hiding something. I thought back to the black flash I'd seen in the woods, just before I found the first bottle.

And then she'd been hanging out by the bridge when Crash and I were gathering acorns.

Was Grace leaving the bottle messages? But that didn't make sense. She was just as convinced as I was that my father's identity would be revealed during Autumnfest.

Before I could pepper her with pointed questions, Lemon and Chai Hardly showed up.

Dressed as village criers in matching leggings and tunics, they waved at me, then had the nerve to stand on the money table. Some fool had given them a megaphone, not realizing that even at six, they had fully developed Hardly lungs.

"Witch hanging!" Chai called into the megaphone, her clear, high voice making it sound like a garden party.

"We're hanging another witch at three o'clock sharp in Town Square!" Lem shouted with glee. "Fifteen more minutes, then we'll hang her till she's dead, dead, dead!"

"Come and heckle her all you want!" Chai boomed. "She's a dirty, nasty witch!"

They hopped down and hurried toward the hay maze, leaving both shell-shocked and amused tourists in their wake, and leaving me feeling uneasy and slightly full of dread, as though I were next in line at some sort of big, unknowable gallows.

Nobody came the entire day. Scratch that—plenty of people came, just nobody with life-changing news for me. I considered the short list of Gilbreth fathers once again.

Mr. Willis kept pushing bread on me, Mr. Mackenzie let us have free meals and had studied abroad, and having Will Wharton as family would keep things nearly the same as they already were. But if I was being really honest, Mayor Ripty, with his black hair and olive complexion and large nose, looked the most like me. Maybe Grace was wrong about him.

"You've still got the full list of names and addresses," Crash pointed out, offering me a sweet potato fry.

"Yeah." I took it and munched at the salty sweetness.

"And you've still got tomorrow," Grace pointed out.

"Yeah." I took another fry from Crash. "There's still time for a miracle."

"Speaking of miracles," Uncle Theo said, appearing at the main stage, where we'd agreed to meet, "do I get an early peek at your miraculous junior artisan project?"

I smiled weakly. "That," I told him, "would take an entirely different miracle."

The next day had the same bright, brisk, beautiful fall weather, with just enough breeze to send the festival's smells my way, taunting my pumpkin perch and making me start to resent the bottle message leaver. If anyone managed to show up, I might have to give him or her a piece of my mind before asking for a loan to keep me and Uncle Theo in Gilbreth.

Soaked and squished inside a big orange squash, I scanned the crowd and chanted "Minna Treat's life will change at Autumnfest" to myself like some kind of secret wish mantra.

I got desperate, calling out to almost everyone who walked past. I had no way of knowing who'd been leaving the bottles, so I focused on anyone who made eye contact, making an extra effort with every male of the rightish age:

"Hey, did you go to Camden College?"

"Hey, do I look familiar to you?"

"Is your pointer toe longer than your big toe?"

"You! You with the black hair and big nose! Get over here!"

Grace, lounging in her pumpkin costume in a lawn chair beside me while counting money in the cash box, suggested maybe I was getting water in my brain and offered to be my scout for an hour so I could at least do the hay maze. But I'd specifically said in my bottle message that I'd be at the Punkin Dunkin' booth.

"I didn't mean to get you all excited." She sneaked a millionth look at her backpack. "I feel like it's my fault. It's just that this whole thing is completely out of a mystery book, and I expected . . ." She sighed. "I guess I thought you'd get a big reveal here. I mean, why would the person just ignore you after leaving that last message?" She frowned.

"There's still time," I pointed out. "What on earth do you keep looking at that notebook for?"

"Nothing," she chirped. She studied me again, her eyes lingering on my cheeks, my ears, my nose.

Crash had gone missing for a four-hour stretch to help Mr. Abel move the final boxes from his shop to Will Wharton's truck. He'd been weird the whole day, sneaking glances at me and looking a little sick to his stomach. Maybe he'd eaten too much pumpkin brittle.

Will and Mr. Abel and Mayor Ripty and Uncle Theo all tried to engage me in chatter as they passed by during the day, paying a dollar to dunk me, munching on apple tarts and barbecued pork sandwiches and funnel cake, sipping on barrel-pressed apple cider and lemonade, all of them openly speculating about what glorious entry I'd created for tomorrow's Bonfire Night presentation and wondering why on earth I had dedicated myself to drown over and over when a simple four-hour shift would have been enough.

"I like the costume," I told them through gritted teeth. "And the water."

Darian came by to collect his three free turns, sinking me into the small pool each time with tremendous glee and then apologizing profusely afterward.

By six o'clock in the evening the booth needed to be taken down, and I was finally shivering and exhausted enough to give up. But I couldn't believe it. Two full days of waiting, and nobody had announced himself or herself as anyone other than someone who wanted to pay to throw an orange ball at a target and try to drop me into the water.

Grace offered to wait with me, but I told her to go home.

Crash stood beside me in a tight buttoned jacket with elaborate trimmings and goofy poufs at the bottom that looked like bee-stung shorts. Beneath that he wore dark leg hose and low-cut shoes with buckles. The outfit he'd changed into after his final shift was another repeat from last year—William Shakespeare.

Shakespeare took my hand and squeezed it. "Minna,

I'm sorry about your dad. We'll find him, if that's what you want."

"Thanks, Crash." All of a sudden I was really tired. "At least we didn't get smacked with giant hail or fire or misshot cannonballs."

He laughed, but it sounded shaky. "Listen, I've been wanting to talk to you about . . ." He paused and cleared his throat, looking down the road where Grace was just disappearing from sight.

His stupid crush—Crash wanted to talk to me about liking Grace, to make sure I wouldn't feel bad about it. Well, I didn't want his pity. Not right then, anyway. I'd had about all of the adrenaline rushes, dashed hopes, and nervous talk I could take for one weekend. "I'm gonna go home, okay, Crash? I'm tired."

Without waiting for an answer, I slumped over to the Village Green, limply accepted a pumpkin pastry from the Willises' booth, and watched Uncle Theo take the gallows apart. He piled its wood into the circular, low-walled garden enclosure where the village bonfire would be lit the next night.

We waved at Will Wharton, who was leaving a Torrey Wood trailhead with a soft smile on his face. Uncle Theo and I walked home on the road, Uncle Theo with the easy stroll of a man with a shop-winning chair in his barn workshop, and me with a slouch of defeat. The thought of Bonfire

Night made me feel like there was a piece of cheese puff stuck in my throat.

He kissed me at the top of the porch stairs and unlocked the front door. "I'm going to bed, Minna. I'm beat."

I followed him inside. I felt beaten too.

When I got to my room, the diary was lying on my desk as though it was waiting for an explanation about being ignored.

Unable to sleep, I wriggled into jeans and a hooded sweatshirt, lifted the closet plank and grabbed the list of potential dads. Then I picked up Mom's diary and slipped down to the barn workshop.

I filled and lit the oil lamp and read through Mom's entire diary, feeling . . . I don't know what. Maybe I was getting sick or something. Her words were soft and hard and funny and boring and curious and whiny. Her words were so close to my face that I could almost sense a voice speaking them, but from somewhere too far away to ever hear.

She'd complained about Uncle Theo's foot odor. She'd written a poem about her favorite thing in Gilbreth. She'd brought Mrs. Abel a pot full of flowers on Grandparents Day, probably because she felt bad about the fact that Mrs. Abel had no children, let alone grandchildren.

I placed the diary on top of the list of father names.

I took it off again.

Then, as though my body belonged to someone way

more brave and way more well-adjusted than I felt, I found myself taking the list and setting it on Uncle Theo's special chair, which was right beside the worktable nearest my Minna nook.

Tomorrow was Bonfire Night.

I had no project, other than a mediocre, confused-looking frame made of bits and pieces of broken wood. And even that was locked in the school, where it was useless.

There was no way I'd win the money to buy stamps and envelopes to try to find my father, not to mention the trip to New York City to show off Uncle Theo's portfolio.

I had lied to my uncle big-time, in more ways than one.

I at least had to show him something honest. Lots of the parenting books talked about treating mistakes with understanding. By listening. Maybe Uncle Theo would reconsider the idea of searching for my father and help me. Maybe he wouldn't.

Either way, I was tired of hiding.

I turned off the lamp and went to bed without bothering to put on pajamas, falling into a fitful sleep full of dreams starring lists and pickles and pumpkins and gallows and diary pages and carved wood and horseshoes.

I woke in the middle of the night to muffled but horrified yelling and the smell of woodsmoke.

Ashes and a Wild Thing

The Treat family suffered a heartbreaking loss in 1728 when Tobias Treat fell off the schoolhouse while helping Elias finish the roof. Tobias was fifty-four years old, the father of eight children, and still adamant about using the skills of his trade. He had lived his life, Elias Treat wrote in the eulogy for his favorite brother, with a smiling heart and hoping eyes. Elias had always thought that Elizabeth Maybeck's death would be the hardest thing he would ever endure, but the day Tobias fell to his death was one of his darkest times.

–From **Gilbreth History: Founding Families & Artisanal Traditions** (Gilbreth Welcome Center, $16.99)

Thick legs thundered down the steps, and my uncle called my name over and over. He thought the screaming coming from outside our home was me.

I sprinted down the path he had blazed through the house

and out the back door to see flames through the barn window. My uncle's huge silhouette rushed to the barn and surged inside, like a flood hoping to smother the fire. The panicked yelling I'd heard changed to a wild scream of pain.

Without stopping to think, I tore back into the house and grabbed the fire extinguisher.

By the time I reached the barn, Uncle Theo was frantically flapping a towel over the flaring floor near my corner nook, where a large, moaning lump was curled up on the floor. The only live flames left were isolated to a single object just feet from him.

I aimed the extinguisher the best I could, and within a minute all signs of fire were gone, other than soft smoke rising from the places where the oil lamp had splattered its contents.

I stared in horror at the remaining scene, all shadows and ghosts, lit only by moonlight through the window. It was then that I realized that the moaning lump was Crash.

He was lying on the ground with a nail embedded in his forearm. I ran to him and took the arm gently, turning it to see the metal up close, piercing the skin so forcefully that there wasn't any blood yet, just a large amount of swelling. "Oh no."

He cried out and pulled the arm back toward him and said, with rattled breath, that he was so sorry. "In my pocket," he said. "From the apothecary's wall." Hand trembling, he pulled a long leather cord from his vest pocket and held it out to me. "It's the bottle message. It goes with the horseshoes." He looked behind me, and a fresh hurt filled his eyes. "Minna, I'm so sorry." His head fell back and he cried out again.

I took the necklace from his hand. He'd stolen the horse pendant from Mr. Poppy's shop, the one that he always tapped remedies into. And now he was talking nonsense. "Quiet," I told him. "Crash, you're gonna be fine." More short speeches raced one another through my brain as I searched for something to say that would make the pain fade. "Maybe just another tetanus shot—hey, the first one turned out okay, right?"

Too busy gritting his teeth and wiping at the tears pouring down both cheeks, he declined responding.

Uncle Theo breathed heavily as he hurried to Crash's side. "Minna, turn the lights on and get the first-aid kit."

I reached for the light switch and pulled the kit off its spot on the wall. Hands shaking, I searched for the antiseptic wipes and gauze.

Uncle Theo grimaced at the wound. "It's not too deep. I'm going to pull it out now. Okay, Christopher?"

He nodded, then howled at the fresh sting of cleaning and bandaging, but the pain on his face changed into something deeper as he turned to see the other thing that had been damaged. I followed his hollow gaze and finally realized what I'd been spraying with the extinguisher.

Uncle Theo's Town Square shop–winning chair.

Charred beyond repair.

A large chunk of blackened mess sat on the seat—the pile of paper I'd placed there just hours before.

I paced slowly to the blackened paper. When I tried to lift the list, it disintegrated into ash. Nothing more. The list containing my father's name, a list that I'd never see again now that Lorelei had switched jobs, was gone forever.

The world shrank and my tunnel vision focused on the disaster. I might as well have written a bottle message that said, *Inside the Treats' barn.*

Something in me tore open at the sight of the burned chair and papers. I turned slowly, feeling myself catch fire.

I stepped over to Crash, the blaze inside me building with painful pressure, blasting outward when I reached him.

"What is wrong with you! You ruin everything you touch! Do you know that? Now we're going to have to move!" I jabbed an angry finger at the chair. "And you see that big wad of nothing on the nothing chair?"

Crash tilted his head to see around me.

"My father was in that pile of ash!"

His eyes widened. His mouth opened. He shook his head. "Oh no! . . . Minna, *no.*" But as his eyes drifted over the mess, I could see that he knew I was telling the truth.

Uncle Theo finally noticed his chair.

I saw a piece of his heart break off.

I stuck my face in Crash's. "*Yes.* That's the list. You've got a million brothers and sisters and two parents, and I've got

NOTHING!" I flung a wild arm in the direction of the chair's ruins. "No wonder your parents don't want you around the shop." I flicked his fancy jacket buttons. "I figured it out. You wear stupid costumes of people who were actually good at something because you're horrible at the one thing you're supposed to know how to do. Now *get. Out.*"

Slow, fat tears were sliding down his cheeks while he looked between me and Uncle Theo.

"What were you doing here, Christopher?" Uncle Theo's voice was steady, but I saw the anger and frustration beneath his skin, shimmering to the surface, making his neck and face red from the effort of holding it in.

"I was . . ." Crash looked at us helplessly as he stood, jaw flapping in the air. "I was in the tree house and I wanted to borrow a tool from the workshop. I swear, Mr. Treat, I didn't think you'd mind, and then I lit the lamp to look around, and I tripped over the stool and the lamp fell and the oil spread and . . ." He gestured to the burned remnants of Uncle Theo's chair. "I'm so sorry."

I stuck my face in his. "Why were you in the tree house?"

Scrambling up to a sitting position, he tucked his hurt arm close to his chest. "It's where I've been keeping my . . . you know what, never mind." Using his free hand, he leaned on the bookshelf and hefted himself back up.

"Keeping what?" I demanded.

"You wouldn't even care," he said. "You don't think about

anyone but yourself." He took a step forward and his voice began to tremble. "I have secrets too, you know! And I need to talk about them with someone, and if you weren't so caught up in your stupid Minna bubble, maybe you'd notice stuff and ask me about it!"

Another step, and his tearstained face was inches from mine.

"You're right," he said. "I used to dress up like people who did important things because I suck at glassblowing. And there's more to life than what your parents want you to do. But I dress up now because I want to, so back off! And I don't like Grace Ripty," he whispered. "I like *you*—or I did before you started acting like you know everything. I left that bottle on the stakeout day. *Me*. I was going to tell you how I felt, and then ... and then ..." His face changed into something harder. A stone face, just for me. "You think you know everything, but you *don't*, Minna."

Crash had never shouted at me like that. Ever. It was like he'd turned into a whole different person.

Enraged and confused and not knowing what to do, I picked up a fistful of wood dust and flung it at him. "So you just let me believe my father was going to magically appear when you knew he wouldn't? What's wrong with you! Why don't you just GO!"

Uncle Theo put an arm on my shoulder. "Hey," he said gently, pulling me back. "Minna, it's okay. At least nobody was hurt too badly. What list are you both talking about?"

I whirled on him, stepping within inches of his beard. "Nobody was *hurt*? Are you kidding me? You're not going to get a Town Square shop and we're going to have to move! I know all about it, okay? You telling Will we can't afford the house, you checking out apartments in Vickerston, us getting calls from real estate agents."

My nostrils flared like a ready-to-charge bull, just waiting for Uncle Theo to deny it. "And there's no junior artisan project! I didn't make anything except a stupid frame, okay? So I'm not going to win and we can't go to that stupid party in New York to get you clients. That chair was your one chance!"

"Minna . . ." His hand flopped off my shoulder and he blinked, openmouthed.

"And that burned pile on the chair there," I choked out. "That was a list of all the men who attended school with Mom her junior year—the year she got pregnant with me."

Taking parenting-book-recommended deep breaths and visualizing a calm light-blue sky, I tried to tell myself that it was okay. That maybe I didn't need the list. Maybe my father was right here in Gilbreth, and if he was, surely my uncle would know *something*.

"Uncle Theo," I asked slowly, evenly, breathing in and blowing out for eight seconds before I asked the question, "is Mr. Mackenzie my father?"

If my uncle had been drinking water, it would have sprayed

all over the barn. "What on earth are you talking about?"

I pressed on, raising my shaking voice. "You heard me—why does he give us free meals every week?"

Astonishment filled his eyes and he shook his head back and forth. "Because I do repairs for him free of charge. You're not thinking straight."

"What about Mr. Willis? He made us free bread and he went to school with Mom. Is he my dad? Is he? Tell me the truth!"

"Minna, absolutely not, I—"

I cut him off, yelling directly up into his face, screeching another Gilbreth name. "David Ripty!"

Looking startled and almost frightened, Uncle Theo kept shaking and shaking his head. "*No*, Minna. I have no idea who your father is, but he's not in Gilbreth, I guarantee you that. Your mom had a lot of boyfriends her freshman year, and then she stopped dating altogether. She must have met someone her junior year, but nobody knew who. She never told anyone. And that didn't matter to us." His voice softened. "I guess it's time we talked about this."

The air was too thin. I tried sucking it down, but something blocked my breath and I gasped, panicking until the lump freed itself. "Will Wharton was in there! You're always saying he's family. Is Will my dad? Is he?"

Stepping back, Uncle Theo tripped over my bookshelf and clutched the nearest worktable for support. "What are you talking about? Of course Will isn't your dad. Will is . . . is part of our lives—mine and yours." Uncle Theo looked lost, then came toward me, his arms moving out for what I knew was going to be a firm but gentle hug—a tactic I knew too well from *Smother the Crazy with Love: Dealing with Drama During the Teen Years*. "Minna, it'll be okay," he said again, his stress vein popping up on his forehead.

He was giving me an "it'll be okay" speech? I slapped his hands aside. "You don't get it! You can't fix this with something you learned in a book! I've been living and breathing every single one of your books my whole life, and now everything's falling apart!"

Crash looked between us, not knowing what to do.

Uncle Theo shook his head, his huge fists opening and closing. "You think I want to move?" he asked. "You think I haven't tried everything I can think of to hang on to this house?" He paced back and forth, raw and wide open in a way I'd never seen. "I didn't tell you anything about having to move, because I was trying to fix it, okay? I was trying to fix everything so you wouldn't have to worry!"

It was like looking in a mirror. I'd been trying to fix things for us too. And I'd also failed.

Uncle Theo pounded an open palm into his chest, his voice cracking as he spoke again. "I—I'm the captain, remember?" He leaned his back against the worktable and bent over, elbows on knees, hands clutched together. "I'm supposed to be the captain." His head fell limply onto his woven fingers. "You think I haven't lost things? Sometimes things fall apart, Minna." His voice was softer now, his eyes wet and broken as he looked up at me. "They get destroyed, right under your feet, and you get knocked down, and you have to decide."

"Decide what?"

Crash reached out his injured arm and held his pocket handkerchief in the air with a wobbly hand.

Uncle Theo shook his head, rivulets wetly running down his cheeks before he wiped them aside with his hands. He was tired and angry and sad, and I wasn't sure which he was most. "You have to decide whether you want to rebuild what was lost, with whatever you have around you to build with."

I backed away. "There's nothing left."

He came closer. "There's you, Minna. There's us."

I closed my eyes, trying to shut out his words to keep them at a distance. The hurt inside me was still strong enough to do that, if only I fanned its flames. I took a good look at the chair and the burned-up names.

I ducked his arms and stomped over to our ruined dreams. "My *father* was in there! Lorelei got me a list, and now she's switched jobs and I'll never get it back!" I felt my dented Treat chin tremble, on the verge of giving in to the sad that was pushing against my mad. "It was my one chance. And now it's gone." Feeling unsteady, I stumbled back to Crash. "And *you* burned it."

"I'm so sorry." He said it with hoping eyes. He wanted me to forgive him.

"Shut up. I didn't get a chance to send a single letter," I whispered. "I hate you." The last three words were so quiet that Crash had to lean forward, as though unsure of what I'd said.

Then, like a crazed, stereotypical example out of one of the most ridiculous parenting books I'd ever read, *KaBOOM: Rage Fests During Adolescence, When to Defuse and When to Find a Bomb Shelter*, my body spun like a possessed doll and I screeched at Uncle Theo and the world in general. "I hate you, too! I hate EVERYTHING!"

I snatched up Mom's diary, ripped one of my old twig frames from the wall and stomped all over it, and went running out of the barn.

I ran back to the house and up to my room. Within seconds I'd grabbed my backpack and stuffed a few things inside, shoved Mom's diary into my sweatshirt's front pocket, and sprinted off toward Torrey Wood like some kind of wild thing, my heart torn to pieces, just like my life in Gilbreth.

Under the Bottle Bridge

Whistler Bridge, be warned, be warned,
There wait souls of maids unmourned,
There wait souls of maids unmourned.

–From **Gilbreth History: Founding Families & Artisanal**
Traditions (Gilbreth Welcome Center, $16.99)

The smell of burning clung to the air, gusts of bitter wind blowing into my back as I ran along low stone walls, my flashlight catching the rows of piled rock until I cut into the forest, where the branches and leaves groaned and murmured and bashed against one another overhead.

I found the path to Whistler, and my legs pumped along with my broken heart, thumping over stones and fallen acorns, pounding out a cluttered rhythm.

In the beam of light ahead I saw my bridge. The sight of it brought both relief and a fresh round of anger and grief.

Just as I neared the entrance, my foot caught a root. The horse necklace I clutched in one hand went flying and I tumbled sideways, then down to the center of the place where a strong creek once ran, knees crashing into a half-buried boulder with a solid bang. I cried out, and the bridge answered, the sky's whirling drafts and Whistler's loose planks howling with haunted moans and high-pitched cries that faded into a thin, reedlike song.

Rising gingerly, I heard a faint clinking sound near my foot. Aiming my headlamp toward it, I saw another bottle, the message inside poking just above the opening. Tearing it out, I read the words:

Under the bridge.

I didn't need anyone to tell me what disaster had happened at this bridge. I stuffed the stupid message back where it had come from. Rain began to drop straight from the sky, not harsh, but steady enough to make me crawl under Whistler for protection, into the thickest part of the wilting forget-me-nots.

Exhausted and cold and clutching the bottle, I huddled within my hood, my hands stuffed into the large front pocket, where I could feel the diary. Rocking back and forth, I thought of all the things that had gone wrong in the last three weeks:

I had no junior artisan project.

Uncle Theo's chances of winning a Town Square shop were gone.

The list that included my father's name had been burned to ashes before I'd used it.

I'd told my best friend that I hated him.

We were going to have to move away from Gilbreth.

The rain let up, and I took off my hood. The rustling nearby sounded strange, and when I turned the flashlight toward the trees above the ravine, I realized that the turtle-doves were flocked and huddling near the feeding boxes. Watching me.

I threw the bottle hard at the group of them. "What do you want from me?"

One flew straight for me, dodging my head, then hovering below Whistler's woodwork. Fluttering across the underside of the bridge, it found an awkward perch near a crossbeam. The dove flapped and flapped, its wings banging against the wood.

"Stop that!" I called. "You'll hurt yourself!"

I stood to shoo it away from the bridge. My hands swiped upward, and near my fingertips a dark spot caught my eye. It was a smidgeon of . . . was it carving or weathering? A beam was blocking it.

Half-buried rocks served as footholds along the ravine wall. Gingerly testing my weight, I climbed higher until I could see the marks:

ELIAS, TOBIAS, SAMUEL, JAMES TREAT. BROTHERS ALL.

1702

The turtledove flapped over to the other side of the beam. There was more carving.

Scrambling up the steep wall, I shifted my weight onto a thick root that acted as a tiny platform. Holding on to a trunk that grazed the bridge's side, barely able to breathe, I lifted a shaking hand and touched the crudely formed lines.

ELIZABETH TREAT WAS HERE

There was a month, day, and year underneath it. I did quick math in my head. She'd been twelve. The diary entry. My twelve-year-old mother had been in this spot and had somehow carved her name under the bridge.

"Did you know this was here?" I asked the dove.

The bird moved to the other end of the bridge. I scrambled off the tree root and followed it, shining the light on a crossbeam on the other side to see another etching:

E. AND MINNA TREAT

The date beside it was one week before she'd died. Uncle Theo had told me how she loved to walk through the woods with me strapped to her chest in a carrier, singing and whispering and pointing things out to me. Loving me. I'd pushed that story aside. I had no memory of it, so it wasn't real.

But there were our names, carved deep into the wood.

Right beside each other.

I closed my eyes and imagined being strapped to her chest as she carved her last entry into the wood, declaring that she was here and that I'd been with her, our hearts beating against each other under the bottle bridge.

With that, with the idea of my heart pressed against my mother's and with an impossibly faraway memory that I could somehow feel the echo of, I stepped back down to the flowers and knelt, burying my head among them.

She'd been real and we had been together. She'd named me and cared about me in my purest, simplest, most Minna form. She'd held me close and whispered songs and secret words to me that were ours alone. She hadn't loved me for existing as a Treat—she'd loved me for existing. The diary pressed itself firmly against my chest. I pressed back as hard as I could, knowing I'd never be able to get close enough.

For the first time in my life, I wanted my mom.

The strangest thing about the last few weeks was that I had really, truly, absolutely thought that what I was looking for—what I needed in order to find out who I was as Minna and to feel good and prepared for whatever lay ahead—was my father. And maybe I did want to find him.

But I think what I really needed was to find my mother.

Even as my heart felt like it was being squeezed and twisted apart, it was as though something slipped into an empty space inside me.

Wiping wetness from my eyes, I touched the letters and numbers again, thinking of the four names and dates we'd found carved near horseshoes: above the cooper's door, behind the baker's oven, within the miller's wheel, in the tavern's barrel room.

On those dates, in those places, four different Treats had touched something in Gilbreth. They'd left their marks behind.

I sat back down and peered at the beams and planks of Whistler, which had held for hundreds of years. Each of those planks had its own scars and worn sections. Each was patterned with different whorls in their wood. Each one was necessary for the bridge to exist, and each one was a piece of something larger than it would ever have been on its own.

My mother's plank had been missing from my life's bridge, and I'd been wobbling on unsure footing, with empty spots both behind and ahead.

But I could feel her resting in place just behind me now, holding me steady with invisible arms. Holding me gently, the way the walls of the covered bridge cradled those who passed through its middle.

"I like what's in the middle," Mr. Poppy had said about my twig frame in his shop.

"Frames are important," Mr. Abel had said, "but *their purpose is to protect and celebrate and hold together what's inside. . . . That's the essence."*

"I love framing old houses," Uncle Theo had said.

Bits and pieces of conversation I'd heard around town fluttered around my mind like turtledoves, like feathery wings of possibility swishing against one another.

The dove under the bridge was staring at me, looking a bit scrawny. Maybe he was the one I'd rescued from the school. If so, he'd been eating food from the cafeteria garbage. Mrs. Willis had mentioned that the flocks were coming into town, hungry.

I stood up, shining my light at Whistler and the dove boxes and Torrey Wood.

Slowly, like the flavor of Gilbreth's wild mushrooms whispering a secret truth, an idea grew.

I knew what I would make for my junior artisan project, how to save our house so we could stay in Gilbreth, and how I could fit into the Treat legacy—on my own terms.

Resolved, I crawled up the ravine wall to retrieve Mr. Poppy's horse necklace from the ground. A brief search revealed that it had landed on a moss-covered stone about fifteen feet from the bridge, right along the dry creek. When I picked up the leather cord, a scrap of moss was brushed away.

It was a curious stone to be near the river. It looked almost like a piece of chimney brick from the old settlement—the kind on display at the welcome center.

The rumbling clouds burst open in a sudden, violent

downpour. Startled, I slipped on a pile of soaked leaves and practically plunged beneath the bridge, where there was nothing to do but cower from the rain for what seemed like hours.

Then the lightning started. I counted one, two, three bolts.

Five.

Ten.

I stopped counting. I'd never seen anything like it before. If I hadn't known better, I would have said the lightning was searching for the right place to strike. My entire body buzzed with electricity.

An unearthly bolt lit up the night, breaking the sky in two on the other side of Torrey Wood, striking with a furious, deafening crack. It was as though a mountain had been blown apart. Something had been hit hard.

A low, ominous moan sounded over the storm, followed by a strange rushing noise.

The sound came closer.

Closer.

I looked far down the ravine.

When the disaster that Grace and Mrs. Doring and Mrs. Poppy had predicted became horrifically clear, I had only a few moments to wonder why I hadn't thought of it as a possibility. It wasn't a fire. It wasn't an explosion or an earthquake or a freak accident.

The disaster was a flood. There was no stopping it. I couldn't move. I just stood there trembling. Waiting.

I knew what the lightning had been searching for and what it had finally struck. The natural dam near the mill had been blasted to nothing. A wall of water had been released, heaving and hungry, racing to fill the ravine that had been dry for three hundred years.

And it was about to swallow me whole.

A Hand in the Night

"There are moments," Elias Treat *wrote, "in everyone's life when crossroads are reached—when risk and dreams and danger and discovery all converge—when one season ends and a new one begins."*

–From **Gilbreth History: Founding Families & Artisanal Traditions** (Gilbreth Welcome Center, $16.99)

There was a moment just before the water slammed into my face that I saw the turtledove, still huddled in the bridge eaves.

A familiar rough howl boomed over the remaining thunder, over the flood that was about to carry me away. It sang into the night like a rescue siren.

"It's going to be okay," I whispered to the dove. "Beastie is here."

Then the world turned to swirling madness, and the last thing I remember before fully blacking out was a flash of pain and the firm grip of a hand around my wrist.

It was a large hand, missing a pinkie finger.

Bonfire Night

A month after his older brother's untimely death, Elias Treat did a most surprising thing, which he hadn't done since the death of Elizabeth Maybeck; he began to seek opportunities, traveling to large cities to showcase his work as a craftsman. He began, his brother James noted in a letter to a distant cousin, to live again.

–From **Gilbreth History: Founding Families & Artisanal Traditions** (Gilbreth Welcome Center, $16.99)

THE PAST TELLS US WHERE WE CAME FROM, WHAT WE ARE, AND WHO WE WANT TO BE. The motto of Gilbreth hung in a banner across Town Hall's front porch, where a podium and microphone had been set up for the junior artisan project presentations and Mr. Abel's tale.

The Village Green was packed with milling Gilbretheans. I walked around the bonfire, looking for Crash and dodging question after question as ten-foot-high flames blazed from the base of the cobblestone circle.

Everyone had heard about the flood and my accident. Both had turned out fine.

My left wrist had been fractured and was covered in a cast that hung from a sling decorated to look like a tree log. The pain hadn't stopped me from getting Mr. McConnell to let me into the woodshop at school, or from getting my project finished on time. And the force of the water had burst through the natural berm on the other end of the creek. By the time the residents of Gilbreth had gathered on the Village Green late that afternoon, the water level was so high and flowing that it was as though the empty ravine had never been there at all.

Darian smiled at me across the lawn, setting his tray on a nearby card table and wiping his hands. He pointed to his entry basket, which was a little messy but truly impressive. I'd never realized just how much Torrey Wood could feed us.

For the last hour judges had been walking back and forth along the roped-off space dedicated to the junior artisan projects: ironwork sculptures, buckets, quilts and blankets, spools of hand-spun thread, pottery, glassworks practical and decorative skills that were all more visually impressive than my entry. Most of the judges eyed mine with puzzled expressions before picking it up and studying it more closely, at which point their expressions changed. The rest of the town would have to wait until I went to the podium to present.

There were twenty-one entries altogether, and to my extreme surprise, Crash was listed as number fifteen. But his display area was empty.

I hadn't seen Crash anywhere to apologize or to show him my project or ask about his. I'd asked Tommy and Jane and Adam where he was, and they didn't know. I asked his parents and they just shrugged, secret smiles on both of their faces.

Lemon was chasing a shrieking Chai around, or Chai was chasing a shrieking Lemon, it was hard to say. One of them was dragging an ecstatic Beast along by a rope, the handkerchief saddle and stuffed monkey they'd tied to my dog threatening to come off.

Michael Willis was surrounded by a group of high school girls who wanted to play with the puppy he'd gotten earlier that day. He met my eyes briefly when I passed by, and didn't insult me or sneer, making me think he was on his way to becoming more well-adjusted.

The announcer tapped on the microphone, then introduced the mayor, and the presentations began. An hour later Crash's name had been skipped and I was the last person to be called to the Town Hall steps.

Shaking only very little, I left my frame where it was and picked up the essence of my project. I managed to get up the steps without tripping and handed my project to Mayor Ripty, who stared at the neat pile of papers and gestured to the microphone.

"Care to explain for those of us, myself included, who haven't gotten a closer look at your project, Minna?"

My mouth felt like it was stuffed with cotton balls, but with a deep breath, I leaned over. "It's a proposal." I tapped the paper. "I know it was supposed to be something made of wood, but it's written on Mr. Lee's paper, and we all know that's made from wood pulp from fallen trees in Torrey Wood. I did make the pencil, if that helps. Okay, last year, so I guess that doesn't count. But it's the words that are really my junior artisan project."

Mayor Ripty studied the paper for a small forever and looked at me with an expression I couldn't read. It was either puzzled or admiring. I was hoping for admiring. "Are you serious about this?" he asked me.

A curious murmur swept through the onlookers.

"For the love of Gilbreth glass, what does it say?" Mr. Hardly asked, his voice booming through the night.

Straightening my shoulders, I lifted my chin an inch and adopted what I hoped was a businesslike tone. "The mayor wants our town to be more profitable. He's suggested we modernize by bringing in more commercial franchises, like chain restaurants and stores."

A slightly muffled round of boos echoed around the green, and the mayor shifted anxiously beside me.

"Get to the point," he murmured.

"He's suggested subdivisions," I continued.

Now the cries of protest weren't even muffled.

"He says that towns like ours end up like ghost towns. Young people like me and my classmates won't want to stay in a place like Gilbreth, he says." I turned to the mayor. "But modern's not what we're selling here."

Raising both hands, I gestured to the Gilbreth motto, flapping in a small evening breeze. "We still embrace skills of the past, and we still talk about successes and mistakes and . . ." My voice broke. "And accidents of the past so that we can do better in the present and future. But *not* by forgetting where we came from."

I tapped my project. "It's all in there. My team will start to rebuild as soon as Gilbreth approves it."

Mayor Ripty's eyebrows shot up. "Your *team*?"

"Rebuild *what*?" someone in the crowd shouted.

I pointed to Uncle Theo, who cringed a little but waved at the stage. "That's my team."

"Approves *what*?" yelled another.

"A ghost town!" I yelled back.

Silence bloomed. All I heard was the crackle and pop of the bonfire. Furrowed brows slowly gave way to chuckles and snorts passed among the crowd. I was losing them.

I tapped the microphone. "Okay, not exactly a ghost town." I swallowed. "I'm proposing to rebuild the settlement ruins and have them be a living history museum, open year-round. Everyone would contribute and . . ." I gulped down a thick wad of nerves. "And it would be good for everyone."

The laughter faded. I wasn't sure what that meant, but at least I had their attention.

"It could bring in more school and tourist visits year-round, and all of your businesses would be better off for it. It could create jobs, and students could even dress up and be part of the settlement on the weekends. It could be like Autumn-fest and the other festivals every weekend of the year. And we could have workshops and those retreat things that adults like to have and . . . and . . ." I looked over the papers. "And I think we should have more dove boxes built so the flock can stay in the woods and not have to come into town for food."

"Anything else?" the mayor asked, a hint of disbelief in his voice.

Smoke from the bonfire drifted toward the podium. My eyes watered. "One more thing. I think we should give Whistler Bridge a restoration and put a medical kit and emergency call button in all of the bridges, in case . . . in case . . ." I looked for Uncle Theo.

A few tears spilled down my Captain's cheeks, into the crevices of a sad smile. He nodded for me to finish.

"In case someone ever needs it. That's all. Thank you."

I held my breath and counted. Everyone was quiet for exactly three seconds before Grace and Uncle Theo led the clapping. Timid at first, the noise grew stronger until I stood looking over the crowd, hearing rowdy calls of encouragement and whistles. Gilbreth was whistling for me. I whistled back.

Mayor Ripty raised his hands for silence, then spoke into the microphone. "A project of this caliber would require a tremendous amount of planning and organization." He leaned down. "Young lady, you may just have something here," he whispered. "I'll be speaking to the town board about this at our next meeting. But for now, why don't you go find Gracie and settle in for a story." He turned back to the crowd. "While the judges make their final decisions in our contest for young artisans, Gene, please come on up and tell us a story."

The evening had grown cooler. As Mr. Abel made his way up the steps, blankets were passed around, children were smothered with hugs and leftover kettle corn and threats to remain quiet, and Gilbreth's eldest citizen took the stage.

Grace was waving from one side of the bonfire, and she patted the ground next to her.

"Where's Crash? Why didn't he present a project?"

"Shh," she told me, her face gleaming. "You'll see. By the way, after the story I need to talk to you, okay? It's sort of important."

Before I could demand an explanation, Mr. Abel began to speak, his thick, rustic, aged-barrel voice stretching over the Village Green like homemade hearth milk taffy.

Uncle Theo appeared on my right and sat down beside me. His eyes were still a little misty in the firelight, and he simply wrapped an arm around my shoulder and nodded. I snuggled my head into his neck for a moment, breathing in his sweat and deodorant, soaking in the night.

"Before I begin my story and introduce a special guest, I want to say that, as many of you know, I am the last Abel in this village. My family has been making candles in Gilbreth for three hundred years. I'm ninety-four years old and will die with no relatives. I've come to terms with that. Sometimes endings are endings. And sometimes"—Mr. Abel stepped aside, revealing his special guest—"they are a new beginning."

The guest was Crash. It was my best friend, Christopher Hardly, standing there dressed up like . . . like himself. He wore jeans and a gray sweater that looked just a little too small, like he was growing out of it. In his arms was the largest, most beautiful candle I'd ever seen. Layers upon layers of wax in a beautiful pattern.

"This young lad," Mr. Abel said, his voice breaking while he smiled down on Christopher, "with the blessing of his parents, has agreed to be my apprentice. He's chosen not to enter his project, but it's far too meaningful not to present along with my story." He gestured to the candle. "This candle is made of two hundred and fourteen waxed layers, representing the number of years that Abels have resided over the shop that I'm now unable to run. I couldn't be more proud of this project if Christopher Hardly was my own son. I'm so . . ." He wiped at his eyes and shook his head, not finishing.

He clapped a trembly hand on Crash's shoulder, and

suddenly all of the times my friend had disappeared or been spotted in our yard made sense. He'd been using our old tree house to hold candlemaking supplies—that's what he'd meant the night before. I'd missed it completely.

"I will still be losing my shop, but I will be gaining a student. And together we'll create something new from the old. A rebirth." Mr. Abel pointed to me in the audience. "Something this young lady has also wisely and respectfully proposed."

The crowd turned to me, but I kept my eyes straight ahead, waiting for my best friend. When he met my eyes, I placed one hand over my heart, then the other. It took a forever moment, but he smiled softly and saluted me.

Mr. Abel cleared his throat and wiped his eyes. "And now a Bonfire Night tale for you, full of old superstitions, lost souls now passed, and hope for those who still feel as though they're finding their way in this world." He located me in the crowd again and smiled, pulling a worn book from his back pocket. "I hope you'll all like it.

"About three weeks ago Theodore Treat was helping me with a few boxes from my attic. The boxes were filled with photographs and papers from the past that I thought I might visit with one more time. In doing so, I came across a curiosity that I'd never seen before."

He held the book up to the crowd. "These are the words of my ancestor. In 1704 John Abel, the first of my ancestors to come to Gilbreth, became the best of friends with founder

Elias Treat. John Abel was a learned man and kept this journal, which has been passed down among our family.

"Thankfully, though my hands aren't always as steady as they used to be, my eyes are just fine. I began to read. The things I learned about our town and its people could fill a book."

He held up a finger. "In fact, my Evangeline always thought I should gather all the resources I could and write a history of Gilbreth's families and traditions. Maybe I will, once I get young Christopher up to speed in the art of being a chandler. There's really not much to it, other than making sure you've got a steady supply of burn balm."

The crowd laughed softly.

"That said, here's what I'd like to share with you tonight."

He opened the journal and read a few entries from the beginning. Some were lighthearted, even funny, but the words took on a serious tone as 1718 approached, the year of the Gilbreth witch hanging.

"So Elias found himself in love with a girl named Elizabeth Maybeck, the woman who was wrongfully hanged as a witch right here in Gilbreth. The horse Elizabeth Maybeck was said to have bewitched and stolen was put to death. John Abel discreetly removed the horse's shoes, gifting them to Elias as a keepsake of something Elizabeth Maybeck had healed.

"John was the person ordered to bury the body with no

gravestone. He discovered a necklace that Elizabeth had secretly brought with her to her hanging, a simple leather cord holding a small wooden horse, a trinket she'd received as a girl. He recognized the horse as being his best friend's handiwork and gave the necklace to Elias.

"John was the last one to see Elizabeth, and the only one to know the grave's location. He wrote only that he subtly marked the spot with a plain brick. It's never been found.

"After secretly keeping the items for years, Elias Treat placed the horseshoes on building projects completed by each of the Treat brothers. The locations were all places where tragedy had called for a new beginning. He placed them both for luck and to honor his first love.

"Elias gave the necklace to the local apothecary, who happened to be a distant relative of the Maybecks. The man had become frightened for himself and his family when he saw what the villagers had done to Elizabeth in the name of witchcraft. After all, herbalists had been accused of similar things for centuries. He hung it on his wall, hoping Elizabeth's memory would help protect his family."

Mrs. Poppy let out an audible gasp nearby, then kissed the cheek of a wide-eyed Mr. Poppy.

"After Elizabeth's death John Abel, who knew his friend Elias's heart, suggested the chosen mourning method of his family, casting bottles into the sea with messages for lost loved ones. Elias took it to heart, tossing his messages off all of the bridges of Gilbreth, even Whistler, which had no water flowing beneath it.

"Later in Gilbreth's history hidden bridge bottles became important message holders during times of conflict and war, but they were also used to send messages of love."

Mr. Abel described several hilariously botched love message stories from his high school years, ones where unintended bottle gatherers got the wrong idea, leading to one unfortunate incident where a boy found himself with eleven angry women on his doorstep on the evening of a dance, all of them demanding to be taken to dinner.

"My own wife and I left each other messages on that same bridge while we were courting, and at times during our sixty-three years of marriage when we needed to reconnect. Only once did a message go missing." He held up a pot of blue flowers that matched the ones under the bridge. "It was taken by the same child who brought these pretty things to my Evangeline one day.

"A single packet of forget-me-not seeds, taken by a curious child and spread along the ravine near Whistler. As soon as they first bloomed, the poor child showed up on our doorstep, her eyes red, confessing all sorts of things, from carving her name beneath the bridge to snarfling her brother, whatever that means.

"And then she handed over a small patch of the stolen forget-me-nots to my wife, in this very pot. They'd been lost, then returned. Evangeline kept this pot nice and warm inside, to trick them into thinking it was forever spring so they'd stay in bloom longer. But she didn't have to. They're perennials. If you take care of them, they never die. They simply hibernate until it's time to bloom again.

"This summer, on my wife's birthday, I bought a large amount of forget-me-not seeds and scattered them from each window of her favorite covered bridge. I thought there was a small chance that they might bloom in autumn. They did."

I held my breath. That explained the flowers. What else would Mr. Abel reveal?

"Three weeks ago, when my heart was breaking from grief as the anniversary of my wife's passing approached, I threw a bottle from Whistler Bridge, into the forget-me-nots, to communicate with my Evangeline. Seeking comfort, I suppose.

"I lingered after leaving my second message, one that confessed to my love that I was no longer able to do my work. A young girl appeared. Minna Treat—the daughter of the girl who had found one of my bottle messages years ago.

"I had learned that there was a chance that the Treat family would be leaving Gilbreth, and since four Treat ancestors were original town founders, I wanted to send Miss Treat on a little adventure, to revisit her roots and to perhaps find a piece of her more recent past. I knew that she had lost something irreplaceable on that very bridge. I wanted to help her find it."

Mr. Abel waved at me. I couldn't believe it. *He'd* been leaving me the bottles.

"Sometimes," he continued, "what we go searching for isn't what we find. The most important thing we strive to find in this world is ourselves, and our place. And one of the biggest lessons I've learned in my ninety-four years is that those things can change as the seasons go by—that life is an ever-changing journey—one step, one surprise, one miraculous occurrence at a time.

"When I threw a message bottle into the ravine from Whistler three weeks ago, I was missing my wife. I wanted to talk to her, to let her know that I'd come to an end. And now," he said, clapping a hand on Crash's shoulder, "I'm not so sure about that. Happy Season, Gilbreth."

Every voice on the Village Green echoed him. "Happy season."

"Happy Season," Uncle Theo murmured softly.

A glowing, moon-kissed warmth spread all the way to my fingertips as I joined in the applause.

An hour later pockets of people and conversation were floating around Town Square as the last of the smoke drifted up from the dampened bonfire. Malia Johnson's two silver spoons had won first prize, and both Crash and I had congratulated her with all sincerity. She deserved it.

But there went my chance to attend that fancy party and get Uncle Theo new commissions.

I could only hope the town board would actually review and approve my proposal. Soon.

Uncle Theo was a few feet away, shaking hands with the ecstatic winners of Mr. Abel's shop, two fishermen who had been making fly rods and snowshoes out of their garage for years.

Mayor Ripty waved good-bye to several people and walked over to where Grace and I were admiring Crash's candle.

"I need to talk to your uncle about your proposal," said the mayor.

"I need to talk to you," whispered Grace.

Uncle Theo stepped over, a wriggling grin on his face. "The Schwartzes are going to hire me to carve their shop sign. They're calling it Seasons. *And*"—he held up a finger—"I think they want to join the book club."

"That's great! I hope they like parenting books."

"Very funny." He pinched my elbow lightly. "I'm thinking of branching out, actually." His smile faded to a line. "Hey, listen, I need to talk to you about something, Minna. I wanted to wait until the evening was over, but . . ." He took in one of his Zen, jumping-into-the-deep-end-of-a-pool breaths.

My own breath caught in my throat. Was this it? Had he sold the house or something like that? And what did Grace want?

"What is it?" I asked Uncle Theo.

A hand appeared on his right shoulder. "I think I need to talk to both of you," said Mr. Abel.

Will Wharton came up behind Uncle Theo, scratching

his head in an apologetic way. "I guess I should be here too, seeing as I've been an accomplice."

Good Lord, I was surrounded. "Is this about the bottles?" I asked them all.

"Yes," said Mr. Abel and Will.

"No," said Mayor Ripty.

"No," said Grace, blushing.

"No," said Uncle Theo. "I went to the post office today and . . ." He looked at a piece of paper in his hand with a couple of words scribbled on it. "Minna, who's Abram Peralta?"

I shook my head. "I don't know."

"Well, he's sent you a letter. And he left two phone messages last week—ones that you apparently didn't manage to erase along with the real estate agent's calls."

"Whoops." My toes curled up against the insides of my shoes, cowering for me.

"His messages were brief, just asking me to call him back. I thought it was a client, and was going to call this week sometime. But, Minna, who would be writing you?"

"Abram Peralta?" A puzzled look crept over the mayor's face. "That's the name of my roommate in college."

"He was on Minna's list." Grace Ripty's lips twisted to one side. Her hands looked twitchy, and I could tell she wanted to reach for the notebook in her back pocket.

I was confused. "My list? But I didn't send any letters. And the list is gone."

She squirmed a little under her father's serious expression.

"I was at your house, and when you mentioned roommates, I realized why you look so familiar. That's why I got all weird. There's a photo in my dad's office at home, from when he was in college. It's of my dad and his roommate. He looks like you, I swear he does. So I . . ." She trailed off, biting her lip and looking nervously at Uncle Theo.

I shook her arm. "What did you do, Grace?"

Mayor Ripty frowned down at her. "Yes, what did you do, Grace?"

"I copied down his address. And I mailed a letter." She cowered away from me a little, like a kid about to get yelled at. "Not just any letter. *The* letter."

"Which letter?"

"The one on your desk—it said something about long toes on your feet? I copied it down and didn't change a word. And he wrote you back!"

I felt light-headed. "Probably just to say he's sorry, but he has no idea what I was talking about."

Uncle Theo's head jerked back and forth between me and Grace, then settled on the mayor.

"Theodore, I'm so sorry about all this," Mayor Ripty said. "Minna certainly does resemble Abram, now that you mention it. But I'm sure it's a coincidence. I'll call Abram and explain the mistake. He once mentioned being smitten with some girl he'd been spending time with, but then he left to study abroad. He met another girl in Spain."

Studied overseas. It fit.

"A nice Spanish girl. He ended up staying an extra year there, and they got married and moved back to the States together. I haven't spoken to him in a few years now." He looked at Grace. "My daughter should never have gotten involved."

I felt hollow. Mom's heart hadn't broken for the first time at Whistler Bridge. It had been broken before she even had me. That's why she never told anyone who my dad was.

Grace hung her head, but when she looked up at her father, there was a spark of defiance to her voice. "You're right. I shouldn't get involved with anything. I shouldn't even make friends, should I?"

For a moment I thought Grace was about to let her father have it. But then the battle fell away from her, and she slumped against him.

"Because we'll just be leaving again, won't we, Dad? That's the plan, right?" She said it sadly. Matter-of-factly.

Bending, the mayor dropped to one knee and held Grace by her shoulders. "I'm trying to help places. Fix them. That means we move on when we're done. That's what I do, honey."

"That's all you ever do," she said quietly. "You're so busy trying to fix places, you don't even realize that I'm breaking every time we go somewhere else."

The mayor's jaw flapped helplessly as he stared at his daughter.

Grace's voice came out strong as she took a step back. She gathered the long necklaces around her neck together in a ball and held them to her chest. "Just because you don't care about me having a mom anymore doesn't mean I can't help Minna find her father. I just thought that maybe . . ." She let the sentence melt away, like suddenly she wasn't so sure she'd done the right thing.

Mayor Ripty looked at the ground and shook his head, lifting a single hand to rub at the back of his neck. He stood and stepped forward slowly, relieved when Grace leaned into him. "Where's the letter?" he asked Uncle Theo.

"I left it on the kitchen table." Uncle Theo nodded at me. "Minna, do you want to go home and read it?"

Dizziness washed over me, and I felt my uncle reach out his arm, like an anchor holding me in place, while Gilbreth worked its strange magic, making the past, the present, and the future all blend into one. A moment passed and I blinked myself back. "Okay. Yes."

Crash just stood there, watching all of us and holding the beautiful candle. He was the very picture of an autumn change. My friend had altered his colors so gently, so gradually, that nobody had noticed he'd become different until he stepped onstage to show us.

I took Crash's hand and gave it three quick squeezes. "Will you come with? But by the way, you can't ever 'like me' like me, because I'm obnoxious and we're blood brother and sister, and also because it would ruin our friendship and I could never stand that."

"Me neither," he said. "PS, I think I like Malia Johnson now."

Oh *Lord.* "Crash, no liking *anyone.* At least until next year. Please?" I sighed. "We'll have to discuss this later."

A finger tapped me on the shoulder. Darian stood there, holding out a bouquet of edible greens with red-streaked white stems that ended in bulbs. He smiled shyly. "Your project sounds great. These are for you. They're ramps. Wild leeks."

"Oh . . . thanks." I took the greens and sniffed them, before remembering that they weren't flowers.

Crash's frown matched his piercing eyes, which played Ping-Pong between me and the leeks.

I cleared my throat. "I'm sorry, Darian. I can't like you right now because even though I'm self-anchored for the deluge of volatile changes ahead, I just want to stay friends with my friends and not like anyone. Like *that*, I mean. But you're nice. You can be one of my friends too—the kind you *don't* like. Like *that*, I mean."

Darian wiped his hands on his Three Dogs Tavern apron. "Gotcha. I was just giving you the ramps because your uncle asked me to get him some last time he was at the tavern."

Poopsidaisy. Was it just me, or did the ramps join me in drooping with embarrassment? Hot blood flooded my cheeks while Crash snickered to himself. "Oh, right. Thanks."

Darian grinned. "Friends?" He held out a hand.

I shook it, grateful when he turned and walked away fairly quickly. "PS," I said to Crash, "I feel like maybe there's a teeny-tiny chance that I've been parent-booking everything we've been doing for . . . well, maybe for a while."

"You think?" Crash tilted his head, widening his eyes.

And just like the time I poked him with a rusty nail and forced our blood to become one, Crash forgave me. "I'll come with you to open the letter," he said. "If you forgive me for burning up your barn."

"Deal. And I take it back. I like candles, even the smelly ones. And I still owe you one."

"Deal."

Hovering

In 1731 Elias Treat, who had lived as a bachelor his entire life, met a woman during a furniture delivery trip to Philadelphia. He married her, brought her back to Gilbreth, and had one child, a girl. He named her Elizabeth Virginia in honor of the woman who'd hanged in the village thirteen years earlier, a fact that he confessed only to his closest friend, John Abel. The young girl would grow up to be a teacher, a woman of opinions, and an important historical figure in the village of Gilbreth.

She was known by her nickname, Minna.

–From *Gilbreth History: Founding Families & Artisanal Traditions* (Gilbreth Welcome Center, $16.99)

I am a legacy.

That's what I told myself while I looked at the possible life changer on the kitchen table. It was just sitting there, drowning on the frayed and faded ocean-with-goldfish centerpiece I'd woven at summer camp years ago. I wanted to pluck it from the cloth water, from the flat, blobby yellow fish and forgotten food flecks that time had worn into the blue. I wanted to, very badly.

And I also didn't.

One of the few memories I have of my grandmother is her voice telling me that woodworking floods our family history with such richness that Treat veins flow with magical wood dust disguised as blood. Over and over she'd chatter and sing and whisper those strange, wonderful words, stirring them into homemade stews and tucking them around me with my blanket at night.

Part of me always believed her.

And now I could almost feel my Treat blood pause, trapped and hovering between some kind of before and after. Pulsing steadily in a caught space between here and there.

Uncle Theo stood, tapping his callused palms and long fingers over the stone hearth, keeping his eyes off me, letting me have the moment to myself. From the corner of my eye I saw Crash's arm move, before feeling his hand squeeze mine.

"It'll be okay," he told me.

"That's right." Uncle Theo looked at me and nodded. He said the words firmly, but his fingers were still drumming, itching for something to do, something to work on, someone to need them.

"Go ahead, Minna," said Crash. "You've been waiting for this."

"Can I have some hot chocolate first?" I asked Uncle Theo.

He let out a breath and grinned. "Definitely. Christopher, you too?"

Crash nodded.

My uncle nearly leaped to the stove, then grabbed the kettle, filled it, and cranked the stove knob to its highest setting. I could see the relief in his hands' steady motion, how they were as nervous as me and were glad to have a task. Then he reached his large arms up to the top of the cup cabinet, taking down three enormous mugs that my mother had decorated by dipping my baby hands in blue paint and smushing them on opposite sides of the clay surface, then placing her own painted hand in between. Minna hand, Mom hand, Minna hand. We'd never used those mugs before.

"Might want to rinse them out," I told him.

He nodded. "They've been gathering dust." Flipping the faucet on, he gave one a rinse, then scooped in three heaping tablespoons of hot cocoa powder and handed me the mug.

I traced my own tiny fingers, then pressed my twelve-year-old hand against my mother's. I watched air dust sparkle in a shaft of low oil-lamp light. I waited for the water to boil.

The phone rang.

Uncle Theo went to the front hall to answer. He spoke in

a low voice for a few moments before returning, an unreadable expression on his face.

My chair scooted back with a sharp scratching noise as I stood. "Who was that?"

"It was the mayor. He'd just gotten off a long phone call with an old friend." Uncle Theo poured water into each of our mugs and stirred. "Go ahead and open that envelope, and then we'll talk."

A million feelings flooded through me, so many that when I opened my mouth to speak, all that came out was, "Okay."

"Christopher can spend the night if you need him."

"Uncle Theo, can you *please* just call him Crash? I've told you a million—"

"Actually," Crash said, looking a little embarrassed, "I've been meaning to tell you, Minna. I kind of . . . I mean, I'd like to . . . can you just call me Chris from now on?"

I couldn't respond. Crash wanted to be called by his . . . his name? Well, hmm. I guess I could maybe relate to that. Still, it was a bit too sudden for hearty endorsement—"Crash" was too catchy for that. I took comfort in knowing that—while I, as best friend, would of course loyally follow his wishes— Lemon and Chai would have difficulty giving up the nickname. Somehow I managed a squeaky affirmative.

Uncle Theo smirked at me. "Good choice, Christopher. I can respect that."

I kissed my uncle's chest. "I'm sorry for keeping secrets, Captain."

"You're a woodworker. It's to be expected." His head fell down over mine, tucking me closer. He was a mother swan the size of Paul Bunyan. "I'm sorry too," he said. "I'll do better."

"You're already the best. We do pretty good together, us Treats." I gave his beard a tug. "Though I am going to have to leave you one day to be on my own. What'll you do then?"

"Cry. Then get another dog. Name it Minna. Boss it around. Will and I have been planning for years. It'll be one of those labradoodles that do whatever you tell them to. It'll be just like having you around, but with less hair shedding."

I kissed his cheek and eased back into my chair. "Excellent plan. I approve."

His smile faded. He nodded at the letter. "You ready?"

Was I ready? It was a good question. The thing is, you can't ever prepare for the future, even if you've read sixty-two parenting books.

But I think in the best cases you can try to surround yourself with one or two or more people—people who try too hard or post ridiculous vocabulary sentences, or people who don't tattle when you try to make them blood brothers, or people who bring you good farm milk and butter or leave you bottle messages, or people who are missing the same kind of people you miss—and I think that's about the best kind of bridge materials you can have on your journey to wherever it is you're going next.

"I'm ready," I told him.

And with that I opened my letter.

They say that if you run the five bridges of Gilbreth backward under a full moon, you'll meet up with the past. But it turns out all that running isn't necessary, because sometimes a piece of your past shows up on the tabletop and sits there politely, waiting to be acknowledged.

Waiting to become part of your present.

When it does that, you should pick it up and open it and think of Gilbreth's motto: "The past tells us where we came from, what we are, and who we want to be."

It's a Hokey motto, no doubt about it.

Which was fine by me. Treats tend to like that Hokey stuff.

And though I, first and foremost, am Minna, I am second and . . . aftmost? Next most? Behind-that most??? Ugh, I need more Uncle Theo vocabulary words. . . . Oh, got it!

I am first and foremost Minna, but second and *also* a niece and a friend and a woodworker and a million other things that I haven't even discovered yet.

And *always, always, always*...

I am a Treat.

PS

On Wednesday, Grace got a nasty tick on her ankle, and she let me and Crash get it out with matches and a pocketknife. Crash has stuck firmly to candles but changed his mind about his name again when Malia said she liked "Crash" better, which is completely predictable teenage behavior, but I am fully supportive of whatever he wants to go by, and also I'm glad he's back to being Crash. Anyway, Lemon and Chai found out about the pocketknife use and threatened to tell Mayor Ripty. Now Crash and Beast and I have to be in their talent show entry as bridge trolls.

—From *Journal of Minna Treat's 13th Year (KEEP OUT, Uncle Theo!)*

. . so after the whole argument about whether or not to let The Bigfoot Show use Torrey Wood for filming, everyone FINALLY talked about my proposal. I'm pasting part of the summary they printed in the paper here (I guess this journal can double as a scrapbook—I guess it wasn't that cheesy of a birthday present after all—but if you're reading this, Uncle Theo, I swear I'll find the biggest beetle in Torrey Wood and stick it in your spaghetti):

The town board discussed the terms of building five new dove boxes, restoring Whistler Bridge, and developing the settlement ruins as a living history museum.

The Village of Gilbreth commissioned cost quotes and plans for the entire project from Theodore Treat & Co., a newly formed company focused on woodcraft and historic homes. The lead foreman listed on the contract was Theodore Treat, and his one permanent employee, Minna Treat, was listed as the labor force and head creative consultant.

Citing a voting statute in the long-unrevised village charter, the town board spontaneously and unanimously elected David Ripty, the temporary town mayor, to a five-year term of office, contingent on his overseeing the financials and ensuring the planning and safety of the new "settlement."

Oh! And Uncle Theo also won a contract to build a test settlement home right away and got a fat advance paycheck that'll keep us in our house for the foreseeable future AND buy the best paper towels Readi—Mart Grocery has available.

Which is nice.

Okay, that's it for journaling today. Crash and Grace are coming over. Grace's mom wants to fly her out to Italy really soon for some big, monthlong vacation, and Grace is freaking out a little. Her dad doesn't want her to miss that much class time, so now we have to figure out how to get the school to officially close for a few weeks in February. Our first idea is to somehow break the electricity and plumbing in the entire town of Gilbreth. But part of me thinks the people living here might not mind that too much.

Even if Grace has to wait a little longer to see her mom, I'll tell her not to worry.

You can always find a way back to things that are part of you.

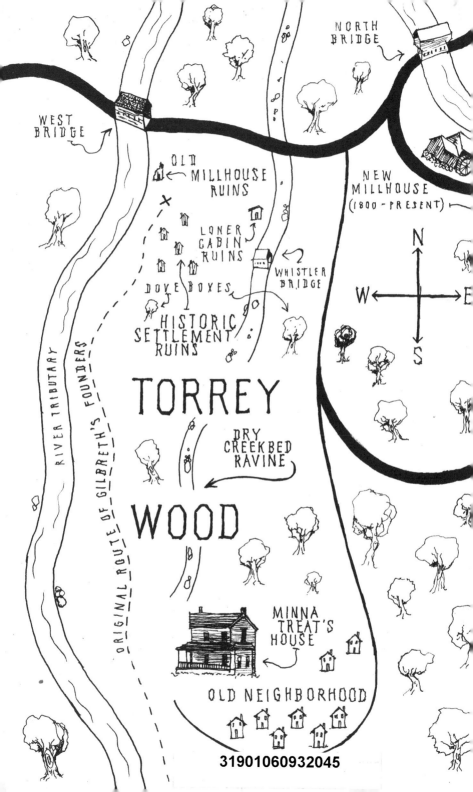

NORTH BRIDGE

WEST BRIDGE

OLD MILLHOUSE RUINS

NEW MILLHOUSE (1800-PRESENT)

LONER CABIN RUINS

WHISTLER BRIDGE

DOVE BOXES

HISTORIC SETTLEMENT RUINS

N
W   E
S

TORREY

DRY CREEKBED RAVINE

WOOD

RIVER TRIBUTARY

ORIGINAL ROUTE OF GILBRETH'S FOUNDERS

MINNA TREAT'S HOUSE

OLD NEIGHBORHOOD

31901060932045